ZEKIAL

A NOVEL

ZEKIAL

A NOVEL

DUSTY

THREE-TIME SPUR AWARD WINNER

RICHARDS

TIREE
PRESS

an imprint of

OGHMA CREATIVE MEDIA

OGHMA

CREATIVE MEDIA

Tiree Press
An imprint of Oghma Creative Media, Inc.
2401 Beth Lane, Bentonville, Arkansas 72712

Library of Congress Cataloging-in-Publication Data

Names: Richards, Dusty, author.
Title: Zekial/Dusty Richards.
Description: First Edition. | Bentonville: Tiree, 2018.
Identifiers: LCCN: 2018947722 | ISBN: 978-1-63373-367-1 (hardcover) |
ISBN: 978-1-63373-368-8 (trade paperback) | ISBN: 978-1-63373-370-1 (eBook)
Subjects: | BISAC: FICTION/Thrillers/Historical | FICTION/Westerns |
FICTION/Historical
LC record available at: https://lccn.loc.gov/2018947722

Tiree Press trade paperback edition December, 2018

Cover art by D.A. Frizell
Cover & Interior Design by Casey W. Cowan
Editing by Regina Hankins, Tommy Hancock, and Dennis Doty

FOREWORD

AS MOST OF YOU ARE no doubt aware by now, my pal Dusty Richards left us this past January, a few weeks after a horrific auto accident that also claimed the life of his beloved wife, Pat. As an early sponsor and author in the enterprise that has become Oghma Creative Media, his loss has left a gaping hole in our ranks—to say nothing of our hearts—that can never be filled. This is especially true for me, as one of the last people to see Dusty and Pat before their accident. Between social media, writers conferences, magazines, and private conversations, I've eulogized my friend and mentor at least a couple of dozen times by now. It never gets any easier, either, no matter how much time passes. This has only happened to me once before. I suppose that's how we know how truly important someone is to us. They may no longer be in our life, but they're still a part of everything we are, everything we do.

That's certainly the case with our dear departed Ranch Boss. Especially when I open up one of his last emails to me talking about the front matter for this book, only to find that he's dedicated it to me. That one made me cry.

What can I say about Dusty? That he was larger than life is the grandest of understatements. He was an irresistible force and an unmovable object all rolled into one, a personality wider than the western skies he wrote about. He was an eternal optimist, a man who woke up each and every day renewed and ready for the next job, the next challenge, the next good fight. He was a father, a patriarch, a mentor of the first order. He toured the country teaching and encouraging new and experienced writers alike, challenging them to follow his lead, tell the next inspiring story, pen the next Great American Novel. He was a fighter, a lover, a joker, an entrepreneur, a canny businessman, a television and radio personality, a famous rodeo announcer, a cowboy, and, perhaps above all else, a master storyteller. Dusty was everything under his trademark ten-gallon hat and so much more, and I could keep writing for a year and not do him justice. He was a legend, and one that touched the lives of many, many thousands—possibly millions—of people.

And this is why you hold this book in your hands today.

Dusty published over 160 books under his own name and various pseudonyms over a career spanning almost 30 years. This is common knowledge. What's not is the fact that he also left behind a wealth of material that has never been seen before... and may well be some of his best work.

Zekial is one of these.

Like *The Mustanger and the Lady*—the novel that won the 2017 Western Writers of America Spur Award for Best Traditional Western and was adapted for the screen as the movie *Painted Woman*—*Zekial* was penned sometime in the mid-1990s. According to Dusty, the book's focus on slavery and race was too controversial, and the plot too far afield of his normal work—ranch-building, cattle-driving, gunsmoke Westerns—no publishing house wanted to touch it. As a result, this manuscript and a few others were left on the shelf collecting dust for the next twenty years.

If you knew Dusty at all, though, you know he was the type who never quit, never gave up on finding new opportunities and avenues to get his work out to the public.

When I approached Dusty in 2014 about publishing with us, I was a young maverick full of piss and vinegar, running an upstart company with an unproven product. Making a play for Dusty—a bona fide legend, the most successful living Western author in the country—was shooting for the moon. Had I been in his shoes, I probably wouldn't have signed with us, concerned that taking such a risk could damage my sales and reputation. Dusty, though, saw something in me and in Oghma. He saw potential, opportunity. A new trail to break to try some new things. So, we shook hands, he signed on the dotted line, and we became partners—something I will always be grateful for.

Our plan was simple. We would start out by publishing some light, classic, loosely-connected ranching and gunsmoke westerns that had either not been released to the public, or had been previously published in limited markets. This is The Brandiron Series, which has—seemingly against all odds—seen great sales success and garnered multiple honors, including the Spur Award for *The Mustanger and the Lady*, and Will Rogers Medallions for both *A Bride for Gil* and *Gold in the Sun*. As we proceeded with that series, we would also start and build a new magazine focused on Western fiction, building a platform to showcase the work of both new and established writers of the genre. This project became the award-winning magazine *Saddlebag Dispatches*. Once we had tested the waters and shaped our market sufficiently with these projects, Dusty wanted to change gears and finally release his "tougher" work that no other publisher wanted. Darker, grittier works like *Zekial, The Texas Badge*, that explore the shady underbelly of the Old West, and take on social issues that still resonate in our world today—slavery, racism, human trafficking, rape.

Dusty may no longer be with us, but his spirit lives on, as does our love for and dedication to him. For that reason, we, at Oghma Creative Media and *Saddlebag Dispatches,* will honor his legacy by following his wishes and publishing these great books he left behind. If you miss Dusty as much as I do, don't worry. There are plenty of his great Western stories still to come. Watch for them in the months—and yes, even years—to come.

As for Dusty himself, I'm certain that he's sitting around that big ol' campfire in the sky right now, Pat at his side, swapping stories with the likes of Zane Grey, Louis L'Amour, and his old friends Jory Sherman and Cotton Smith. He was not one for self-pity, grief, or taking his foot off the gas for a second. He wouldn't want to be grieved but celebrated. He'd want us to keep his memory alive by following his lead. By chasing the sunset with all that we've got, pursuing our dreams, living with passion, and cherishing the ones we love. And that's what we'll do, how we'll honor our beloved father. Keep fighting. Keep telling stories. Keep doing what Dusty did until we can't anymore.

—Casey W. Cowan, President & CEO, Oghma Creative Media
Bentonville, Arkansas
October 4, 2018

This one's for Casey.

I

NOVEMBER 10, 1818

CHOCTAW LANDING, TENNESSEE

THE AUTUMN SUN, IMPRISONED BY a brace of gray clouds, shone weakly down on the chilly midday. Screaming birds dove for scraps left behind from recent repasts on the water among the flotilla of flat-boats docked at the rickety wharfs. Amid the stacked barrels and cotton bales, a half-dozen black men, their backs bent under heavy sacks of corn, plodded barefoot, back and forth on the gangplank from the wharf to the docked vessel. Armed with a short whip, a white overseer strutted about on the dock like a well-fed rooster, growling for them to hurry.

Zekial Broome turned his head away from the scene. He considered the matter of slavery unjust, a conviction that ran deep. Disgusted at the plight of the stevedores, he quickened his pace down the crowded street, away from the small keelboat that had ferried him a half-mile across the choppy brown Mississippi River from land rumored to shortly become Arkansas Territory.

In his leather clothing and wide brimmed hat, he hardly fit in among the gamblers and cutthroats wearing pantaloons and blousy shirts, as he passed amongst them. The entire lot was not worth a thin dime, by Zekial's personal calculations. The uneasy feeling crawling up his spine reinforced his reason for making this trek. He needed an extra pistol to carry into the wilderness.

As he worked his way through the congested street, his eyes narrowed, watchful for glimmers of steel or fast hands. Men of all sorts were subject to danger in towns like this one, even those less innocent, like himself. He would not return to this smelly, crowded shantytown that clung to the escarpment above the wide river for a long while after this trip, he decided. Sharp odors of rotting garbage, night buckets, sweaty men and tobacco smoke hung in the air, making him even more sure of his decision as he neared his goal just a short way up the hill, Shade's Gun Shop.

"Mister, do you want me?" a thin girl of perhaps fourteen asked, holding up her skirts as she ran to keep up with his long strides.

Dirt streaked her face and the bits of clothing hanging from her body amounted to nothing but rags. Nits dotted her matted brown hair like dirty snow. Zekial counted her as just another loathsome pest in this nest of tangled humanity, shaking his head to dismiss her as he walked faster. Her small hand took light hold of his arm.

"Mister, I'm only a dime. I'll please you. I promise I will."

"Not interested." Broome again started forward.

"But, *sir.*" Her dirty fingers tightened their grip. "Me mother is on her death-bed with consumption and the babies all need bread. I swear, Mister, I'll do you good. I'm young and I'm real tight."

Not wanting to literally drag her along behind him, Broome stopped where he stood. Eyes fell heavy on him. He knew that. Every rogue and scoundrel bustling about him took note of anything conspicuous, especially someone making themselves a prime target by standing still. He leaned on his rifle, striking a pose meant to intimidate while he dealt with the beggar child once and for all.

"I really need the money, sir. I can do you good."

"If you're lying to me, girl, I'll tan your butt."

"Oh, no!" She twisted her body around and bent at the waist, presenting her posterior to him. "I'm real tight. Here, you can feel me ass."

"Put that away," he ordered, angered by the offer. "You spoke of children needing food?"

"Oh, yes," she said, a tinge of relief in her voice. "They're so hungry all the time. T'is the only reason I do this sort of thing, sir. It's just me mum and the babies—and me."

"Your father?" Zekial slid thick, rough fingers into the cowhide pouch hanging on his left hip.

"Run away." She dropped her head. "A no-good whiskey drunk."

"You'll be buying food with this money?" He held the small silver coin from the purse between his thumb and index finger beyond her grasp.

"Oh, yes, sir. Food." The thin line of her mouth softened, and her brown eyes glistened at the sight of the silver. "If it weren't for them crying hungry babies, I wouldn't be doing this...."

He put the coin in her grimy palm. "Don't you waste it."

"Oh," she said, her fingers closing about the coin like a bear trap, "I won't." She took hold of the shreds of dress she wore and rewarded Broome's generosity with an awkward curtsey.

A flurry of motion erupted to Zekial's left. He reached out as a fast-moving pony bore down on them, grabbing the girl's thin arm and jerking her out of the way. A dray rumbled past, drawn by a small horse. Standing in the front of the wagon box, the red-faced driver pointed at the girl with his whip as he passed them.

"Screw her for me, mate. She's a sweet tart to do it to."

"You're a blathering liar!" she screamed after him, stomping her foot. "I never done it one time with you!"

Zekial turned her around to face him. "Never mind that. I better not catch you lying to me." He nodded toward her still closed hand holding the coin.

"I swear, sir. I am going home right now." Zekial let go of her arm and she smiled a dirt stained grin and turned away, diving quickly into the ever-shifting crowd.

He watched her disappear in the crowded parade of riffraff that clogged the town's main artery back to the river. An angry knot formed in his stomach. He hated civilization and what it did to people like that child. Between the slavers and the beggars, he wanted to shut his eyes to the whole matter and escape to somewhere in the quiet mountains to the west. Yet, there was still business to attend to. He set off toward the gun shop, but he passed a clumsily built shack just to his right bearing a roughly painted sign which read, "Fine Spirits and Company."

Zekial pushed inside the tavern and hardly drew a stare. A thick fog of tobacco smoke cradled the noisy gathering. The sharp stench of nicotine, unwashed bodies, horse sweat, sour booze and cheap perfume stung his nose. He eased his way down the crowded bar behind the backs of the noisy drinkers until he reached an open space.

"What'll it be, mate?" the bartender asked in a loud voice to be heard over the clamor and shouting of the crowd.

"Four fingers of good whiskey."

"You crazy? All we got is hooch in here."

"An ale then."

"One ale. Be a nickel."

Zekial nodded. It was too much to pay for ale. A sharp, pained scream interrupted his thoughts. Whirling at the outburst, he spotted a large white man near the center of the room flailing a black boy cringing on the floor with a many-tailed quirt. The man's lashes were unmerciful for man or beast.

"Here's your ale—five cents."

Zekial turned back to the bar and paid the bartender. He took the pewter mug in his right hand and grasped his rifle barrel in his left. Facing the abhorrent scene again, he watched as the whipping continued. No one around him made any move to stop it.

The small boy shrieked again. Having his fill, Zekial shoved through the throng. He twisted and turned, weaving his way through the crowded chairs and tables full of bodies until he drew himself up behind the man whipping the black.

"That'll be enough." Zekial ordered, his voice rumbling like barely contained thunder. As he spoke, he looked at the whip's victim. It was no boy at all, but a girl.

"Who the hell are you?" The big man turned with a look of disbelief scarring his red face. His cheeks on fire with the flush of exertion, he towered over Zekial, enraged at being disturbed.

"I said that is enough."

"Who the hell do you think you are?"

"Zekial Broome."

"Well, Broome, this here," he angrily pointed at the cowering girl with his whip, "is a runaway slave, and a poorly behaving one at that. I aim to teach her a lesson."

"Not like this, you won't."

The crowd's interest in their encounter was growing. Whispers became hisses as faces crowded in around him, no one wanting to miss the excitement. The hair on the back of his neck stiffened. He was a stranger in a river-town tavern, and maybe the man he'd confronted wasn't. His touched the pistol in his belt, feeling, too, the weight of the tomahawk sheathed behind his back and the large knife in his right boot—no way to know how many people he might have to fight to get away.

The man with the whip stood up straight, rising to well over six feet tall. "My name is Grissum McCord and I am authorized by the state courts of Alabama to return such runaway chattel to its rightful owners." Like an angry bear showing off, he stepped toward Broome. "If a runaway is a threat to society, unwilling to submit, I may use whatever force is necessary to subject them to their place."

"Don't matter to me who you are. Don't hit her again." Zekial never raised his voice. He was not impressed by the slaver's size or his violent posturing. His eyes scanned what part of the crowd he could see. No one moved, which meant the slaver and Broome had one thing in common. They were both alone in town.

McCord glowered at him through cold, blue eyes. "Mister, don't you go and interfere in Alabama business. This is none of your affair."

"Don't hit her again." Zekial said, unmoved by the angry excuse of a man before him.

"What you going to do about it?" McCord threw his head back and laughed.

Zekial did not bother to reply. He glanced at the girl, still huddled on the floor. Angry welts had begun to rise on her skinny black arms. She held her head bent down, her hands balled up in her stomach, as if expecting more of the same treatment.

"We're done here. You're messing in where you don't belong, Broome. I'll whip her all I want." McCord turned to look down on the girl again, raising the whip over his head. Vengeance twisted his sweaty face as he swung it down hard on top of her.

The girl screamed as the leather lash burned across her arm. Zekial stepped forward, his right hand raised, and struck the big man over the head with his pewter mug. Ale erupted, raining down on McCord as his knees buckled. Zekial slammed the mug down on his head again like a sledgehammer. The crowd whooped and cheered as McCord collapsed, then dropped face down onto the filthy sawdust-covered floor.

Tossing the mug away, Zekial switched hands on his rifle and took hold of the girl's closest arm, sweeping her off the floor. Her eyes widened in shock as he jerked her along after him. The awed crowd parted for them as they left, no one wanting any part of Broome or what was to come.

In the street, Zekial looked up and down for an escape route, any consideration of finding a gun shop tossed aside. "Let's go," he said sternly. "He won't be down for long."

The girl didn't move immediately. Her dark face wore a look of shock and disbelief. Broome shook his head and started off downhill. To his relief, she fell in beside him, matching his long strides as they dodged vendors and people in their path, setting some squawking chickens free in a cloud of feathers and leaving the owner cursing them.

"Cut this way," Broome said, pointing. They darted into an alley to their left. Shouts echoed behind them, but street vendors were a noisy lot and he was relatively certain that McCord was not that close on their heels. They spooked some thin-sided sows nosing through the piles of garbage as they threaded their way between buildings. With wild surprised grunts, the pigs scurried out of the way. Catching his second wind, he glanced over at her as they ran side by side.

Hardly more than a girl, she wore a red rag on her head and her clothing was tattered and ripped. He tore his eyes from her, looking forward again as they burst out into the next street. A team of high-stepping draft horses spooked at their approach and the teamster cursed and shouted for them to move aside.

Dashing past the prancing horses, Zekial took hold of her hand and leapt to the right, leaving the hard dirt street and landing on the wharf. His large hands touched cold metal, forcing his eyes to look at her wrists. Black irons circled each one. He led the way from one rickety dock to the next, searching over the edge of each one for a possible ferry.

Very nearly at the wharf's end, Broome discovered a small craft with two powerful blacks at the oars and a white man manning the tiller about to push off. Stealing a quick look over his shoulder, he found no pursuit. Still....

"Wait! I need a ride across the river," he shouted, out of breath, to the gray-haired white man on the tiller. "To the next settlement down river."

"How much ye pay?"

"How much you asking?" He bent over trying to refill his aching lungs. Beside him with her hands held tight to her stomach, the girl coughed and fought to get her breath as well.

"Two dollars."

"Robbery," he said, again looking behind them. A group of people appeared several docks down, but no one he could clearly recognize. "But I'll pay it."

"Come on," he said to her as the powerful rowers brought the small vessel back around to the dock. She nodded, and like a cat, scrambled down the ladder, stepping aboard.

Zekial took a last look back. That crowd hadn't moved. He lumbered down the rungs into the boat to join her.

"Turn it about," the man on the tiller said and the blacks laid on the oars.

"Here's your money," Zekial said, handing bills to the gray-haired man as the craft began to ply the choppy waters. He watched several flat-bottom boats go by, headed for the lower reaches of the river—Natchez, New Orleans, all downstream. The fishy odor of the Mississippi reminded him of the better smelling French perfume of a Madame Rebareau, also down river.

The distant shore looked over a half-mile away. Broome leaned forward as if to urge them to row faster, as he sat on the first board-seat and clutched the ribbed side with his left hand, the other gripping his rifle. The girl huddled in a fetal position under the bow of the boat, almost hiding, afraid to be found.

After a minute, the gray-haired man on the tiller left his station. "We're well on our way. Name's Henson." He moved up between the two blacks.

"Broome's mine."

"She yours?" Henson waved at the girl

Zekial nodded once. It was easier than explaining. He glanced down at the girl but could not see her eyes. She reminded him of a pathetic cur pup. He looked back, still half expecting McCord to be coming for them, walking on water maybe. The docks grew smaller, each stroke of the oars taking them further and further away.

"You had her long?" Henson asked, standing at his back.

"No."

"Kinda skinny, ain't she?"

"Kind of." He didn't care what shape she was in.

"She's probably got the clap." He looked her over speculatively.

"Probably."

Henson took a step back, studying Zekial from behind. "I know you mountain men don't care what they've got. Black, red or white, you boys will rut between the legs of all of them, won't you?"

"I reckon," he said to put the man off. His most urgent concern rode with getting to his horses and mule that he had boarded with a farmer west of the river and the two of them being on their way.

"You must be in some kind of an all fired hurry to pay two dollars to get across this river." Henson pinched his scruffy chin whiskers like he was thinking on the matter.

"I've got business to take care of." He hoped his short reply would silence Henson's questions.

"You in trouble with the law?" The boat owner raised his bushy eyebrows.

"Nope." Zekial glanced back at Choctaw Landing, the shacks and buildings clinging to the escarpment like moss to a tree. That wasn't exactly true, he realized, if what McCord had said was true. But it didn't matter, not when he kept the girl from being beaten further and not now.

A gun. He'd gone to that hellhole for a second gun and left with a girl he didn't need and no pistol. At least his furs had sold for a fine profit and he already had his powder, lead, and supplies cached with his saddles on the farm.

Broome knew he'd likely came away from Choctaw Landing with something else as well, mainly a tough enemy in McCord. That wasn't a concern, though. Few white men knew the western wilderness beyond the upper White River. If McCord did give them chase that far, Zekial would soon lose the slaver in the trackless land.

Henson peered hard at the girl, still pressed up under the bow as far as she could get. "I'll give you a hundred in gold dollars for her."

"No."

"Get up here girl, I want to see you." Henson waved his hands for her to stand up.

"Are you deaf?" Zekial tensed. "She ain't for sale."

Henson started to step over the seat. Zekial stood and turned in one fluid motion, his rifle rising with him. The muzzle of the gun stuck in Henson's face froze the old man where he stood. He looked at her for a long second, then as if he had considered better, he stepped back. Wordless, he drew a deep breath, hitched up his pants, then went to the rear of the vessel.

The boatman sulked. Zekial ignored him, becoming more anxious as the tree line drew closer. In a week, they'd be beyond McCord's grasp. They'd be in the vast Boston Mountains to the west, far from those foul stinking night jars and the den of thieves and slavers called Choctaw Landing. Then, he'd have to figure out what to do with her.

Waves slapped the bow as the rowers finally eased the nose onto the muddy bank. Zekial stood up, hefted his rifle, and motioned for her to get off. She swiftly rose and obeyed him. He looked back. Henson still pouted in the back. Zekial thanked the blacks, then stepped off onto the soft land.

"She's probably got a double case of the clap," Henson shouted as the oarsmen pushed the boat off into the water again. "What you buy out of them cheap nigger whore houses over there."

For an instant, Zekial considered blowing the old bastard's brains out with his rifle but ignored him instead. He motioned for the girl to walk on. With her beside him in a half lope, they headed for the small community ahead. It was a place Broome had been before, one of many with no name, just people, and across the river from Choctaw Landing.

They dodged the mud holes and wet ruts. Rough-built log cabins and buildings sat on a high spot above where the water lay in rows between dried cornstalks. Bent over and stripped of their nubbins, their brown leaves rustled in the soft wind.

The sun rode low like a great fireball on the western horizon and stained the sky pink and purple. Zekial stopped before a shop with coal smoke spewing from its chimney and its open front wall. Sounds of a hammer falling on steel reverberated from within. With a wave for her to remain there, he ducked under the low header and went in.

Inside the crude log structure, Broome found a broad-shouldered man at work. Stripped to his waist despite the cool air, he hammered on the cherry colored rod drawn from his forge. Beads of sweat matted the curly black hair on his barrel chest. He beat and shaped the rod until he was satisfied, then plunged it into a vessel of water with a great hiss of steam. That finished, he set it aside.

"Howdy." He wiped some of the sweat from his face with the back of his hand. "Much obliged for you waiting. What can I do for you?"

"I need some irons cut off."

"Off you?" The man frowned as he swiped at the beads of water on the end of his nose.

"No. She's outside."

"Is she white?" the smithy asked.

"No." He waited, angry that the color of her skin mattered to a blacksmith.

"That's all right, bring her in. If she was a white woman, I'd put on a shirt."

"How much do you charge?" Civilization had proven an expensive thing. He'd been robbed of a dime by a slip of a whore, a nickel for a two-cent ale that he never tasted, and the ultimate robbery of two whole dollars for them to cross the river.

"Ten cents."

"I'll get her." He walked outside, only to find the girl gone. Remembering how she behaved on the boat, he searched around the smithy's shop and discovered her cowered on the ground to the right of the building, huddled up against the wall.

"Come on. He'll cut those cuffs off you." He extended his hand. Still holding hers close to her stomach, she rose to her feet without his help and stood with her head bowed before him.

"Inside." He indicated for her to enter the doorway. She nodded woodenly and obeyed.

"Let's see them," the blacksmith said as they entered. He patted the anvil with a broad hand.

"Do it." Zekial nudged her back. His fingers slid across her sharp shoulder blade under the cloth. She was thin.

Still undecided, she looked at him for help. He motioned for her to go ahead. He would have to be patient with her. With dread written on her face, she stumbled forward and placed her left arm on the iron. She turned her head, trying to look somewhere far away from where her hand lay.

"He won't hurt you." Zekial tried to reassure her. She nodded, but still leaned away from her hands.

"They're riveted," the smithy said after looking the irons over. He took a large file and began to rasp away at the head of the one on the anvil. Then he chose a punch and tapped the rivet out. The cuff fell open like an eggshell. With her free hand, the girl hitched up the waist of her skirt and then placed the right one on the anvil for him.

A few passes of the file and the other rivet fell out. The smithy held up the bracelet with a grin. The girl looked, and as if in shock, backed away and rubbed her freed wrist. She gave him a grateful bob of her head, her eyes never looking up to meet his.

Zekial paid the man.

The smithy held the irons out like a prize. "You want them?"

"Yes," he said as he stepped and took them. He undid the flap of his possible sack and dropped them into it.

"Here's two rivets that'll fit them in case you ever use them," the man said, finding them on his bench. He passed them to Zekial. "They're soft enough you can even brad them with rock."

"Good." He opened the sack again and slid the rivets into it. "How much do I owe you for them?"

"Nothing. You paid enough for such a small job. Have a safe journey."

"We will. Thank you."

The smithy nodded his welcome and reached over and began to pump his bellows. The coals in the center of his forge glowed ruby red. A sharp smell from the burning coal filled the shop.

"Come on," Zekial said to the girl. "Time still ain't our friend."

They had miles to travel. He wanted plenty of territory between himself and McCord. Somewhere out in the vastness of the Ozark Plateau, he planned to winter. And for that he needed to get to his horses and load the packs.

The girl used her left hand to hold the waist of her skirt up and the other hand to raise her hem high enough to clear her bony black knees. As they walked, Broome hissed at barking dogs that rushed out at them from their home places. His tongue borne sound was enough to make the most vicious mongrel turn and head back for the safety of the porch.

"You all right?" he asked, breathing deep as they closed in on the farm where his stock was boarded.

She nodded. Her dark bare feet matched his moccasin pace.

At last, he could see the zig-zag rails ahead, the way he knew the farm. They were both out of wind when he fell into a long walk to replenish their lungs, the girl following suit. The sight of the farm settled some of the turmoil inside him. He hoped perhaps he'd feel easier when they were loaded, and on their way. Maybe then the skin on the back of his neck would stop crawling.

Beyond the rail fence that lined the wagon tracks, he spotted his black mule, Jim, who raised his head from grazing. The sorrel horse, Red, threw his head up, too, and studied them. The bay pack mare went on gathering the brown grass. Then a dish-faced gray mare named Eagle nickered at him and loped over to greet them.

"These are my horses," he said to her as he held out his palm to the snowy-coated Eagle who came to the rail fence.

"She sure be pretty."

Her words struck him like the slap of an open palm. He whirled and looked at her as he drew in a deep breath, and then exhaled. She could talk.

"You can ride her," he said and patted the mare's muzzle. When she did not answer his offer, he turned to look at her

She trembled, tears spilling down her face. Words failed Zekial in moments like this. A sense of helplessness consumed him as she dropped to her knees in the road and began to sob into her hands.

He knelt on one leg beside her. She cried for a full minute and he knew nothing else to do but let her. As her breathing slowed back down, he said, "What's your name?"

She raised her head slowly. Two wet rivers shone on her dark face in the twilight. "M—Matilda.... Tilly."

"You're safe with me, Tilly."

She nodded sharply. "I know. I just can't believe it."

"You will," he said, squeezing her bony shoulder. "You will, gal."

II

HIS HEAD HURT. HE SPIT filth and sour sawdust from his mouth as he rose up to all fours. The raucous laughter around him sounded like magpies. Grissum McCord was mad clear to his pounding heart. He growled and swung himself to his feet like a raging bear. The roar came from deep in his guts. He blinked his bleary eyes and searched about with murderous intent, anything, anyone who dared to get in his way, a likely victim. Men scrambled from their chairs to escape his wrath.

Forcing himself to stand upright, he searched the room again. They were gone, both of them. He bellowed again, flipping the closest chair to him across the floor with one swift swipe.

"Where's she at?" He blinked his eyes to focus in the smoky haze.

Men drew back, and he roared again for effect, then demanded, "Which way did they go?"

"They run out the front door." An older man at the bar pointed toward the opening. Like a great bull, McCord staggered across the room tossing tables and chairs aside.

He exploded through the door and into the street. As cooler air overtook him, he stopped and looked both ways up and down the thick stream of hawkers and passersby. He'd not drug that bitch back to Choctaw Landing to have her stolen by some buckskin bastard from the frontier. He scrubbed at his whiskered mouth with his hand and tried to clear the cobwebs from his pounding head.

No sign of them existed in the filthy mass choking the street. They had a head start on him—he needed to think. Go get Judson, his man, and get him to scout this Broome guy up. The man wouldn't go far, Grissum figured, having himself a black girl. He'd likely have his fun, then celebrate his way to the bottom of a whiskey jug. That would be when Judson would find him. Then he would step in and beat that bastard until he couldn't shit or puke ever again. Maybe he'd even do worse things than that to him. Grissum McCord wanted this Zekial Broome to damn sure rue the day he interfered in someone else's affairs.

Grissum massaged the knot on the back of his head again while he rambled through the street traffic. He had to find Judson and knew full well where he would be. With that whore of his.

Grissum came to a stop, three buildings up from the tavern on the other side of the street. A two-story house of sorts, thrown up quickly to accommodate a boatload of working girls coming into town a few years back before it was called Choctaw Landing.

"Judson!" Grissum bellowed. The long traces of sundown began to sweep the street where he stood on sea legs. "Judson, get out of her bed and answer me!"

"Hush!" A man with a head of uncombed black hair stuck his head out of a second story window. "What's wrong, McCord?"

"Wrong?" McCord wailed. "Me half-killed and that wench stolen. You're asking me what's wrong?"

"Who stole her?"

"Hi, Big Grissum," a woman said as she perched herself on Judson's shoulder. He narrowed his eyes in the too bright sun's glare. She looked as if she wasn't wearing a thing, but that might have been his own wishful thinking. He could only see her bare shoulders and her pudgy face framed by red hair as she huddled over Judson's back.

McCord ignored her. "Get dressed, Judson. Get down here. We got a frontier bastard and that bitch what he took from me to find." He held his hand to the back of his scalp. The damn headache had to stop, and soon.

"Coming, now."

Grissum grunted, then looked around for a place to sit while he waited. He had had all the standing he could take. With some effort, he took himself a place on the log sidewalk and put his back to the building. He touched the top of his skull again and winced at the two tender bumps. Why didn't Judson get down here? He closed his eyes.

Minutes or maybe hours later, he didn't know nor care, something jabbed Grissum repeatedly in his side. Opening his eyes painfully and slowly, he found Judson standing just to his left, poking him with the tip of his boot.

"When did all this happen?" Judson asked, out of breath and pale looking standing before him.

McCord shook his head at the effort he needed to exert to get to his feet. Maybe he'd just sit there. A gagging flowery smell filled his nose. He frowned at the powerful aroma while he fought his way to his feet. Deep in his throat he tried to hack up the taste and spit it out. He tried to swallow away the disgusting flavor and shook his head when he couldn't get rid of the odor. "You stink like hell."

"Perfume. French perfume."

"Jesus, did you have to take a bath in it?" He said as he backed up to the wall to support himself.

Judson grinned. "No, just washed myself with her. All over. Now what is this about a frontier bastard and the girl?"

"His name is Broome." Grissum drew in a deep breath. His shoulder pressed against the wall for support, he wondered if he could stand alone without the aid of the building. He drew himself up. With his palms, he scrubbed his fevered face.

"How did he do it?" Judson asked, jarring McCord from his confusion.

"Jumped me from behind, knocked me out, took her and ran...."

"Where did he go?"

"Damnit, Judson, how should I know?" He took two ragged breaths, the pain about to overtake him completely. "But he can't go far. You go down on the wharf and find him. I'm going back to our room. You come up there when you find him and get me. I want to strangle him with my bare fists." He squeezed his hands together, demonstrating just what he intended to do to the buck-skinner's neck.

"What if he's gone further?"

McCord poked him in the chest. "You find out where he went."

"I hate that we lost all that work. Going clear to Kentucky and all, I mean." A look of disgust spread over Judson's face as he spoke.

"Hell, we ain't lost her. That leather-stocking bastard will get his fill of her skinny butt and then he'll get drunk and we'll swoop him and her up."

"You sound like you know him."

"Never saw him before he came up in that damn McGuinison's gin mill—but I know how them frontiersmen do."

"What's his name again?"

"Broome's all I recall. About six-foot-tall, dressed in buckskins. Light hair. Hell, he looks like all them woodsmen do."

"I'm going to the wharf and look for him," Judson said and stared at McCord with a concerned frown. "Can you get back to the boarding house by yourself all right?"

"Sure, I can. You think I'm a baby?"

"I think you've had lots too much to drink."

"Not near enough, for the pain in my head." McCord stood, weaving a little from one foot to the other, then shook his head to dismiss Judson's concern.

"Go find the buck-skinner."

McCord sent Judson off with a push and turned the other way, starting for the boarding house. A few hours' sleep and he'd be all right. Damn, he could lay down anywhere and rest a little while, he glanced in thoughtfully as he passed an alley between two buildings. He decided against it, thinking the town watchman might put him in that pigsty jail, even with him, an officer of the court, too. His Alabama badge wasn't worth much around Choctaw Landing. Feeling queasier than before, he stopped and leaned on a building.

"Hey, mister—"

Grissum blinked at the brown eyes of the young girl standing before him.

"You want me?" she asked.

"Huh?" he asked, acting dumb, but already figuring on what to do next. She was young and tender stuff, not some loose worn out deal. Not like the fat fishwife he'd had two nights before when they first reached Choctaw Landing. He'd been drunk then, too.

"I mean you want my body." She lowered her voice. "I'm real tight."

"Yeah," he said with a small grin. "Come here. I want to feel you."

"Not here on the street." She shook her head with an impatient frown from outside the reach of his hands.

"Where then?"

"We can go in the alley."

"How much you charge?"

"Ten cents."

"Ten cents, huh?" He followed her as she kept looking over her shoulder at him. Twice he had to raise up to his full height to clear his head enough to walk some more.

"That's dirt cheap, too," she said with an impatient look cast over her shoulder at him.

"Cheap," he mumbled. Damn, he kept getting drunker and could hardly focus on her. Or maybe it was the ambush he took from that damned woodsman. It had been an hour since his last drink. Unsteady on his feet, he used the corner of the house to lean against at the entrance to the alley. He couldn't see across to the next building.

When he could see again, they were sitting on the ground. Him and her side by side. His head swirled, and he knew she was pulling on his root. Why didn't it work? It always worked. Why had he paid her ten cents to screw him? She wasn't worth two cents. Or had he paid her yet? His fault? No. He fainted and came to again, lying on his back.

Do something. It always works. Damn you.

"Honey," he mumbled at her kiss as he half awoke and reached for her. Then he stopped. It wasn't a woman at all, but the snoot of a damn pig sniffing in his face.

He struck out with his fist, smashing the sow on the side of the head and hurt his hand. The pig barely withdrew, and then as if curious, she sniffed at him again while he cursed at her. With his toe, he repeatedly kicked her until the beast rushed away, squealing.

It was still nighttime, dark and cold to the bone. Something rotten, a bad odor rushed up his nose. He felt around in the darkness and discovered his pants were undone and his privates exposed to the night air. He quickly put them away and buttoned his britches. Had he been robbed? No. His money belt was still there around his waist. At least that tart hadn't rolled him in his drunken state.

He lay on a refuse pile, probably had been the whole time and not in her bed at all. Overhead, he could see stars in the sky. He was in the alley she'd first led him into. He rolled over on his side and reached out. His fingers touched chilled flesh and he drew them back. In the pearly moonlight, he sat up, trying to focus on the still, cold body beside him.

It was a naked girl. No, not plumb naked, but her dress was wadded up to her chest, so that her belly, legs and hips were exposed. McCord touched her again. She was too cold to be living anymore. He swallowed hard and tried to see her face. Her eyes were open—staring at nothing.

It was the girl who only charged ten cents.

Last thing he recalled, he'd been on the ground in the alley and couldn't get hard. Too soft to stick it in her, he could only remember trying.

Something flashed in his memory. He'd been angry with her. That's why it hadn't worked.

His head hurt like hell as he struggled to his feet. What time was it? How had she died? No time for that, he'd sure get blamed if anyone found him around her corpse. He had to get moving fast and not be seen.

On his feet, he glanced back and began to run. He half stumbled while he made his way past the dark houses, his eyes now set on a tree line he could barely make out in front of him. Frowning at dogs that barked at him in the inky darkness, he made the woods. No one had seen him, he was grateful for that.

He rushed downhill through the brush and timber until he splashed into a small slough. Fully dressed, he plowed into the waist deep water despite the cool night air. He needed to get rid of some of that stink or they'd sure know he was the one that had been with her.

How had she died? He could barely recall getting real mad at her. That was all. The cold water he cupped on his face and the chilly air surrounding him sobered him to a new awareness.

He'd chocked her a little for not getting it up. That was it. But he hadn't killed her. He swept up more water on his sleeves and soon saturated his clothing and the cold wetness sought his skin. Damn, he'd probably die of pneumonia. Better than to hang for murder—someone had killed her. They'd sure lynch the killer.

With hands full of the swampy water, he washed the back of his neck; it woke him further. A cold shiver brought goose bumps on his arms. He'd probably freeze to death before he got back to the boarding house. It was a mile away or more on the other side of town.

Shaking with a bone deep chill, he considered his next move. An alibi. It must be ironclad. What if someone had seen him with her? He'd been too drunk to know if they had or hadn't. With another shake of his head at the troubles this might cause him, he climbed up the slick bank and headed for the boarding house.

———

YOU FALL IN THE RIVER?" Mrs. O'Day, a buxom woman, asked when he entered the back door of the boarding house. Then she snickered up her nose. Her broad form filled the chair at the table in the kitchen. A flickering candle waved orange light over her full face. Shadows accented the fine black mustache on her upper lip.

"Had a little accident."

"Where's that black prize of yours?" she asked.

"Run off."

"Guess you won't be needing the key to the shed, huh?"

"Oh, I will come morning. She won't get far."

"She run off to Kentucky again?" O'Day laughed aloud. "That's where you got her from wasn't it?"

"Judson's looking for her now."

"No, he ain't. He looked for you until an hour ago. He's upstairs asleep."

"Good," McCord said. "He mention her?"

"Nope. But he sure stinks with damn perfume. Why he'll have folks thinking I run a bawdy house if that smell lasts long around here."

"Why are you up for?"

"Can't sleep." She shrugged her thick shoulders and folded her arms under her full bosom, as if considering him.

"I can."

"I bet you can. You can change in the back room. You'll track that mud all up the stairs otherwise."

"I haven't got any clothes down here."

"Who cares? I been married four times. You see one butt, you've seen them all."

"I guess so."

"My first husband was a Scot like you. Big man he was. Drank a barrel of whiskey at a time. Got drunk one night, on his way home to me, and fell in a hog pen. They ate him."

"That's horrible," Grissum shook his head, remembering his recent encounter with a pig.

"Ah, the second good man in me life got kicked in the head by a mule on our honeymoon. Poor boy never even got under the covers. Happened outside the parson's house. Took him five days to die."

"What happened to the next one?"

"I guess the Injuns got him. He was out wandering around where he didn't belong. Neighbors was his name, Matthew Neighbors. We lived in east Tennessee then and Injuns was bad about that time. A Captain Buckley brought me his knife. Had *M-T-N* on the blade. They got it off a buck they killed down on the river. It was his knife all right."

"O'Day? He die, too?"

"Yeah, I guess he did. He fell overboard in the river, never come up. He was ferrying over one day and plop, he went in the drink. Guess the catfish ate him."

"It sounds to me like it ain't healthy to be married to you."

"Think what you want. I own this house. Got me savings. A man could do worse." She raised her double chin so the flap of skin under her jaw shook.

"I'm going back to take off my clothes."

"Go ahead. Leave them clothes back there, that scrub girl will wash them. Don't need that mud all over." She scowled, her upper lip curling.

"Good enough."

McCord staggered into the darkness of the back room and pulled off his soggy boots. Water ran out of them. Cold clear to his soul, he peeled off the wet clothing that stuck to his skin. He used a cloth towel he found on a wall rack to dry himself and finished on his shriveled privates. He hated for any woman, even an ugly one like Mrs. O'Day, to see him in such a condition.

As he dried himself, he touched the top of his skull. The two knots were still sore. He owed that Broome.

Barefoot, he plodded down the gritty floor and past her. She acted occupied and busy sewing something. Self-conscious in his nudity, he stepped through the candle's lit circle with his hands covering himself. Ignoring her, he started up the stairs.

"McCord."

"Yeah?"

"You see one, you seen them all." She cackled at her own joke.

Upstairs in the small room, he rummaged in their gear until he found his extra pants and shirt.

Judson sat up on his bunk. "Where you been?"

"Never mind. Did you find her or him?"

"No one's seen them."

"Aw, the hell," he said, pulling on his pants.

"I was all up and down the dock. I talked to lots of folks. No one remembered a Broome nor seeing a colored wench with someone dressed in leather."

"He's gone to the Territory then."

"What are we going to do about that?"

"After I get some sleep, we'll go after him."

"What if he gets her pregnant? That man ain't going to want to give no big reward for—"

"Shut up in there!" someone shouted down the hall.

"Yeah. I'm trying to sleep, too," another added.

"What we going to do?" Judson hissed.

"Do like everyone else in this damned house," McCord ordered, "sleep a while. I can't think right now myself."

He crawled into the lower bunk. Starlight streamed in the small window. When he closed his eyes, his mind replayed the image of the girl, lying on her back in the alley, bathed in the same grayish light, her dress shoved up to expose the small mound of her belly and legs. Hard as he tried, he couldn't shake the sight of her. Like a great fish, he flopped over in the bed and tried harder to lose the vision of her blank eyes staring into death. Nothing helped him forget it; not being mad at Broome nor his upset over the loss of the girl, not one thing made it fade away. He lay awake, unable to close his eyes, for fear of seeing that little whore, dead.

III

"L EAVING AT NIGHT, ZEKIAL?" BARLEY Whit, the farmer who had boarded his horses, asked in dismay. Light from inside his cabin illuminated his outline in the doorway.

"I need to get on my way."

"Wait. I'll get a lamp, so you can see, and I'll help you."

In a minute, Whit was back. Behind him, his small children filled the lighted doorway whispering about her.

"He done got him a nigger boy now!" a sure voice among the youngsters said. The others sounded equally impressed with his companion as their father led the two of them to the shed.

Whit held the small candle reflector, so his boarder could sort out his saddles, bridles and gear from the pile. The light cast great shadows of Zekial on the wall like a giant pilfering in his things.

"You're sure welcome to stay the night," Whit said, shaking his head ruefully. "You may ride off into a ditch in this darkness."

"We'll be fine. We need to get going is all." Zekial swept up the first rig and pads, then carried them to the gray horse, the one she would ride. He had traded a Cherokee out of the saddle a month earlier. Hardly more than a seat, girth and stirrups, he'd used it to tie on his packs of furs. It would serve her, if she could ride. If not, she would have to learn how. There would be little time in his plans for much training.

Blankets in place, the saddle on right, he laced the cinch leathers and tightened them. She stood back in the dark shadows.

"I guess I did something impulsive," he said while he bridled the gray.

"Her?" the tall farmer asked with a head toss toward the black girl.

"Yes. Some slaver named McCord was whipping her in his drunken stupor and I took her away from him."

"Took her away from him? My Gawd man, that can get you prison time in Tennessee. You can't take slaves away from their owners."

"I did, and I expect that McCord will be coming after me. He's a slave chaser from Alabama. I can't undo it, right or wrong."

"Oh, hell, you are in a peck of trouble. Leave her here and I'll give her back to them. Then you can go on out west where they'll never find you. Chances are, if they get her back, they won't even file charges."

"I can't do that." Zekial went for his saddle. He hefted it over his arm and started for his horse.

"My Gawd, man," Whit followed Zekial to the sorrel, "they'll lock you up in prison for the rest of your life for taking her. They don't treat slave stealing with no light hand."

"I don't care. They'd only beat her some more if I gave her back." He stared out into the night.

"Yes, but she is chattel property and she belongs to whoever owns her. He can do whatever he wants to her. She is his, period."

Zekial turned sharply to look at Whit. "You got girls. They're your daughters. If someone beat them, what would you do?" He smoothed out the blanket pad, then set the fork of his saddle up on the red horse's withers, measuring carefully, he needed no saddle galls from a sloppy saddling.

Whit shook his head in disapproval. "First, they ain't colored." He frowned as Zekial seemed to ignore him. "Zekial Broome, you've lived out in the wilderness too long."

"I never said they were nothing than what they are. They're nice girls. But someone goes to whipping on them, what would you do?"

"Probably kill them or try to."

"That's how I felt when he beat on her and no one, mind you, no one in that whole barroom made a move to stop him."

"She's a slave. Wasn't none of their business."

"That's why I'm leaving in the middle of the night."

"You'll never get away. They'll hound you to hell."

"If they do, they might end up there."

He still had the packs to put on the bay mare and the mule. No matter, he was closer to being away with the riding horses saddled than he had been since they reached the street in front of that gin mill. He picked up the cross-buck packsaddle for the mule.

"You ever do anything in your life you had to do, Barley Whit?"

"I guess I have. I left a perfectly good farm in Pennsylvania to come to Tennessee, then I moved here."

"No, I mean done something that you couldn't really help yourself—that you had to do?"

"No. I married Marthie. Knowed her since we were wee ones. Had them children. I always farmed. Always hoped to find better land—this ain't bad, if the river don't get up too high in the spring. Land's rich enough. No, I never did nothing like you're doing. I always kind of stayed, you know, inside the law."

"Let me tell you something. I never liked to look at the butt of a mule." Zekial reached under and drew the girth up. "I went to trapping at seven, bought my own first gun at nine, I went and lived with some Cherokees when I was twelve."

"But you aren't an unlearned man." Whit turned his head to the side as if doubting him.

"I read the Bible. Mother taught me how when I was small. I read Shakespeare, too, about them kings and queens. I still don't know why I did that."

"I can barely sign my name. Marthie can read some from the Bible. Like to hear her read—amazes me. Never heard of no Shakespeare though."

"It's kinda highbrow, now I think about it," Zekial said. "I guess rich folks talk that way. 'You there,' 'my good man' sort of talk. More British sounding than even them officers we captured at New Orleans."

"You didn't get any land script from the War of '12?" Whit asked. "You told me before that you were with Jackson there at New Orleans."

"I told you, too, that I don't like mules in harness." Zekial hoisted up the first pannier to go on the mule. Tilly ran in and struggled to lift the other one before he could tell her not to. He hung his on the cross bucks, then hurried around to take it from her.

"That's too heavy for you," he said as he took it from her and hooked it in place. She nodded and slunk back out of the candle's ring of light.

"I sure will worry about you," Barley said. "Marthie and I kinda liked seeing you come by here in the spring and again in the fall. We talked all summer about you coming back and telling us what it was like up the Arkansas River and all. I ain't never seen no buffalo."

"Just a wooly cow."

"Yeah, but I heard eating their meat will put the stuffing in your old peter." He looked around like he was trying to locate the girl, or maybe his children, when he finished. Then he held the lamp up high for Zekial to fix the next pack-saddle on the bay mare.

"Can't say I know any difference from eating it. It ain't bad. But I like elk better."

"Seen a few of them elk in Tennessee years ago. But I'd bet they've all been killed out across the river by now."

"More than likely. Things are going fast, game in these parts will be all gone before long." Zekial slapped on the packsaddle and cinched up the mare. Disappointed with his speed, it seemed to him it would take him forever to get under way. By daylight, he wanted to be long gone up country, leaving McCord waiting across the river and wondering where he went.

"I can't talk you into leaving her here for them?" Whit asked, looking down at his bare feet.

"No, she's going with me."

"Can't tell you how bad them folks hate a slave stealer."

"They'll have to hate me then. I can't abide by slaving either. Ain't no one another's master, white or not." He wrestled the smaller pack up to his knees, then balanced it for a few seconds on his knees before he hoisted it onto the packsaddle crosses.

"You sound like a New Englander talking," Whit said as if he had a bad flavor on his tongue. "They talk like that, but they've got chin whiskers and straight backs and talk about Calvin and the Bible. I think they're too cold to do anything."

"I don't care for them either. Everyone's going to hell, is what they say. I don't believe that." Broome struggled to load the last one of the buffalo-hide packs on the mare. The final pannier in place, he straightened his stiff back in relief—ready to go—finally.

"You sure may be going to hell now, and it'll be of your own doing taking her along," Whit said.

Zekial stuck out his hand and clasped the other man's in his grip. "I appreciate your caring for me and my stock. You're a fine man, Barley Whit, and I hate to not abide by your advice. But me and her, we're getting out of here."

"God be with you, Zekial." Whit shook Broome's hand heartily. "Me and Marthie will worry about you. You ever can come by again, you look us up. And thanks for that knife you gave me. It holds a keen edge and I got me a real Injun one to show off to my neighbors at butchering time."

Broome nodded at Whit. "Here," he said, waving the girl over and holding both hands in a cradle for her foot. Following his direction, she stepped in it and sprung aboard the gray mare. When she gathered the reins, he could see she knew her business about a horse. Satisfied, he hefted his rifle and went to get on the sorrel while Whit untied the two pack animals.

Mounted on Red, Zekial picked up the leads. After a quiet goodbye to Whit, they rode out and headed west on the dark wagon tracks called a road. The animals, freshly rested and fed, pranced some, but they soon settled into a long single file walk with Tilly in the rear. Zekial moved them along with all the speed he dared as they entered some dark woods, barely seeing the cleared path in the starlight. He allowed the sorrel to shy from the mud holes and ruts as they went.

"How's come you didn't left me back there?" she asked as the soft pad of unshod hooves broke the night's silence.

"You want to go back with McCord?" he asked over his shoulder.

"No, but I heard what that man said. You be breaking the law, risking your neck for me."

"I heard enough of that talk from Whit. Don't you start in on me now."

Tilly sighed a heavy breath for such a slight girl. "I ain't going to nag you. I don't like to be nagged myself. I just wonder why you be so set on taking me away."

"I ain't sure, right now. But if I get an answer, I'll tell you all right."

They rode on in silence.

———

DAWN SPREAD LIKE A SLOW blanket across the land. First, a gray light shone on the yellow and red leaves that still clung to the maples and oaks. An occasional grove of bare walnuts with clusters of nuts weighing their branches dotted the countryside. Zekial studied the tall stately pines that towered above them as they passed through this land.

He rose in the stirrups and set the sorrel into a trot. The pack animals followed, and she came along on the gray. He was hungry, and reckoned she was as well, but they would eat later. They had many miles to cross. He guided the red horse around the mud holes where wagons and sleds had been mired.

He had a spot in mind where they could rest a day. An old army buddy, Kelsey Davis, had a place close to the lower White River. Zekial would be glad to see him and his lovely wife, Betty Lou, and their children again.

They rode until midday. Coming to a full stop, Broome dug out hardtack and cheese for them to munch on while the horses grazed. The sun had warmed the air and the chill was gone. A strong south wind blew with intensity and Zekial wondered if that meant rain coming up from the gulf. They drank from the stream and she washed her arms, face, feet and legs in the water. He found a towel buried deep in his pack and gave it to her. The cloth brought a grateful smile. Neither spoke. He remained deeply engrossed in his plans to escape the slaver and she didn't offer anything while he inspected the gear and made sure the cinches were on proper and tight enough again.

"You get cold in the night?" he finally asked, realizing that her arms were bare.

"Not bad."

"You get cold, you take a blanket and wrap yourself in it."

"We going to ride all night again?" She looked at him, worry knitting her brow.

"No," he said, then realizing his mistake. "I mean if you're cold, you wrap up in a blanket, night or day."

"I be fine."

"You hear me?"

"I hear you. I'll wrap in one of your blankets if I be cold."

"Good." That settled, he pointed to the horses. Time to move on again. In another day's ride, they would be at the Davis's. Maybe he dared to rest there.

He glanced back down the wagon tracks that disappeared a hundred yards into the woods. No sign of McCord or any pursuit. Maybe there wouldn't be, but Zekial knew better. He'd known men like McCord, those with jobs to do, vile duties. Also, he knew men who didn't like to be embarrassed in their work, just as Zekial had done to him. Yes, he would come. It was just a matter of when.

———

THEY PUSHED THEIR MOUNTS UNTIL dark. He shot a hen turkey for their supper. She took charge of it while he unsaddled and put out the horses in a wide meadow of grass. Busy hobbling and stacking his things, he knew the Jim mule would stay with them through a major earthquake or Indian attack. Especially an Indian raid. Jim hated Indians and usually he set off a series of alarming brays when they came close. Zekial hobbled the bay mare and the gray. His sorrel gelding wouldn't go far from the two mares.

The turkey meat sizzled in the pan over her fire. Obviously, she had found some bacon in the panniers to melt for her grease. He also noted she had deboned the bird and the cooking meat smelled delicious. He could not recall the last time he had eaten anything substantial.

"I wasted some," she said, seeing his interest in the pan.

"There's plenty more turkeys."

"I'd sure never got it cooked in the whole." She held up the ragged carcass she had been whittling on. With an underhanded pitch, she tossed it into the brush.

"It would have taken a long time to cook whole. I'm hungry, been a spell since I ate. How about you?"

"That cheese and them crackers you give me?"

"Yeah."

"That be the first I eat in three days." She dropped down and sat cross-legged on the ground facing the fire. The short skirt barely covered her knees when she leaned forward and stirred the turkey with the long wooden fork.

"Why?"

"Didn't care if I lived or died if I had to go back there."

"Alabama?"

"Yes, sir."

"I understand. We're going kinda northwest tomorrow and stopping at an old Army friend's place on the White River. They're nice people."

She nodded her head. "Good."

"Be a long day's ride, but we can rest there. McCord, he won't find us there for a while."

She waved the fork absently and looked across the prairies to the west. "Don't you ever go to thinking he can't find you. He done found that Quaker's house in Kentucky where I was hiding. That man, he said, 'Oh, that slaver won't never find you here.'"

"He did?"

She nodded. "There I was sleeping down there and that man of his, Judson, he drug me out of the root cellar like a coon done been treed. McCord, him beat that old man up, too, for hiding me. That Grissum McCord is a mean one."

Zekial agreed with a nod. McCord was a senseless, cruel person. Seated on the ground, his knees drawn under his chin, Broome studied the setting sun. When the time and place came, he'd decided what he must do about that man. He watched the orange sky turn to purple, until the glow settled under the horizon.

"I think we can eat it," she finally said. The night wind fanned the red-hot coals under the skillet. "You sure do have the pots and pans. My, oh my, you nearly gots a house full of them in them packs."

He nodded. No sense going halfway. Besides, he'd found most of them two years before in a long-deserted camp far out on the Arkansas River in the tall grass country. Why the owners had gone off and abandoned such valuable things he never knew, but their fire had been dead for days and no signs of life were about the place.

The turkey meat filled them. With few words, they turned in, wrapped in their individual blankets and slept.

———

SHE WAS UP BEFORE DAWN and had the fire going. He found her some tea to boil. Huddled under the blanket, she used it for a coat and squatted beside the fire. They had the rest of the bird and hot tea in the nippy air. Finished, he rose to go for the horses and she joined him.

While he loaded the pack animals, she saddled both horses. He watched her, concerned about her knowledge, but her efforts under his close inspection satisfied him.

He hoisted up one of the panniers "You do that before?"

"All my life, I be watching men saddle horses."

"You watched good." He hung the pack on the mule.

A wide smile crossed her face and showed even white teeth. If it was the first time she'd ever done that, she'd done it right. He finished packing, took his rifle and mounted up. She followed suit and they both gathered the leads and headed up the two ruts that he decided folks called a road.

Clouds closed in and Zekial wondered if they would beat the rain. He had expected it all day as the south wind pushed them along. They had left the main road twice at the approach of wagons. No need to give McCord fuel to keep him coming. He knew that the slave catcher would ask anyone he came across if they had seen them. The oxen outfits lumbered by as they watched them from afar each time, then they resumed their trek.

The first drops of rain fell on them when they rode up the deep ruts that led to the Davis claim. From all the fresh tracks in and out of the lane to Kelsey's place, Broome decided something had happened there. Maybe a community gathering like a corn shucking or something had taken place. The sorrel had trouble finding his way to avoid the water filled holes and ruts in the primitive road. Zekial wondered about the reason for such heavy traffic, but the smell of wood smoke pleased him when they drew closer.

He rode up to the front of the two-story log house and hissed at the barking hounds. In the doorway, with the light of the room behind her, Betty Lou was dressed in black. Her long face looked drawn. Something bad had happened. He slipped from his horse and raced to her.

"My God, what is it? The children?" he asked, his voice rumbling deep in his throat, pinning the anxiety deep inside.

"No. It's Kelsey, Zekial. He's dead." She threw herself at him, burying her face in his leather shirt. Her forehead pressed to his chest. Great sobs shook her body while she cried.

IV

DAMNIT, HE CAN'T JUST DISAPPEAR."

As Grissum McCord rubbed his hand over his mustache, he still smelled that stinking garbage odor from the alley on his fingers. An image of the girl lying on her back in the filth forced him to swallow hard. No way, by this time, that they could ever prove it was him that killed her. He didn't think he had anyway, only choked her a little because she couldn't get him up.

Judson snorted in disgust. "They've done just that, disappeared. Ain't no one seen him ride out east on the road and no one at the docks seen him go over into the western territory."

"Maybe he got on a flatboat?"

"No, no one's done seen him, I told you"

"He couldn't vanish into thin air." His head hurt as he sat on the edge of his bed. The pounding at his temples was like a drum roll. They needed that slave girl back and the reward money. They'd been clear to Kentucky to find her, came back by St. Louis with her, looking for another runaway. But they'd never found that buck, so all they had to show for their work was her.

"He's plumb vanished."

"Bullshit! We're going to find him and her today!"

"Not here, you ain't."

———

AN HOUR LATER, GRISSUM'S STOMACH still churned like hell and the pounding headache rode his temples. He and Judson squatted on a rickety dock and spoke with a short older man named Henson.

"I took a buck-skinner called Broome across the river last night," Henson said. "I kinda figured he was stealing her when he paid me two dollars to ferry him over there."

"Two dollars?" Grissum exclaimed. "He say where he was going?"

"No, but I'd suspect he denned up with that girl over there." Henson pointed to the bank. "There's a village over there. They call it New Castle. You ever been across the river?"

"Not here. We been across at St. Louis," Grissum said and looked beyond the wind-rippled, broad river at the brown tree line. His molars tightened, and the pounding inside his skull deepened. Zekial Broome owed him plenty and he planned to extract every bit of it out of him—real slow like.

"I'll be going over there in an hour," Henson offered. "Take both of you over for fifty cents. I hate a damn slave thief worse than anything."

"So do we." Judson looked at his boss for approval of the statement.

"We'll get our things from the boarding house." Grissum never took his stare from the far shoreline. He didn't bother to acknowledge Judson's remarks, he had more important things to think about. "And we'll be ready to go with you by then."

———

MIDAFTERNOON, HENSON AND HIS OARSMEN delivered Mc-Cord and Judson to the far shore. They unloaded their rifles and gear on the bank. Filled with confidence, Grissum expected to quickly locate them. He had made little provisions for supplies. In a day, they'd round them two up and be back to Choctaw Landing with that black wench in irons.

Along with their rifles, powder and lead, their bedrolls consisted of a wool blanket and a backpack with small items. All that a soldier needed. Grissum carried a small pistol in his belt, a hunter's knife and a hatchet. Judson carried a knife and hatchet on his person, too.

McCord paid Henson, pleased that men like him considered slave stealing so offensive. They sure made his and Judson's job much easier. As he put the pack on his shoulder, he drew another whiff of that damn perfume his man must have bathed in. He would remember to stay up wind of Judson.

They strode up the rutted road, each of them wearing a felt hat that the south wind threatened to blow away. Grissum observed the harvested corn-stalks beside them. The settlers had had a good crop year. Ahead, he could see the cooking fire smoke and raw cabins of the settlement strategically placed on a small knob above the farming ground. In these bottoms so close to the Missis-sippi, a man would want even higher ground, McCord decided.

"We'll stop and talk to the blacksmith. Them irons might have got in his way," Grissum said, when they reached the shop. Wheels and wagons for repair were parked all around the business.

"Good afternoon," Grissum spoke to the large man at the forge.

"Good afternoon, gents." The smithy looked up as he worked the bellows to fire up the coals.

"We're the law from Alabama. We're looking for a colored girl and a fron-tiersman. He's tall with fair hair and blue eyes. You seen them?"

"Two like that have been here," the smithy said as he continued pumping with his powerful arm.

"Did they seek your services?" The man's reply warmed him. A wave of confidence spread through his body. For a moment, even his headache less-ened somewhat.

"Yes, I undid some cuffs on a girl for him."

"They say where they were going?"

"No, they went west is all I can tell you. Close to dark last night when I saw them going that way."

McCord narrowed his eyes. "Does this man live about here?"

The smithy shook his head. "I've seen him pass here several times before, but doubt he lives here. I know most of the farmers. He's not a farmer."

"No," Grissum agreed. "He's a wanted felon and she's a runaway. Where would this man stay around here?"

"You might try the tavern. It is up the road a small way."

"They were on foot?" Judson asked, looking over the various things the man made from iron.

"They were when they left here."

"Did they have horses?" Grissum asked.

"I can't tell you." The smithy shook his head as he shoved a strap of metal in the fire.

"Appreciate your help," Grissum said and they left the shop.

"Reckon they have horses?" Judson asked when they reached the road.

"I don't know. Let's go to the tavern and see what they know there."

The River Inn, the sign announced as the two men walked up to it. Liquor and boarding were listed on some crude hand-painted slabs tacked to the log wall. Grissum set down his pack on the rough split pole porch. He kicked at an over-curious, thin nosed mongrel interested in his pack. Aided by the force of his boot toe, the dog yelped and leaped aside. Grissum indicated for Judson to wait there and watch his things. He set his rifle against the side of the door and entered the tavern.

"Aye there, what'll be your pleasure?" a full busted woman of perhaps mid-thirties asked. Long blonde braids twirled around her face. Her rounded, exposed cleavage shook with a firmness that made him forget his purpose for a split second.

"An ale and some information." He took a place before the short bar.

"Tell your friend to come in. An ale I've got. Be two cents, the information is free." She drew him a mug and put it on the counter.

"Judson, bring the gear and rifles inside." The man quickly obeyed.

"I suppose he needs an ale, too?" She tossed those shoulder-length braids in Judson's direction.

"Of course."

"What can I do for you, now?" she asked, looking at the pair.

"A man named Broome, dressed in leather, tall, blue eyes, you seen him around here lately?"

She smiled slightly and nodded. "I have. His name is Zekial Broome, comes by here in the spring and fall to sell his skins. I guess over at Choctaw Landing. Nice gentleman for a mountain man. But I've not seen him in two days. Must have took his pack train back to the west. A fine man, he is." Her smile indicated something, as if she might have taken some pleasure from the man. "Do you need him for a guide?"

"He have a pack train?" Judson asked, his eyes widening.

"A fine one. Big sorrel horse and some mules, I think. He would make a good man to lead your party west."

"We ain't—"

Grissum's scowl cut off his assistant's words. He didn't want her to stop talking about Broome. So far, she didn't know they were Alabama lawmen, but his hopes were fast sinking that Broome was denned up in this village. Damn, they would need some stock to ride after him if he had left with his animals. Provisions, too. That, he had not even considered in his drive to rush over to this place and capture them. Obviously, if he had animals, Broome had used them to leave on.

"He have a place here?" he asked her.

"Broome?"

"Yes."

"Not him. He makes his place out under the stars, boys." She looked whimsical, then nodded as if she had digested a bit more. "Zekial Broome ain't going to live under a roof anywhere for very long. That ain't his kinda thing."

"He ever mention where he was going next?"

"Up the White River, I'd expect. You two know him very well?"

"Oh, we've heard about him." McCord frowned at Judson to keep him quiet. That dunderhead might say anything and throw her off telling them all she knew about their man.

"More ale?" she asked.

"Yes. Do you have food here?"

"Got deer stew on the stove."

"That will be fine. My companion and I will take some."

"Coming right up. Ale and stew."

"What are we going to do now?" Judson asked under his breath.

"Eat stew and drink this pretty lady's ale." Grissum raised his glass and speculated on her shapely body.

"I mean about him?"

"Follow him up the White River." He silenced Judson with a firm glare before she returned with their steaming bowls of stew in each hand.

"Your man about?" Grissum asked as they followed her to the rough table.

"I ain't got no man," she laughed. "Died, not two months ago, they tell me."

"Tell you?" Judson paused, a spoon of stew close to his mouth.

"Yeah, they tell me he drowned when the keel boat struck a rock up on the White River."

"This White River a wild one?" Grissum asked, blowing on his second spoonful after the first one seared the roof of his mouth.

"Dangerous enough. But then, Mike Turpin might have been drinking, too. He did that often and staggered around. They said he fell overboard when the boat hit the rock. I'll never know. He's gone."

"You run this inn by yourself?" McCord continued, motioning to the room around them.

"I did before he died and I'm doing it now."

"I can see you are very capable." He exchanged a smile with her.

"Capable enough. Here comes a customer." She went back of the bar and waited as a tall farmer came in. His homespun linsey pants and shirt were the mark of a man of the soil.

"Ah, Barley Whit, these men were just asking about your friend Zekial Broome—I never got their names...."

The man's eyes widened, and his jaw sagged. "You must be the law from Choctaw Landing."

Grissum swore to himself. Their cover was gone. And so, he now knew, were Broome and that damned girl.

V

"**HOW—HOW DID HE DIE?**" Zekial cleared his throat and looked at Betty Lou as they went inside the house. He could hardly fathom such a thing ever happening to his friend. They'd shared some good and bad times in the march with Old Hickory to New Orleans. A sourness rose in his throat at the mention of her loss. He could hardly keep it down.

She wiped away the tears on her linen kerchief and tried to regain her composure. He waited, feeling awkward standing on the puncheon floor before her. Wanting to comfort her, he was unsure how to do it. She was not a person he had ever felt comfortable hugging, as if she had an aura about her to hold him at arms' length. Even as they stood inside her doorway in the soft light of the fireplace and candle lamps, he wondered why he did not feel completely comfortable taking her into his arms at such a tragic time for them both.

"A week ago. One afternoon, he came in from the fields and just fell over in the yard holding his chest. In a very short while, he was dead in my arms. His heart was always strong, we thought."

"Children, your uncle Zeke is here," she announced and finished wiping away the last tears on the back of her long slender hand while the half dozen urchins gathered around them. Samuel, Gretchen, Mark, Luke, he could not recall the rest of their names, especially the toddler on the floor who waddled after them. This uncle business was new, and he wondered—did she expect him to take Kelsey's place? He had always considered her a very elegant woman. Still very handsome at twenty-eight and all that child bearing had done was improve her figure, putting some padding on her that looked appealing.

"You killed any b'ar lately?" the oldest boy asked.

"Samuel," his mother said exasperated. "That ain't no way to treat our guest."

"Good question for a boy. No, Samuel, but we saw plenty sign of them coming up here."

"There's lots of them around here."

"Good, maybe we can fetch some."

"Can I go? Can I go?" the chorus came from the others.

"Now, Samuel, he may be old enough, but bear hunting is serious business," he warned the younger ones.

"Uncle Zeke, what's that black boy's name that come with you?" one of the girls asked peering out in the dark.

"Ain't no boy," he said. "She's a girl. Her name's Tilly."

"She a real slave?" another child asked.

"Children, you are asking your Uncle Zeke too many questions."

"Can we invite her in?" the oldest girl asked.

"Certainly." Their mother looked at him as two of the children went outside.

"Fine, she's just a mistreated girl."

"Colored girl," Betty Lou corrected him.

He glanced at her and the frost in her eyes. Colored girl. He wondered what she would think about the Cherokee woman, Mary Horsekiller, who he had lived with two years ago. Red girl? Mary died of smallpox. Lucky for him that he had been vaccinated. She should have been inoculated, too. For that, he bore his own scars inside.

"She won't come in," the oldest girl, Gretchen, said.

"I'll tell her to." He excused himself and immediately realized that a greater wall had begun to grow like a post stockade between him and Betty Lou.

He remembered, as he crossed to the doorway, that Betty Lou came from Virginia. Her people grew tobacco and were slave owners. They were aristocracy, if they had such roles in a democracy. Once, after the war, he'd gone back to look up his army companion, Kelsey. At that time, they'd lived on the Cumberland River. He had noticed her ways that very first time when he sat at their dinner table; she was not from common folks. He expected her to have his soldiering buddy wearing a powdered wig any day. Obviously, she resented him having Tilly along with him.

———

THE SMALL BLAZE IN THE raw fireplace drove the chill from the cabin. The children were sleeping upstairs. Tilly had taken the horses to the shed and stayed there. Zekial sat in a ladderback chair and Betty Lou in a rocker beside it while they talked.

"Our cotton did good. Kelsey planned to buy two slaves to help him put out more acres next year." The chair runners squeaked lightly on the rough-hewn floor while she rocked. "I guess all that is gone for now."

"He already sell this year's crop?"

"The cotton, oh, yes. It brought twenty-five-cents a pound and we made two bales. Banker from Choctaw Landing was ready to loan us the money to buy another forty acres and those two slaves."

"Slaves sell pretty high, don't they?"

"Good ones, yes."

"Take a lot of cotton to pay for one."

"Yes, but this land is rich. You can't believe how rich it is."

"Floods, too, don't it?"

"Usually only for a couple of weeks, but not for long. We're far enough from the river. He picked this location because it was much higher."

"I sure don't know nothing about cotton." He shook his head, then leaned forward to study the dancing blue flame in the fireplace.

"You could learn."

"I guess." If he wanted to. The vision of a mule's tail all trimmed down to the bush with a breeching strap around his sweaty butt, lines hung around his neck and two tugs coming back to a plow made him want to gag. He didn't want to know about cotton growing, period.

"I swear." She rocked faster. The squeaking grew louder "If Kelsey had lived, in just five years we'd have built a real plantation here. Big house, fine horses, plenty of niggers to work it, even a big flock of sheep to keep the grass mowed down. Why it would have been finer than any old estate in Tennessee."

"I imagine it would have been," he said to get along. The soles of his feet itched to get up and go outside, but he owed her an audience for a while longer.

"Oh, it will be a real stately place, yet," she said. "I intend to build it."

"Be a job." He glanced at her for a second, then looked away. Clear enough, her words indicated she was possessed with the notion of owning a finer place than she was raised on. In Tennessee, there had been talk about her family's place, this and that. She even showed him a small ink sketch of the pillared house once.

"I guess this here land is better than Tennessee?"

"Ten times better here. We got to the Cumberland too late. All the good land was bought up, but we came here, just right. Folks around here, they plan to ask for statehood in a few years. It will be a slave holding state. My heavens, we are sitting on the greatest frontier land to ever open. Why this soil is ten times richer than any land along the Cumberland."

She drew a deep breath and threw her head back on the rocker to look at the ceiling. "Forty acres of cotton at a bale per acre would earn you five thousand dollars." She clapped her legs under the calico dress and looked over at him. "Can you even imagine that much money?"

"That's a fair piece, honest telling."

"A lot of money, it's a fortune. In ten years, this place will be farming six-hundred and forty acres or more. Half that in cotton." She took a sudden breath. "Maybe I'm going too fast." Her gaze locked on him as she went back to rocking.

He didn't answer her. His insides constricted at the thought—being in one place that long would strangle his very soul to death. Even the thought of having Betty Lou as his wife to share his bed and the wild notion of her eventually birthing him a son or two of his own did not negate his dislike of every day forcing men, black-skinned men, against their will, to farm his land. He tried to suppress the cold chill that ran up his spine. Despite the warmth from the fireplace, he shivered.

"You figure what three-hundred and twenty bales of cotton will bring a man in one year?" she asked, an edge of excitement in her voice.

"Quite a lot of money."

"I'd say quite a lot. Over thirty thousand dollars."

"You need anything done around here?" He wanted to change the subject. The matter of work mules and slaves made his stomach turn sour. He wanted no part of a cotton empire and she could talk all night—he would not be convinced of anything else.

"He planned to butcher nine hogs for our winter food supply that he'd fattened on corn. He was going to sell some of the meat and lard, but I guess I'll need all of them cured since he's not here to shoot deer meat for the table."

He watched her bite her lip and then fight back her sorrow. A knot swelled in his throat. Pretty woman like Betty Lou, widow at twenty-eight with six small urchins; her life wouldn't be easy without her man. He'd butcher the hogs and get them in the smoke house for her—the least he could do was take the time to help her out. McCord must be miles behind him, if he was on their trail at all.

"I'll get that butchering done for you," he said softly.

"Oh, would you?" Her blue eyes opened wider as she looked at him.

"Least I could do."

"Oh, Zekial, I knew the minute that I laid eyes on you tonight that God had sent you to help us."

"I'm not sure about that, but I'll get that meat in the smoke house for you." He waved his hand in an awkward gesture and rose to his feet, then stretched his arms over his head. "We better get some sleep. We've got plenty to do tomorrow."

"Yes." She stood. "I'll see you in the morning." Her eyes averted from his gaze. "You don't—have to sleep outside."

"Oh, I like being out under the stars."

"She's out in the cow shed, isn't she?"

"I guess. See you in the morning?"

"Of course," she said and walked him to the door.

"Good night," he said and headed off the porch. She never said another word. Once, he glanced back. The door was closed, and the red glow of the fire shone on the small glass window. He went to the shed to find his bedding. There would be plenty to do come sunup.

"That be you?" she asked from atop the fodder pile in the shed.

"Where's my bedding?" he asked under his breath.

"I figured you going to sleep in that house. Here's you a blanket."

"Good." He took it. Her warmth remained on the material as he wrapped up in it and settled on the pile of cornstalks. Tilly's faint musk still clung to the threads. He considered Betty Lou's ripe body while he closed his eyes and snuggled up in the blanket to sleep. Piles and piles of five-hundred-pound cotton bales everywhere—he dreamed of them, too.

————

AT DAYBREAK, HE DISCOVERED THE girl squatted on her bare feet in the doorway of the shed. He stretched and tried to shake the sleep from his head. The boy, Samuel, came driving the cows in, two small brindle Jerseys with their udders swaying from side to side. He carried a wooden pail over his arm.

"Morning, Mr. Broome. We going b'ar hunting today? I'll be through milking in a little while."

"Not today. You can call me Zeke, Samuel."

"You reckon my ma would like that?" He narrowed his eyes and waited for the answer.

"It'll be fine with me."

"Want me to help him milk?" Tilly asked Broome, then to Samuel, "You have an extra bucket?"

"Sure do."

"She'll help you."

"Wow, I never have any help to milk these danged old cows. Thanks a bunch for loaning her to me."

He started to correct him and decided it would do no good. He wasn't lending anyone. She volunteered to help him, but he doubted the boy would understand the difference, so he left them to the milking chores and went toward the house. The front door was open despite the nippy air, and he figured that was a welcome intended for him.

"Come in, Zekial. I have some coffee made."

"Morning, ma'am, and you girls and boys, too. I can smell it."

The aroma of home cured ham cooking filled the air along with other fine rich smells. The oldest girl twirled the Dutch oven top around on the ashes with a hook, then set it down to brown the other side. A familiar sound of iron cookware made him recall growing up in a cabin like this and his mother busy bustling around to get a breakfast on the table by the time the early morning chores were done and the mules were harnessed to go to work.

"How about some sourdough biscuits and redeye gravy?" Betty Lou asked, looking fresh as a new rose. Her snow-white apron shone as she hurried about and brought him a cup of coffee in a real china cup.

"Sounds like you aim to fatten me."

"I would if you'd let me," she said under her breath before she hurried off to supervise the younger girl frying eggs.

"Can Tilly eat with us?" the older girl—Gretchen—asked.

"I think Tilly would feel very uncomfortable eating with regular folks," Betty Lou said. "Why don't you fix her a plate and serve her outside?"

"Can I eat outside with her?"

"I guess, if you must."

"Thank you, Mother."

Betty Lou shook her head like she couldn't understand her daughter's reasoning. Undisturbed, Gretchen began fixing two plates. She set the cast iron oven on the table and drew out some steaming brown biscuits from it. She looked at Broome with a warm smile.

"Can you catch one?" she asked and before her aghast mother could stop her, she tossed one to Zeke.

"Gretchen, where are your manners?"

"Just like Dad, he caught it good, Ma."

"Thanks," Zekial said with a nod. Changing hands with the hot roll to save burning himself, he tore off a bite to eat. The sweet-sour rich flavor drew the saliva rushing to his mouth.

"These are wonderful," he said.

"We made them special for you, Uncle Zeke," the girl cooking the eggs said. "We usually eat grits for our breakfast."

"Millie, now don't you tell Uncle Zeke all our secrets," her mother tried to admonish her.

"The truth comes from the mouth of babies," Zeke said and patted the blonde-headed girl on the top of her head.

"They don't need to tell everything." She looked a little red in the face.

"I appreciate you all working so hard on this meal," he said, watching as she set the food out.

"No trouble. Sit down and fix yourself a plate. We have fresh butter to go on that bread. Millie, dear, get some for Uncle Zeke and some of those blackberry preserves."

He took his place, taking his hat off and hanging it on the back of the chair, still impressed with the rich taste of the sourdough. Under the curious eyes of the children, he filled his plate with fried eggs, ham, biscuits and thick gravy. Betty Lou refilled his coffee cup.

"Aren't you going to eat?" he asked looking them over.

"After you, Uncle Zeke," Millie said.

"That will never do. Get up here and dig in."

A cheer went up and the four younger ones clambered up on the benches opposite him and began to fill their plates despite their mother's warnings for them to behave and act like little ladies and gentlemen.

"Millie, use your fork, you aren't an animal. Clarence, don't pick up that ham with your fingers. Will one of you children cut up his meat for him? And save some for your Uncle Zeke. Oh my, that is why I didn't want them eating until you were through. They are like barbarians, I swear."

"No, just real healthy children," he said.

"Milking's done," Samuel announced as he entered the kitchen. "Tilly helped me. Her and Gretchen are eating on the porch."

"Join us," Zekial offered.

"Yes, sir, Zeke."

"Samuel!"

"Ma, he said I could call him that."

Zekial busied himself eating. To him, it looked like Betty Lou had her hands full making proper folks out of this army of kids. He didn't envy her any at that, but they were healthy and had good color. They took after their father a lot, stood straight-backed like the rest of the Scotch-Irish. Sharp eyes didn't miss a thing. Not stoop-shouldered and acting afraid of their own shadows. They'd all make real folks when they grew up, even if they didn't have all their manners by then. That wouldn't be because Betty Lou didn't try to teach them better.

"What're we going to do today?" Samuel asked, fixing his plate.

"Lay in the wood we'll need to butcher and get ready," Zekial answered. Sharpen knives and all that."

"When we going to kill them?"

"Samuel," Betty Lou chided, "butchering hogs is not something we talk about around the breakfast table."

"Yes, ma'am. I'm sorry."

"Tomorrow," Zekial said, "we can start."

"Good." Samuel turned his attention to his food.

Full to the brim, Zeke needed one more roll with butter and blackberry preserves. He prepared it with care, and then leaned back and savored each bite. "Mighty fine cooking, Betty Lou."

"Usual fare here." She began gathering up the children's plates. "Well, most of the time." She snuck a look around to see if one of her own would dispute the fact.

"No matter, I haven't had a meal like this in years." He leaned back in the chair, his stomach packed so tight that he wondered if he could even budge from his seat.

"You ever miss civilization out there?" She motioned to the west with her head as she picked up his dishes and utensils.

"Good food, sometimes."

"Don't you ever want a home, a wife, and children of your own?" Her gaze was inches from him.

"I guess all men dream of the like."

"Do you dream of all that, Zekial Broome?"

"And then I wonder if my soles would itch so bad I'd not sleep one wink in a feather bed."

"I could rub that out of them."

"Don't doubt it." He cleared his throat and rose to his feet.

She turned her attention to the table clearing and he thought he had escaped final captivity by a hair's breadth. Damn, she sorely needed a man—deserved a good one, but he wasn't cut out of the material necessary to cultivate cotton and live in one place.

Ready to go to work, he drew in a deep breath, amazed at the pounding of his heart. He went for his hat. The children, Samuel in the lead, followed him out, most of them leaving plates unfinished.

Betty Lou damn sure had her cap set for him to remain there, he'd seen that clear enough. He'd have to tell her about McCord and how he came to have Tilly with him. No way that he could stay there. Sooner or later, someone would come looking for them.

For the moment, though, getting things ready to butcher was his plan, he'd almost forgot about it, back there at the table facing her. He dried his palms on his leather pants. The cool wind swept his whiskers when he stepped out on the porch. Wouldn't hurt to shave either, he decided. Might make him feel halfway human again.

Everyone chopped or stacked wood at Zekial's direction. He and Samuel swung axes felling hickory and small oaks for the fire. It would take lots of fuel to heat the barrels of scalding water and later the fires for the lard rendering pots. Youngsters piled the sticks and wood they split into the wagon while the sun rose across the pale sky. Grateful the rain had been light, he swung the ax and chips flew.

Twice Samuel and Tilly drove the mules back to the house with a heaping load of wood to the killing bar and unloaded it. The site, marked by a thick pole hung between two great walnut trees, was where they would kill and scald the pigs. Then, they came back for more.

The colored girl worked beside the boy tossing wood with the fury of Samuel's I'll-show-you-spirit. Zekial listened while they talked about St. Louis and Choctaw Landing, her the guide and the boy asking questions until finally he asked if she'd seen the steamboat he'd heard had come up the Mississippi River.

"No, never seen that." She shook her head.

"Wish I'd been there when she steamed up," he said wistfully, then they resumed their wood-tossing competition.

"Time for a water break," Betty Lou announced, walking amongst them carrying a wooden pail and gourd dipper.

Zekial strained against his sore back muscles and set aside the ax. He smiled and waved her to the two hard workers at the wagon to be first.

Tilly deferred to Samuel. "You go first."

"No. Ladies first."

His mother crossed her arms and frowned mightily. "Samuel, she said for you to go first."

"Yes, ma'am."

The wind cooled Zekial's face, and with the side of his finger, he shaved off the sweat from his forehead. He had not missed the woman's words and their implications. Raise that boy so he knows where he belongs and that blacks come after him. Betty Lou couldn't help herself, she'd grown up with slave servants. She knew where they belonged. By her thinking, it was lucky she even let the wench drink at all.

"I'll bet you're thirsty?" Betty Lou asked bringing the pail over after they drank several dippers apiece.

"Yes, ma'am." Zekial took the dipper, watching her look about as if to be certain they were alone enough for her to speak.

"He's too young," she said under her breath.

Wide-eyed, he looked at her. What did she mean? The water choked him going down. He fought for his breath.

"I don't want him lying with her." Her dark frown punctuated her words.

"No problem."

"No, but there will be. No telling what diseases she has."

She glanced aside at them, and then impatiently turned back.

"Put your worries aside about that happening."

"I can't."

He dipped the gourd again. The little ones, stacking limbs, were too close for him to say anything else. This time he sipped the water slower, expecting something else to be said. She looked at him for his promise and when he nodded to reassure her and replaced the dipper, she went on to water the smaller children. Nothing would happen between them.

Zekial Broome had forgotten—white women worried about a lot of shit.

VI

WHICH WAY DO WE GO?" Judson circled his red mule impatiently in front of the tavern, jerking the reins back and forth.

"Whoa," McCord demanded and tried to make his black mule stand still so he could mount it. "We go west, stupid. We can't go east; the damn river is that way. I doubt this cussed thing would swim."

He stuck his left foot in the stirrup and hobbled around chasing the moving mule and trying to mount it. Rifle in his right hand, the reins in his left hand, he was ready to start caving the animal's ribs with his boot toe for not standing still for him. At last, he gripped the small saddle in front and back, hoisted himself up and threw his leg over. His other toe never found the stirrup.

The mule ducked his head between his knees and left out grunting like a boar hog and bucking as hard as he knew how. McCord made the first jump, the second one, he grew looser and the third one, daylight began to show between his butt and the leather seat.

Forced to toss aside his rifle to save it, his free hand shot for the saddle between his knees to find a grip. Too late, the mule's actions had drawn him face down over the animal's neck and threatened to throw him forward over the long, flattened ears. Not the place he wanted to be.

"Whoa, damn you!" he shouted, but at that moment, the mule ran out from under him and he landed hard on the road. The tail pumping action of the bucking animal looked like it mocked him as the mule headed westward kicking his hooves over his back.

"Well, don't just sit there!" he shouted at the wide-eyed Judson. "Go get that damn jackass."

Wincing in pain, McCord struggled to his feet and went to check on his rifle. He picked it up and checked it over with care. To his relief, it looked all right, and he started down the road to catch up with Judson who was lashing his mule to overtake the black one fleeing away.

"Come again," the innkeeper shouted after them from the porch.

"Yeah." Grissum thought again about the woman from the night before, about her deep feather bed and his hand busy kneading her spongy, naked flesh. The thought alone made him feel light-headed. She'd sure gotten excited. A real woman—too much for one night.

He drew a deep breath and tried to shake the curtain of memories and a lingering hangover as he strode westward on the wagon tracks, heading toward a copse of trees. That damn mule. Maybe Judson caught him in the trees. McCord hoped he had. Saddles and mules cost a fortune from that crooked dealer. Nothing he could do but pay it. Fifteen dollars apiece was too steep for wild mules and those skimpy seated saddles he had sold them. He began to hike faster, still no sign of Judson or that mule.

He crossed through the cool woods. Crisp dry leaves filled the wagon ruts. No sign of Judson, but other horse tracks dotted the ground, likely those of Broome and the wench. He had ridden west with a mule and three saddlehorses according to what McCord could learn from the farmer. The set of tracks were obvious; all they had to do was follow them. If that damn Judson came back with his mule, they'd push on and capture them in the next day or so. He knew for dead certain in his bones that they were closing in.

Out in the full sun again, Grissum found no sign of his associate or the mule. With his head down under his pack, he hiked on. Those two couldn't be far ahead. Besides, no sense in him waiting on his man. They'd save some time with him walking on. When he got his hands on that buck-skinner he'd choke him to death.

His shoulders shuddered, and he tried to regain his composure. No, not choke him—he'd hang him with a rope. That's what they did with the bad sorts, like slave stealers and murderers. McCord shook his head at that last thought, as if it tasted like a bad persimmon. Too late, though, his mind had already drifted back to the alley.

That damn little whore—he never killed her—he only shook her hard. She must have died of some disease while he slept. He'd never killed her—just shook her. She should have got his tool up. That was her business.

Grissum walked on, trying to scare off the bad thoughts of her. He needed to figure about this Broome and how to capture him. The man was like a fox, leading him on such a wild goose chase. He flexed his stiff back. The fall from the mule had hurt him and he made a face. Maybe it wasn't the fall off that jackass after all—maybe all that rutting last night with that barmaid might have done part of it.

Impatient for Judson's return, he stood on top of a stump and viewed the country to the west. Smoke from clearing fires streaked the western sky, yet no sign of his mule or the man. All he could do was keep walking.

In late afternoon, a man with a one-horse rig came along. By his black coat and vest over a starched white shirt, he looked like a preacher. When he drew up, they nodded at each other. Sporting a trimmed gray beard, the man sat with some bearing upon the spring seat of his open-topped cart. A dandy brown mare with a stylish small head pulled the rig.

"Gilbert Hankins, sir," the man offered removing his stove pipe hat.

"A man of the word?" McCord asked.

"Indeed. And where be you going, brother?"

"Down this road, a piece. My mule bucked me off and ran this way. My associate is chasing him."

"Climb on. Sugar, my fine mare, and I are going up this excellent road to a place where the Lord has directed me to build a new church."

Grissum put his pack and rifle in the back. He adjusted the pistol in his belt, so the barrel did not poke him in the privates and climbed onto the seat of the light cart. His weight made the buggy list hard toward him, but once seated, it righted itself.

Hankins clucked to Sugar and they were underway. A fine mode of transportation, Grissum decided looking it over. It damn sure beat a bucking mule that he had yet to see sign of.

"I did not catch your name, sir."

"Grissum McCord. I am an officer of the Alabama courts."

"Ah, a lawman. You're out here searching for a desperado?"

"Yes. A felon who calls himself Zeke Broome."

"Oh, yes, and his crime?"

"Assaulting an officer of the law and stealing a slave."

Hankins bobbed his head. "A serious infraction of the law indeed."

"Serious enough to send him to the gallows." Instead of Broome, Grissum's mind dwelled on this fine spring wagon as they skirted mud holes and the light-footed mare jogged on at a ground eating pace. If he and Judson had such a rig they could cover many miles in comfort while in search of this Broome. Then they'd return in like comfort and would have that black wench chained in the back. What would the preacher sell it for?

He wondered how to broach the subject. Obviously, the man liked the brown mare. Why shouldn't he admire the animal, she was well broke, and road hardened for she seldom blew and kept up a great pace. No matter. They needed this rig much worse than some hellfire and brimstone circuit rider. He drew a deep breath and set about considering how they'd take it from him if he would not sell it to them.

McCord looked all four directions—not a single sign of Judson or the mules and at the very moment when he needed him the most. No matter, he would own this outfit before sundown and not ride another bucking mule if he could help it. He winced at the pain in his lower backside. Maybe he'd kill that damn jackass whenever Judson brought it back.

"What faith are you, sir?" Hankins asked.

"Raised Baptist. I believe in river dunking to cleanse the soul," Grissum said.

"Good man. No sprinkling for me, either. Baptizing in the river, oh, yes. For no man shall enter the kingdom of God without being born of the water and the spirit, John 3:5. That's what saves their souls and opens the gates of heaven for them. Praise the Lord."

"Amen." McCord swore at Judson under his breath. When he needed him, he was always off, somewhere. Hell, with that damn contrary mule, he needed to come on right then. They'd take this spring wagon and mare and catch up with Broome in no time.

"I say that we stop here and relieve our kidneys," Hankins said, drawing in the reins. "That will rest Sugar, too. No sign of your man yet?"

"Not a hair."

They stopped under a great oak shedding its brown leaves like a gambler dealing from a deck. Walking on the crunchy carpet, Grissum went behind it to empty his bladder and Hankins went the other way.

"Ah, don't look now, but I believe the Lord has brought us supper, sir."

"What's that?" Grissum asked, busy straining to force a great stream out the end of his tool.

He'd be lucky if he didn't get the clap again between that one in Choctaw Landing and the barmaid the past night. He finished, shook it and put it away—so far nothing was wrong with it. He hoped it remained well—having the clap was no joke.

"Must be a dozen fat red fox squirrels in these trees about us. Perhaps you could shoot some for our evening meal since the Lord has provided them."

Grissum went for the rifle in the rig. Squirrels sent by God. He'd get them. Lifting his gun, he shot a fat one. It dropped from the sky and the preacher went to fetch it. Grissum reloaded and another stuck his head out to scold at them. The rifle shattered the quiet and the angry one fell, shot in the head. Then two more fell to his marksmanship. The fifth, he missed, and pieces of bark showered on them to mark his poor shot.

"We have enough," Hankins said and waved at him to stop as he finished skinning and gutting the last one.

"Got my partner to feed if he ever finds us."

"Go ahead then."

The rifle barked, and another squirrel fell into the leaves.

He reloaded and placed the walnut stock to his cheek and drew a bead in the high crotch. Small ears appeared, then a small fuzzy face. His curiosity drew him a lead bullet and the sixth one came tumbling through the branches.

"Praise the Lord," the preacher said and Grissum echoed an 'amen' and reloaded the rifle. He took lots of pride in his shooting. Nary could a man in his home country beat him. It was at least something to do, shooting squirrels to eat and plotting how to take the preacher's rig from him, to pass the time until he came across Judson.

VII

SHARP SMOKE FROM THE FIRES under the large kettles stung Zekiel's eyes when he straightened his tired back. Their first hog of the day was shaved clean. Tilly looked at him for his approval, her dark forearms and hands covered in wet shaven hair. The long knife blade in her right hand shone in the sunshine. He nodded. Their finished product looked all right.

Samuel scrubbed his hands in a wooden tub full of soapy water.

"Have we got this one good enough?"

"Yes. Time to gut him." Zekial pointed at the large, shaved barrow that lay on his side on the log table.

"I have a pan for the entrails," Betty Lou announced. "There will be fried liver tonight."

"Yes," Zekial agreed and took the two ropes that were tied in the singletree and tossed them over the killing bar that sometime soon he hoped would be lined with nine slaughtered pigs to chill overnight. He wished for a simple wood pulley, then he could have used a mule to hoist them, but there was not a block to be had on the place. He feared without one the rope might break when a mule pulled too hard on it and let a carcass drop onto the dirt. So, the pigs had to be hoisted by sheer human strength. Not gutted yet, he guessed the first pig lay dead at well over three hundred weight, the largest one in the fattening pen. He started with the biggest, because he knew his small crew of Tilly and Samuel would soon tire as the day wore on.

"You two ready?" he called as he tightened the rope thrown over the bar. The two rushed to his side.

"May I help?" Betty Lou asked.

"No, can't get any more on the ropes than three of us." He strained as they pulled and watched the hindquarters raise a few inches off the surface, and then they began to pull hand over hand. The hog's body started to come from the table.

New holds on the rope, his above theirs, together they towed hard and half of the porker came up. Each of them drew a deep breath, and new grips were taken, keeping the ropes taut. They leaned hard enough that the pole over their head bowed until at last the carcass swung free.

"Now, Samuel, quick, tie off the second rope," he said as he and she held the swinging pig in place. The rope threatened to rip from his hard fists as the two of them stood familiarly close. They gritted their teeth and pulled down with all their might.

"I've got it," he said.

"Good." They tested it, real slow-like. He shared a confident look with Betty that the tie-down would hold and they released their grips on the rope.

"Is that the biggest one?" Betty Lou asked.

"Yes—" He backed up, resting his butt against the table while he caught his breath. "I think the others will be easier."

"Good. I wish I could help you."

"We're fine. You'll have plenty to do in the next thirty minutes, I assure you."

"Here's a towel to dry your hands on," she said and handed him one made from a cotton sack.

"Thanks," he said, already busy putting a new edge on his knife while he considered the broad black belly of the hog and how he must slice it open and remove the intestines.

"Can Tilly and I kill and scrape the next one while you do that?" Samuel asked.

"Good idea. Drive another over." He liked the fact that the boy could think ahead like that. Thinking for himself and not wanting to lie down and rest was a strong attribute in a young person.

They coaxed the second porker with an ear of corn to a spot underneath the pole where they delivered a stunning blow to his unsuspecting head.

Zekial stepped in, raised him by an ear, and cut open his jugular vein, letting the red blood surge out. Before the pig quit shaking, they raised him in the air with much less effort than the last one and laid him on the table. Samuel began to bathe it with boiling water that the younger children brought them in small kettles to soak the hair, so they could begin the shaving process.

Zekial turned back to the business of slitting open the first one with his large knife. His incision begun, the sour smell of entrails filled his nose as the green-brown guts spilled into the tub Mary Lou had brought him. He freed the brown-lobed liver and saved the gall separately. He used an ax to split apart the chest cavity and soon the pink lungs were removed and the heart set aside in a pan with the liver.

The pale kidneys were dug out of the snow-white fat of the hog's back. A good healthy animal, he surmised from all he could see, as Betty Lou and Gretchen carried off the tub to sort out the tripe and to wash the intestines for sausage casings.

He dipped water from the oak barrel in a small pan and rinsed down the inside of the pig. The blood had begun to dry on his fingers. He washed his hands. There would be plenty of lard on these hogs to cook with and to make lye soap.

"You like killing hogs, Uncle Zekial?" Millie asked as she brought two small pails of water to refill the supply in his barrel.

"I don't mind. If you want to eat, I guess it is just a job needs to be done."

"I like to eat them, but I hate to wash out their guts. Your hands stink like hog poop for weeks after you do it." She wrinkled her nose at the notion.

"Maybe they'll keep you on the water bucket detail," he said under his breath as he emptied the pails for her.

"I sure hope so." Her shoulders slumped down in defeat as she started back to the spring for more water.

"We about have this one shaved. Want to check it?" Samuel asked.

"No, Samuel, you're in charge of that scrapping business. If that hog is shaved to suit you, I say it is good."

"He's ready. Should I get another one over here?"

"You sure may. You two give me your knives and I'll sharpen them."

"Can I kill this one, this time?" the boy asked.

"Yes, you may."

He caught the sly smile on the girl's face. She knew he was making a man out of a boy. Not much that her brown eyes missed, though she never said much. No lack of effort on her part either. All his life, he'd heard about them damn lazy blacks. No lazy bones like that in Tilly's thin body. He was proud of her as she raced barefooted after this new-found man on the Davis Plantation.

"He needs someone like you. A man to show him things that I can't," Betty Lou said under her breath, wiping her hands on her apron as she walked up.

"Some things you can show. Some things you have to learn for yourself."

Hands clean, she now parked them on her hips. "I know, but he's sure going to need a man the next few years to show him how."

He nodded. Wasn't nothing he could say. McCord was back behind them someplace. He wasn't likely to just leave them be here.

"We may need two days to get all of the hogs dressed," he said to warn her that he feared this was a bigger job than he thought at the start. It had been years since he'd killed hogs.

"I guess we have all fall," she said with a shrug. "I'd like to have them finished in the next few days."

Zekial nodded, not having the words Betty Lou wanted to hear or to explain why he couldn't stay. She waited a few minutes, awkwardly looking at him, then turned and walked away as Samuel and Tilly brought another hog over.

The blunt ax fell on the third hog's head and he assisted the boy by pointing out the jugular on the hog's throat. At last, Samuel's hands were christened in the surging blood when he cut into the animal's skin. A personal smile spread over his tanned face at his accomplishment.

"Is that enough?" Samuel asked, holding the pig up by the ear, ready with the dripping red knife in hand to do more cutting.

"It's enough. Let's hoist this one that you two scrapped so I can gut it."

"Yes, sir."

The copper smell of blood drew buzzards. Lazily drifting on the updrafts, the scavengers circled in great numbers. A few dipped low and stretched their ugly heads out, hoping to steal a bite. Some grew braver and landed. They were driven swiftly into flapping flight by the small children's noisy charges at them.

Samuel looked up from his scrapping. "Must be a hundred of them dang buzzards. I hate those things."

"They's got to eat, too," Tilly said.

"Yeah, but they get what's left."

"They's sure ain't going to be much of that around here," she said.

"You're right, Tilly, not much left around here at all," Samuel said.

Zekial finished gutting the second hog, then straightened the muscles in his stiff back. Betty Lou and the girls had carried off the tub of guts, despite his protest that he would do it for them. His hands washed and dried, he laid the edge of his knife to the stone and drew it slowly across to re-make the edge.

"Maybe you should use more water," Millie said, arriving with her pails.

"Why?" he asked in a quiet voice.

"If you don't use a lot, pretty soon that barrel will be full, and I'll be over there on that gut cleaning detail." She made a face.

"I'll dip some out then," he said privately.

Tilly gave him a private look of approval from her side of the hog on the table. Then she wiped the cut hair from her knife on the table edge, hitched up the waist of her skirt and went back to work.

Zekial used Millie's pails to refill the steaming iron kettles, then dipped more out of the supply to finish them. He handed them back to her with a grin.

"Thanks, Uncle Zekial."

"You're welcome," he said and went back to his knife sharpening.

———

BY NOON, THEY HAD OVER half the pigs slaughtered, moving at a far better pace than he'd imagined they would.

"Samuel," Zekial asked as everyone sat down on the ground to eat, "when we hang them in that smoke house, you know how to keep smoke going so the flies don't lay eggs on them and get maggots in the meat?'"

"Yes, sir. My daddy taught me that. He always said not to burn it down, but keep the smoke going all the time, night and day."

"Good. A man's family counts on him to keep that smoke going all the time."

They ate their lunch of fried liver and bread in silence.

Hard work had a way of taking the talk from people, even young ones. The smallest children kept up their buzzard control, and with the family hounds tied up at the house, things were well in hand.

Zekial knew he would need the carcasses high enough so a bear or wolf couldn't get into them overnight. Plenty of both in the surrounding country. They'd have to be watched over until morning.

"We may need a big fire or two and tend these carcasses all night, so the varmints don't get in them," he said.

"I could watch them with my rifle," Samuel said.

"We may need to take turns watching. All of us will be tired enough to sleep when we get all this job done tonight."

"If they get close enough they can smell them hogs. They'd sure try and get to this meat, wouldn't they?" Betty asked with a disturbed look on her face at the notion of something taking her winter food supply.

"I guess that smokehouse is bear proof?" Zekial asked, looking at the low roofed log structure.

"A couple bears tried to get in, but the hounds woke us, and Kelsey shot one of them."

"It was a boar bear." Gretchen sounded disgusted.

"He was rank tasting," Betty Lou said.

"Bad. He stunk up the whole house when we cooked him," Millie said with her food in her lap.

"We shot a boar hog once, when we were moving here," Samuel said. "Dad worried after he shot it that it would be rank, and he sure was, but he was mild beside that bear meat."

"Bears can be pretty rank tasting at times," Zekial agreed.

"That one we had was worse than rank." Gretchen made a gagging sound that drew her mother's frown.

"I am certain your Uncle Zekial does not wish to hear any more about nasty bear meat while he eats his meal."

"He didn't have to eat that stinking stuff either," Millie added.

———

NINE HOG CARCASSES HUNG SIDE by side on the bowed rail as the sun set on them. A huge kettle of fat simmered on the fire and the girls took turns stirring it. Another towering pile of the white fat trimmings was stacked nearby ready to be reduced into lard. There would be plenty for all purposes and some for Betty Lou to sell or trade for staples that she might need. Lard was a commodity not wasted on the frontier and a two-pound pail of it was as good as a deer hide and fetched a dollar at most outposts.

Samuel tied the dogs on stakes in a wide circle around the pole. Full of entrails and waste, they laid about acting half in a stupor, only able to pound their thick tails on the ground at the approach of anyone.

"They ought to let us know if something tries to get to our meat," he said and Zekial agreed as they headed for the house.

The butchering was over for the day. On the way to the house, Broome enjoyed the cooler wind on his face and hoped the temperature would drop even more as the night progressed. The cooler the meat the better it would keep.

"Tomorrow, I'm going to send Gretchen to Linder's Mill in a cart for some salt. We don't have enough curing salt on hand for that much meat. Could the black girl go with her?" Betty Lou asked. "I don't know of any problems, but the two seem to get along so well and you will need Samuel to help you all day. If you can spare her for a few hours?"

She stood on the porch in a fresh dress and clean apron as he and Samuel approached. Her hair in place, maybe her pride was what he had mistaken for her good looks, not that it looked bad—she always took note of her personal appearance and most women on the frontier with six kids sunk off into slovenly ways. That was it. A man could do a lot worse than have a neat, prideful woman.

"That's fine," he said. "She can go. She's a good hand with horses."

"Good, that's settled. They can go first thing in the morning and get the salt." She gathered up her dress to go inside. "Supper's ready."

"Yes, ma'am."

He looked back in the twilight shining on the eighteen halves swinging on the rail. Tired to the bone, he was pleased with his progress. With some effort, he climbed up on the porch. Somehow, between bedtime and his turn at guard duty, he would sleep well this night.

After supper, he left Samuel to guard the yard until midnight. When the living room clock struck the twelve o'clock hour, the boy was to come and wake him to stand watch the rest of the night. Everyone else turned in right after the meal. He and Tilly lay side by side on the cornstalk pile in their individual blankets.

"You's want to stay here?" she asked in a husky whisper.

"Why are you asking?"

"I ain't so sure. That woman, she needs a man, real bad like. She ain't bad to look at neither and she has a fair place here."

"I ain't no cotton farmer."

"Oh, you could learn to be one I reckon."

"What would I do when McCord came?"

"Kill him like you's going to have to do any way."

"Kill him?" He rose up in the darkness and frowned in disbelief at her words. He had no plans to kill anyone. For a long moment he studied her small dark form huddled under the blanket and then laid back down.

"You going to have to do that unless he kills himself before he gets here. Like if'n he falls in the river and drowns."

"What would you do if I stayed?"

"If you stay. . . I think I go on. She don't like no black female around her men no way."

"Don't you leave without me."

"I ain't going to run out on you. I's only going to leave if you decide to stay here with her is all."

"We both better watch out for McCord."

"I be watching real close."

"Good night."

"Good night."

———

THE DOGS RAISED A HELLUVA racket. The carrying on awoke Zekial from a deep sleep. Panicked by the noise of their angry barks, he wondered what had attacked them. He threw back the covers when the blast of the boy's rifle echoed among the hills.

"Here." Tilly handed him his rifle. Her small hand patted him on the shoulder. "I's coming, too."

"There may be several bears out there, you stay back." He pulled his powder horn over his head as he hurried off the stack. He stepped out of the shed and looked in the direction of the fires and noise of the dogs.

In the light of the bonfire, the boy was using his rifle for a club to ward off a huge black bear. He stopped, pressed a cap on the nipple, drew a bead and cocked the hammer in one fluid motion. The blast caused a mushroom cloud of smoke around the muzzle and the acrid smell burned his eyes and nose as he rushed through it.

His shot knocked down the bear, leaving it unmoving. To his relief, the boy was still standing, but how many more bruins were down there? Beyond the boy who was frantically trying to reload, he could see another dark form on all fours fighting with a tethered hound. Their raging snarls cut the night air.

"Here, take my rifle," he said and handed Tilly the gun on the run. In great long strides he covered the last hundred feet and drew out his tomahawk while he ran. He leaped past the boy, still loading his rifle, and drove his hatchet deep in the fighting bear's skull before he could do any more damage.

"Any others?" he asked, removing the bloody hatchet and searching around.

"Samuel!" Betty Lou cried out in a shrill wavering voice.

Holding up the tail of her white nightgown, she raced from the house. "My God, have they harmed you?"

"I'm fine, Ma. Fine," he said. His hands shook so hard he couldn't finish reloading his rifle.

"The boy did very well," Zekial said, "He defended the meat against two bears."

"Two bears. Oh, God, this wilderness that you brought me to, Kelsey!" White faced in the firelight, she stood holding her forearms together, her face raised looking up at the dark sky in terror.

"Why shoot, you ain't even scratched," Tilly said, examining Samuel as she leaned on Zekial's rifle.

"He got mighty close." Samuel took a deep breath and let it out.

"Too damn close. But Zekial done shot him dead just in the nick of time." They both laughed.

"What's so funny?" his mother demanded.

"They're upset," Zekial said.

"It's not funny to me."

"Come on, you need to go to the house." He started to turn her around, but she shook his hand from her shoulder.

"No. My eldest son was nearly eaten alive by wild animals. I won't leave his side until I am sure he is unharmed."

"I'm fine, Ma."

"Anyone who faces death like that and laughs is not fine. Hold out your arms, I want to see them."

Shaking his head, Zekial went and bled both bears. They had more work to do. The quicker they skinned and gutted them, the quicker someone would get to go to sleep. He had it gauged that he had slept his last wink for that night.

———

ELEVEN CARCASSES NOW HUNG ON the pole and he wondered if their weight would break it. In the cool predawn, he sliced the first hog apart with his knife and hacked bones with a sharp axe to separate the hams and bacon from the carcass. Betty Lou salted each section in a large tub as he handed them to her. With her hands, she rubbed in the coarse salt and then packed it over the bone ends.

"I could do that for you," the colored girl said.

"Why, thank you, Tilly. If you will, I'll go make breakfast and get the girls ready. I may have a dress that would fit you." She looked her over as if measuring her. "I think one of Krettchen's old ones would fit you for you to wear going to the mill with her today. And if I find one, you could keep it. You have done a lot of work here helping us."

"Thank you, Ma'am."

"You are welcome, Tilly. Samuel, go hitch the mules to the cart. Your sister is going with Tilly to the mill to get more salt this morning. Then when he gets that ready, all of you come to the house. By then we shall have breakfast fixed."

"We'll be there." Zekial shared a nod with Tilly. A new dress might be payment enough. It sure wouldn't hurt, even if it had been worn some. It would beat the rags she wore.

———

HIS HANDS SLICK WITH HOG fat, he lost track of the number of pigs left to cut up. The girls had left right after the morning meal to get the salt, Tilly wearing her new white and blue dress. He nodded his approval when she showed him. He could see the elation she had wearing it. If he had to buy it for her he would. Maybe Betty Lou would recall promising her that she was going to pay her with the dress for all the work she'd done.

As it drew close to lunch, Zekial noticed that Betty Lou kept her eyes on the lane while she salted the meat and set it out on the table between them for Millie and Samuel to wrap in cloth.

"They should be back any time," Betty Lou said.

"They'll be coming," he said to set her worries aside.

"You sound like him," she said. "He always tried to brush my frets aside."

"I guess that's a man's job."

"How do you do it, Zekial?" Samuel asked.

"It is a learned thing," Betty Lou said quickly and they all laughed.

Zeke flopped another half a hog on the butchering table. Two more carcasses to go. That made him feel a little elated. It wouldn't be long until her meat would be ready for the smokehouse.

"Something's coming in a hurry." Samuel stood on his toes to look from his side of the table.

"It's them! Tilly's running them mules hard. I told her not to run them."

"Zekial! Zekial!" With the frilly new dress above her knees, Tilly leaped from the wagon and raced to him.

"What's wrong, girl?"

"Grissum McCord! Grissum McCord! He be at that mill right now!"

VIII

THANK YOU, LORD, FOR THIS food you have provided...." the preacher, Hankins, went on and on. Grissum had forgotten how long-winded one of them holy men could be praying over some half-cooked squirrels. Hankins worked hard not to leave out all the lost souls in Africa, India, and Arabia and on the frontier that needed blessed while Grissum sat on a log growing impatient and waiting to say amen and start eating his supper. He was tempted to go ahead and kill him right then.

Not a peek of Judson. He might have lost that dumb scudder. Be a damn shame for a man who had been his shadow for five years to up and disappear chasing a damn mule, dropping off the far edge of the earth out there in no man's land.

"Amen!"

"Amen." McCord reached for the closest bit of squirrel meat he could lay hands on and stuffed it in his mouth.

"What about your friend?" Hankins asked, taking a leg from one squirrel by twisting it free of the browned carcass.

"He's a big boy, guess he can find his way."

"You and him partners?"

"Yes. I was thinking on that," Grissum tossed some bones aside, then went after more. "We been working together for five years now."

"You reckon we should go look for him?"

"Wouldn't know where to start—he's out there, I guess, chasing that mule that got away from me." He took a whole squirrel from the skillet and began to gnaw on the meat. Lucky for him that he shot six. He could eat four himself.

"He'll come along," McCord said between bites. "He knows I'm going up this road. We've been separated before and he came up my back trail like a coon hound."

"My, such trust, sir." Hankins looked impressed.

"He knows we've got to get this slave stealer and then take that wench back to the man who she belongs to."

"Must be exciting work."

"Sometimes, but usually it's like a blood hound running down a possum. They ain't very intelligent, you know. They just run off in the swamp or woods. They get their ass lost, and about right then, most of them want to go back to their home. They get out there with no food, no money, but they can't go back because they're scared they're going to get whipped for running off. See, when me and my partner find them, they nearly hug us." He bit some more meat off the bone and with his mouth full, he continued to talk. "Then they cry, 'oh, please take us home, boss'."

"Like children away from their father?"

"Yeah, like that." He wiped his greasy fingers on his pants leg and reached for another squirrel.

"We can't understand their animal-like qualities, can we?"

"Yeah, pretty animal-like," Grissum replied. He recalled the mulatto wench they'd brought back from Georgia, too good looking for her own good. She went and convinced that white trash boy she'd been laying with they needed to go to Florida and the Spaniards would hug them.

One sunup, he and Judson found the two of them in a hammock under a grove of big oaks with Spanish moss curtains, sleeping like babies. The sun's rays shining across the little opening, birds singing in the tree tops, both asleep with their folded hands for pillows like they'd gone to sleep praying.

He'd grabbed that trashy boy by his uncombed hair, jerked him to his feet, set the edge of his big knife to his throat and demanded to know why he took her.

"I—ah... I ah—"

"Do you know what we do to slave stealers?" he asked in the boy's ear, holding him up on his toes by a fistful of his hair. Meanwhile Judson fastened the chains on her shapely ankles and she cried out for him not to hurt that trashy little boy.

"We cut a slave stealer's throat. You know what I'm fixing to do to you?"

"Yes sir—I mean, no sir. Don't do that to me." His eyes grew larger, fear made him quake.

Grissum laid the knife-edge to the boy's neck. The sharp steel sliced the white skin dirty with crillies and road dust. In a vicious slash, he opened it to the windpipe and that silenced the boy's screams. He tossed aside his kicking body, then deliberate-like wiped the bloody knife on his pants—finished. He looked at the silent girl in chains on the ground.

Her dark eyes glared with a deep hatred at him. Good, he always liked to take on a real mad woman. Somehow, they made better lovers. This one might think she was something, but when he got through with her she'd beg to go home— his fingers fumbled with the buttons on his fly—yes sir, she'd sure enough beg to go home.

"You must see a lot of interesting country, being all the way from Alabama?" Hankins asked, forcing him back from his thoughts.

"Most niggers run north. I been to Kentucky more times than I can count. Damn do-gooders—and they call themselves Christians. They hide them out."

"False prophets."

"Yeah, they sure are."

Hankins got up and put some more wood on the fire. McCord narrowed his eyes and studied the man fussing with the blaze. Whenever Hankins fell asleep he aimed to kill him and take the wagon and horse for himself. Somewhere up ahead, Broome and that bitch were still ahead of them. Before dark, he had spotted old tracks of those four animals he was sure belonged to the buck-skinner on the road.

"You ever been to Frog Gap, Tennessee?"

"I think so," Grissum said to make conversation.

"My wife Alma Mae is buried there."

"Been recent?"

"No, five years ago."

"You never married again?"

"No, she was the love of my life. I courted her at an early age. I was ten and her seven. We were made for each other. I thank the Lord that we had those good years together."

"Any children?"

"No, he never blessed us with any. And you, sir?"

"Got one boy, rest girls. First wife, Tressie, she died of poison."

"What kind of poison?"

"Food kind. Doc said it was poison, he thought it was something rotten she put in the stew." Not true, what he told Hankins, but no one ever found out different. He'd had all her nagging and slovenly ways any man could take. Hogs could have lived in that filthy cabin no better than she kept it. She'd sit on the porch and smoke her damn pipe and rock and wouldn't even change the diapers on her own baby. Then she'd complain when he came home about having to lie for him—hell, all she ever did was lie on her back for him.

"Did you remarry?"

"Yes, a good Christian woman."

"Ah, and she's raising your children in a Christian home?"

"Yes, she is."

McCord's mind drifted to Clara. That dark eyed Dempsey girl, who'd waited up in the woods on the mountain trail to stop him and talk to him. She knew damn good and well that he was a married man. He grinned at the thought of her hanging on those saplings and twisting around showing off her ripe young body in that short calico dress while she asked him all those dumb questions. When he had enough of her talk, he grabbed her, put her on the ground, shoved up her dress, ripped off her sack panties and showed her what happened to little girls that stopped big men in the mountains.

Never mind that she liked it so durn well that soon after that first time he took her, he knew he had to get rid of that trashy Tressie. They met several times in that glade on Willow Mountain. He didn't believe he could live without her body. She was showing big when Harley Northcut married the two of them—two months after his wife's funeral.

"So, you have a Christian wife?"

"Yeah."

"And the children, have they been baptized?"

"Boy was. Rest will be when they're old enough. This place that you're going to?" he asked the preacher.

"Linder's Mill, the new settlement."

"Yes, do they know that you're coming?"

"Did they know the Lord was coming to Jerusalem in the final days?"

"I don't know. I wasn't there."

"Well, of course, none of us were either, except in the spirit and scripture. No, I shall join those good people and then at a prayer meeting I shall announce my intentions to build a chapel in their midst. I am certain the Lord is in their heart as he is in yours and mine. They will welcome a pastor in their settlement and we shall proceed with building a temple for the Lord's worship."

"I see. I'm going to sleep." An itinerant preacher and widower on his way to a place where he wasn't expected—perfect. All McCord had to do now was wait until the old windbag finally went to sleep.

"Shall we pray for your associate who must be lost in the night and for his safe return, sir?"

"Be fine," he said, almost ready to scream at the man. Why didn't he just go to sleep?

"His name is Judson?"

"Yes, Lighe Judson."

The night's prayer for Judson's safety proved longer than the supper one that made the meat cold before he finished it.

"Amen."

"Amen"

At last, after many more words, Grissum laid on the ground in his blanket. Two questions plagued him. How long before Hankins went to sleep? How would he kill him? He needed a club.

A gunshot was too loud, even though no one was likely to hear it. A knife would be too messy. He needed a club.

Somewhere a wolf howled in the distance. His deep mournful cry made the hair stand up on Grissum's neck—that bastard out there knew what he intended to do. Knew it like that witch at home, Maudie Sumpter knew things before they happened. Even when he only had begun to plan how he would poison Tressie, Maudie came by and told her to watch what she ate.

"Damned old witch," Tressie swore when she left, taking the corncob pipe out of her mouth. "She's a trying to put a spell on me. I always watch what I eat."

"I think so," Grissum agreed. Maybe they'd blame Maudie for poisoning her.

Toadstool mushrooms, he'd been told all his life, they was bad poison when they got ripe. The first batch that he fixed and slipped in her food only made her sick to her stomach and crazy in the head. While he watched and waited for her to die, she went around the house babbling and holding her stomach saying that he had gone and got her pregnant again. Later that night, so that she wouldn't go to her death disappointed, he tried to knock her up—funny thing, she even acted like she liked it for once. Amazed at her performance, he about decided that he should have fed them mushrooms to her years before.

A week later, determined to send his sloppy housekeeper to her maker, he had a double dose powdered up and ready to treat her. She never even tasted it in her bowl of stew that night either. The onions she put in it were about rotten, so how could she have tasted anything. In a couple of hours, she got sick like before, but in another hour, she slipped off in a coma. He called for the doctor to show his concern. When Doc Crater got there, he couldn't wake her. After he sniffed the stew left on the stove, he wanted to purge Grissum.

"That's rotten, man. Did you eat any of it?"

"Some."

"You must have a cast iron stomach, that stuff would kill a strong hound. That woman have no sense at all?"

"Not much. Tressie never was much of a housewife. You can look around this house and see that."

"Hmm," Doc snorted out his nose. "You better prepare yourself, Grissum McCord. I'd say in an hour, your wife'll be God's responsibility, the way her heart and pulse have slowed down. You feeling all right?"

"Oh, a little sick." He held his stomach.

"Here, take these pills. They'll purge you and you'll be all right."

"Thanks Doc," he said. After Crater left, he threw them away.

Following Tressie's funeral, the boy and girls went to stay at her sister's; he had to go chase down a half-dozen runaway slaves for their owners. Unbeknownst to him, when he got back in three weeks, Clara and some of the neighbors had scoured that cabin clean.

He put his horse in the corral the first night he came back. His back ached from the long ride and he dreaded going inside that pigsty. Tuckered out, he climbed on the porch and frowned at the open door as he braced himself on the post. Be better than sleeping on the ground, he looked back at the sunset.

Then without a word, Clara stepped in the doorway and smiled at him. The setting sun shone flat across the mountains on her. She pulled a little ribbon at her throat and that dress fell off her like a feather. The golden light danced on her tight apple-sized breasts and her belly beginning to swell with their first one. Her little triangle of pubic hair glistened like polished copper and the spears of sundown shone like fire on her skin as she smiled at him.

Grissum's recollection forced him to sit up. If he'd been this hard in the alley that night Broome stole the wench, why that damn little tramp would still be working the streets. He moved back the covers as he listened to the Reverend Hankins' rhythmic breathing.

He rose slow so as not to wake the preacher and went to the fire. There squatted on his heels, he tested several of the sticks. None felt green enough. He hated a sloppy job. Maybe he would use his knife on the man. Then, feeling around, he found a pine knot.

In his hand, he hefted the club. Good enough. Stealthily he crossed the ground until he stood over the prone, blanket wrapped Hankins. He raised the club over his head with both hands and then delivered the blow with all his force.

One grunt was all the man made. McCord struck him twice more to be certain he was dead. Each time he enjoyed watching the skull crushing effect of his blow. After the third hit, Grissum set the weapon down and began to check Hankins's pockets. In his pants, he found a purse with twenty dollars. A large sum for a preacher, but no doubt it represented his entire life savings. Several letters in his coat pockets which Grissum couldn't read, so he burned them in the fire.

He found a good knife and a compass. Reading glasses in another pocket and of course, a Holy Bible. Inside the cover, it had Hankins' name in it as well as family member birthdays and weddings. He sat cross-legged at the fire and burned its pages a few at a time. There were so many books to the bible, it required over an hour to see them go up in flames. The leather cover burning made a stink, but with added wood it, too, was soon unrecognizable ashes.

Seated on the ground he removed the man's boots and tried them on. They were large, but much better made than his own.

When he dragged the still body out a hundred yards into the dark woods, McCord left his own shoes there with the corpse. Out of breath, he returned and checked around for anything that he might have missed. Nothing. Then he took Hankins's blankets and put them with his own to use against the night chill setting in. He lay down and went to sleep.

For breakfast, as the sun came up, he had hardtack and cheese. No sign of Judson. McCord was done worrying over him. He'd have to find his own way. The capture of this Broome and that girl was more pressing. After a drink from the nearby stream to wash down his dry breakfast, he hitched the mare to the wagon and started northward.

The mare moved out smartly and held her wind. He was beginning to take lots of pride in her. As he drove, he noticed flocks of buzzards in the sky far to the west. A dead cow or pig, no doubt, lay out there to gather that many of those birds of carrion. He rested the mare and wondered how much further to this mill. He checked the load in his pistol. All looked ready—he might need it to kill that buck-skinner. Satisfied, he pushed it back in his belt, clucked to the smooth driving horse and went on northward.

He dodged the holes where rigs had been mired and stuck. Sometimes he was forced to bring the mare to a halt, stand up, and look all around to find a fresh way to skirt the worst ones. Midmorning, the smoke of cooking fires appeared over the trees and the sharp scent carried to his nose. He could hear dogs barking and he grinned. Settlement ahead. And, probably, Broome. He clucked to the mare and she stepped up the pace.

The land opened to more prairie, and farms dotted the land. A mill structure came into view beside a log dam that leaked, but obviously held enough water back because the undershot power wheel turned. He could hear the clatter of machinery—rocks grinding corn, an unmistakable sound. Several riding horses and saddle mules were hitched in front of the mill and their owners leaned on their rifles as was the habit of men on the frontier.

He looked them over, especially the ones dressed in leather for any sign of

Broome. None of them looked familiar. Then he reined the mare up and nodded to them. Dismounting heavily, he drew his own rifle out of the back.

"Don't you move an inch, Mister," someone ordered. "Put your hands up, I've got you covered."

He did as he was told. "What's wrong?"

"I know this wagon, Mister. It belongs to a preacher called Hankins from Tennessee and he would never have parted with that sweet little driving mare for no amount of money."

"You got this all wrong. He was down at New Castle and he rented this rig to me so I could head off a criminal headed up here. I have papers in my pocket to show that I am a lawman from Alabama."

"Move around over there," a gangly man said, looking down the barrel of his rifle at McCord. "Don't try nothing."

After McCord did as he was told, someone took his rifle, powder horn, possible pouch and another cautious-like man removed his knife and pistol, and quickly stepped back. Two other farmers joined the first man and covered him with their rifles. His heart gave a flutter.

"Check my papers. I am a man of the law." He indicated for them to look in the possible pouch.

One man removed his wallet while several more crowded around to see what he had found. None of them could read, he decided, impatient for someone to read it out loud to them. At last one man did that.

"Says here that this is Grissum McCord and he is an officer of the supreme court of the state of Alabama."

"Boys, listen to me," the first one behind the rifle pleaded, "I knowed this preacher for several years back home and he ain't about to loan that good mare to just anyone. This guy might have stolen them papers too, like he did this mare and wagon."

"I'm Grissum McCord. You're all wrong."

"I'm Thomas Jefferson, too. Can you prove it different?"

"We'll lock him up in that storehouse and someone can send a boy back to New Castle on horseback and ask Hankins if he rented him this rig. Then we'll be sure."

"Fine, do that. Waste of time, but you do that," Grissum said. "But I can tell you right now that you're messing with the law of Alabama. I want you to know that."

"Alabama can go eat shit," a burley woodsman said in his face as he took hold of his arm. Another muscular man took his other and they began to drag him across the yard to the fresh chinked building.

"Wait, this is a mistake—"

Then, to his disbelief, he caught a glimpse of her. That wench in a white dress. And he was sure their eyes locked, if only for a moment.

He watched in numb shock as she scampered into a wagon with a teenage white girl right after her. While those two apes drug him away, he watched helplessly as two men loaded some sacks in the back of their rig and that damn black bitch with a look of fear in her eyes took the lines to drive. The white girl whipped them mules and they tore out.

Helpless, he tried to look back and see them. The strong hands on his arms belonged to lumberjacks—he knew they were powerful, so strong he couldn't jam his heels down and stop them or pull free to see which way she went, but the clatter of the wagon leaving told him she was gone, as he protested his imprisonment.

"You can't do this to me," he said. When they did not reply to his protest, he asked, "Who were those girls?"

"Which ones?" the burly one on his left arm asked.

"Them in that wagon that just left here."

"I know that trick. You want me to look away. I never seed no girls. Your ass is going in jail until we learn the truth about that there wagon and horse."

Hurled face first through a rough-hewn doorway, Grissum landed hard on the wood chips on the floor. The door slammed, and his jailers bolted it with a bar on the outside. Dark as a tomb. The only light that entered was at the eaves of the shake roof where some managed to come in.

A fine kettle of fish he'd fallen into. Jailed by partisans, and on top of that, he'd even found that damn girl and she'd gotten away.

With his clenched fists, he pounded the wood chips on the ground beside him. It wasn't fair. Here he was with Broome and that black slut within his grasp and instead of arresting them . . . he sat helpless—a prisoner, himself.

Damn it!

IX

ZEKIAL, YOU CAN'T LEAVE NOW." Betty Lou's long fingers grasped his sleeve and her blue eyes brimmed with tears. "Please don't!"

He swallowed hard, half-sick at the notion of leaving her in such a limbo, but he had no choice. The die was cast. Like the old Indians said, the bones were tossed and his came up, fight or run.

He chose to leave.

"There's things I can't explain with the children here." He looked about at their forlorn faces where they stood in a semi-circle acting hang-dog over the news of his leaving.

"All of you, go to the house!" she said with a wave of her hand. She drew in a deep breath that made her long breasts rise under her dress. With disappointment written on their faces and their heads bowed, they obeyed her and started their trek toward the structure.

Millie paused and glanced back at him. "Uncle Zeke, we still love you even if you to have to leave with Tilly." Seeing the impatient look on her mother's face, she hurried off with the others.

"We have to talk—alone." She looked around for the black girl, but Tilly had gone with Samuel to gather their stock. She couldn't see them anywhere.

"I'm sorry," Broome said. "I can't explain everything that happened, except back in Choctaw Landing, a drunken slave chaser was beating her. I stopped him."

"Oh, my God...." She held her hands to her mouth and her face paled in shock. "You *stole* her?"

"Yes, I did. And this McCord, who I hit over the head, is coming after me."

"What will you do, Zekial?"

"Head out in the Territory. He's no match for me out there. I'll lose him."

"Zekial, don't you know what they do to slave stealers?" Her eyes narrowed with deep concern.

"Not really, and quite frankly, I don't give a damn. She's a human being and he was lashing her—she'd been a horse, I'd have done the same thing to him."

"But slave stealing...." Her gasp of disbelief audible, she looked completely taken aback by the knowledge of his actions.

"Betty Lou, I can't endanger your family by staying here—"

She threw her arms around his neck and began to kiss him. Her hot tongue like a serpent sought his mouth and the fiery need of a real woman came against him. He closed his eyes but resisted the strong temptation to take her in a great hug. As if realizing his intentions were not to be overwhelmed by her fierce actions, she relented, lifting her face from his to give him an instant to reconsider. Then she dropped her arms to her sides in defeat.

"I'm sorry. I've shown myself a hussy and, obviously, to no avail. You certainly must think more of her black ass than a decent woman who would help build your kingdom and have your heirs here on this earth."

"It ain't you. It ain't here. It's the way things have happened, Betty Lou. I don't respect you any less. You have children to raise and I understand about your dreams for this place—"

"No, you don't, or you would stay!" Her face twisted into a mask of flushed defiance. She raised her chin and drew her shoulders up straight.

He began to feel the distance between them. Though they still stood less than a foot apart, the gulf widened and the feeling that he was trespassing in her personal arena became obvious.

Out of respect, he stepped back and glanced around.

"What is taking Samuel so long?" She slapped her hands against her sides. To find four head of stock? If that wench has seduced my son—"

"You always want to think the worst things, fine." Her accusation made him angry. That girl had helped her and done the work of two people the entire time they had been there. If all she could think about was that, he had no time for her petty ways.

"I meant what I said about them."

"She's not an animal."

"She's a black whore."

"Betty Lou, you're upset, and I can understand that. But don't talk about that girl like that."

"Just because you're blind to the truth, I'm not. My son doesn't need to experiment around with a diseased nigger slut."

"They're coming now. I'll hear no more of your vicious tongue." He looked at the woman hard enough to silence her

"I'll talk like—"

Filled with rage, his hands shot out. He grasped her by the upper arms and roughly drew her face to within inches of his. His breath raged out his nose as he glared at her. "You will lower your voice and act decent. We've butchered your hogs for you and they're ready to smoke. That girl did everything we asked of her and more. She's no business of yours nor do you have to tongue lash her to show her your position in life. Am I understood?"

"Yes." Despite her agreement to his terms, her blue eyes were frosted over with anger. He set her down. She rubbed her upper arms briskly where his fingers had dug into the flesh.

Emptiness began to grow in his stomach. He could see the piles of hams and sides wrapped like mummies in white cloth on the table. Salted and ready to go in the smoke house, she and the children would make it until spring. Nothing else he could do for them—it was time for him and Tilly to leave.

"Good day, Betty Lou." He turned and strode rapidly to the barn. He needed to get packed and be on his way.

"They were way down by Hannigan's," Samuel said as they tied them to the rack. "We had a heck of a time finding them."

Tilly nodded to confirm his words.

He tossed the blankets on the mule. "No problem."

"Tilly told me about this McCord. He's a mean man, ain't he?"

"Mean enough." He put the crossbuck on Jim's back and drew the girth up tight.

"Son, you don't understand about slave chasers," Betty Lou walked over, interrupting them. "She belongs to another man. It was McCord's job to return her to her rightful owner. Obviously, she was disobedient, and he was punishing her."

"But he was drunk?" Samuel asked in disbelief.

"There is no great heroism in interfering with a slave and her overseer."

"But Ma—"

"Don't Ma me. Go to the house, Samuel. These people are trying to poison your mind. That nigger wench needs to be sent back to her rightful owner. Go to the house right now!"

Zekial glanced around for Tilly, but she was gone. He turned back and Betty Lou was pointing the way to the house for the protesting boy as they both crossed the yard. He had no time for their nonsense and picked up the packsaddle for the bay mare. With the pads in his other hand, he went to saddle her up.

He looked again. Tilly brought out the saddle and blankets for his sorrel. She wore her old brown rags again. What had she done with the dress? He hurriedly finished saddling the mare and went for the panniers. She could saddle Red by herself. He bucked up the heavy buffalo-hide pack on his knees, and with a heave, hung it on the left side of the mare. The butchering had made his back sore and to lift the packs challenged those muscles.

"You say they'd arrested McCord?" he asked her.

"They sure was dragging him away at gunpoint is all I seen."

"I wonder what for."

"I sure don't know, but I was grateful they had him when I sees him there. Then them men from the store, they load that salt in that wagon and I whip them mules out of there."

"What did you do with that dress?" He started loading the pack mare.

"I hung it up in the barn where they can find it."

"How come?"

"She never gave it to me." Her eyes narrowed to slits as she looked toward the house. "She never liked me, and I sure not be a wanting to be reminded of her all the time I be wearing it, either. You understand?"

"It looked nice on you."

"Maybe so, but it didn't feel that good, 'cause of her."

"I understand." He straightened up. "We better ride. Mount up."

She obeyed, and in the saddle, moved the gray in close to him.

"You and him—her man that died. You was real good friends?"

"Real good friends. We went to New Orleans together with Old Hickory and whipped them British." His rifle in his hand, he mounted the sorrel and took up the bay's lead, hitched the mule to her halter and started out.

He could hear the children shouting goodbye at him from the house. Filled with guilt, he raised his hand to wave and decided not to go up and hug them. Neither Betty Lou nor the boy were in sight. The little ones filed inside—all but Millie, who kept waving until her mother came out, grasped her by the arm and whipped her fanny as she dragged her into the house.

Burn all the bridges behind you, old son.

He sighed. His private war with Grissum McCord had begun. Tilly's stern words in the darkness of the shed that night about killing the man still niggled his conscience. For the present, he chose to run, leave no links to the past.

He rose in the stirrups and set Red into a lope.

———

THEY RODE NORTHWEST AND ARRIVED at Batesville on the second day. Mules, hinnies and horses laden with dead bears filled the streets. Even ox-drawn sleds were piled high with dead bruins that clogged the streets. Red shied from the smelly conveyances loaded with them and the mule took rollers in his nose as he snorted at the strong coppery smell.

"Where did they get all them?" she asked.

"Lots of bears around these parts. We must have seen two dozen live ones ourselves the past two days."

"I know, but they must be a thousand dead ones here," she offered, holding in the gray horse who pranced and acted upset at all of them.

"Howdy, stranger, welcome to Batesville," a tall man in a brown suit addressed him in the center of the street.

"Good day."

"You wouldn't be needing work now, would you?"

"What kind of work you offering?" He halted Red, and then laid the rifle over his lap to listen to the man.

"I see you've got a set of fine stock and a helper. I'm Simon O'Leary and my business is, of course, bear rendering. I could use another hunter to bring them to my plant up the street." He gave a toss of his head to show where it was located.

"What do you pay?"

"A dollar a bear for full-size animals, and you get to keep the hide."

"Fair price."

"You and her could make hundreds."

"We thank you, sir, but we have urgent business in the west that calls."

"Beaver trade, huh?"

"Aye." With that, he booted Red around a high-wheeled cart pulled by two donkeys. His packhorses shied at it and pulled on their leads. Two black men in irons sat in the back wrapped in dark blankets. They smelled unbathed, worse than the dead bears' strong odor.

A gray-bearded man sitting on the front of the bed acted unheeding of the traffic as he tried to drive the burros up the street. Stoop shouldered with age, he barely glanced up from under the edge of his floppy hat when they passed him, but Zekial noticed he looked hard enough at her—like a man did a good horse, appraising its strong and weak points in passing.

The blacks in his possession were either recovered slaves or for sale, for they were not only chained to each other, but to the cart as well. Apparently, they'd been chained that way for some time and this was why they smelled so bad.

"Hold the horses," he said and dismounted before a mercantile store. On the ground, he handed her the reins and headed for the store.

He nodded politely to a lady under a slatted sunbonnet coming out the door, then stepped inside the darker store piled high with trade goods. The scent of vanilla, coffee beans and harness oil assailed his nose. He walked through the wares and found a clerk. A balding man about his own age came forth and gave him a nod.

"Sir, my name is Abraham. What may we do for you?"

"Zekial Broome. I need two good wool blankets. I also want to look at your hats and a pistol. I could use a good one."

"We have several, sir. May I show you the hats first, Mister Broome?"

"Zekial's fine. Certainly, Abraham."

The man led him to the stock of hats. There were cheap ones of felt and better-made ones spun of beaver hair. The quality ones were obvious. He pointed to one with a round top and wide brim.

He tried it on and examined himself in the smoky looking glass that the man held up before him. An expensive purchase, but the hat would stand many rains and snows.

"How much?"

"Two dollars, sir."

A lot of money for a simple hat. He considered his grizzly image in the glass. Setting the hat to the side, he readjusted it to sit straight on his head. Unshaven, his wiry beard spilled all over like wild vines. With his buckskins glazed in dirt and spotted with hog blood and grease, he looked the total part of a wild man. He studied the hat in the reflection. It looked good enough.

"I'll take it. And that small one, how much is it?" She needed some head cover.

"Seventy-five cents."

"Good enough. Let's get those blankets, then we'll study your pistols."

"Have some fine woolen ones we just got in." Abraham said over his shoulder as he led the way through the tables to the counter in the back.

He picked two dark gray ones, thick and well woven. The workmanship was obvious, both hemmed with small stitches by a real seamstress. He had come to learn the marks of good workmanship and their worth for lasting longer.

"The pistols are over here." Blankets on his arm, the clerk guided him to the next counter. "This is a British made gun. It has London stamped on the barrel." He showed him the marking. "It's a .64 caliber. Dependable and the barrel's not badly pitted."

Zeke tried to examine the barrel in the poor light. "Take it to the doorway and look at it in the light out there," Abraham offered.

"Thanks." Zekial walked to the door.

The single shot had well-defined rifling and it was in good condition when he could see down it. He glanced over to check on Tilly. She remained on the gray, holding all the leads. She nodded her approval at the sight of his new hat.

He turned the pistol over in his hand. Good enough condition for a weapon. It would do him fine. He went back inside to the rear counter.

"How much?"

"Two dollars."

He frowned at the man. "High enough for a used pistol."

"That's the price, sir."

"I'll need fifty shot and a mold for it, too." He noted the man acted very firm and he had no time to dicker around all day.

"We can do that. Gunpowder?"

"No, I have a good supply." He looked around, interested in a dress to fit her. He wrinkled his nose at the merchandise. They only had material in bolts, thread and needles. No time for that with them on the move.

"Anything else?"

"Yes, a sack of hard candy."

"We'll give you that for your purchases." The clerk filled a small cloth sack with the glazed pieces from the large jar.

He paid the man and put the candy in his possible pouch, stuck the pistol on the left side of his belt and took the blankets over his left arm and her hat in his left hand. His rifle in his right, he headed for the door.

Outside, the commotion of snarling dogs and shouting men had quickly drawn a crowd. With a frown, Zekial pushed his way through. From the porch, he watched Tilly gathering up the leads as the gray mare skittered and circled in the dust and wild excitement.

"Dogfight!" The man besides him bailed off the porch to join the wary crowd. Blood flew and two large dogs a black and a yellow one, fell on each other in furious combat.

Two men in leather acted as the owners while the fight moved around in the street. First one dog, then the other had the advantage. Fresh, they tore loose from each other's pain filled holds and went back in, raging for more.

"Take our stock to the alley." He tossed his head that direction and put the blankets over her lap. Then with a grin, he held out the hat for her.

Tilly smiled in surprise at the gift and bent her head down with her hands full of reins. He put the new hat on her head.

He quickly stepped aside when the two raging dogs rolled over and over, ending close to their horses in a furious clinch. The yellow dog was fast turning red, while the black only showed a few scratches here and there.

To escape their fury, Tilly drove the horses through the crowd of men, headed for the space between the store and the next building. The onlookers only gave her and the animals enough berth to barely escape the savage bout. Zekial watched to make certain she was clear and safely headed between the store and the next rough-framed structure. Then he turned back to watch the fight.

"Sic 'em," the shorter of the two men shouted, hissing at the yellow dog to jump back into the action.

"I'm betting on Rufus's cur winning this one. The yeller one," a lanky freckled faced man said, "How're you, ah, betting?"

"I just got here. That one the toughest of the two?"

"Yeah, that yellow cur is part Injun dog, rest mastiff. I figure that black is out of Governor Meriwether Lewis's big Labrador. The one he took with him to the Pacific. Good retrievers for duck hunting, but they ain't worth a damn for fighting."

"Get him, Killer," the man they called Rufus shouted and the yellow dog charged back in.

The fury of the pair spilled under the hitch rack and forced men to flee to avoid being in the teeth snapping, growling anger of the two males. The cur managed a death-like grip on the Lab, but all the fur cushioned his bite. In turn, the Lab managed to bite down on the cur's leg in all the confusion. In obvious pain, the cur tried to tear loose from his deep grip in an ear-shattering scream that drew cheers from the Lab's supporters.

Blood flew from the Lab's shredded right ear when the cur took the offensive. He let go of the cur's leg. They charged each other and rose on their hind legs like battling stallions, each trying to get a throat hold on the other. The roar of their growls grew deafening. In the next instance the Lab had the yellow dog by the throat and from his gasping, the black dog would soon have his opponent subdued.

"Rufus, you giving up yet?" The Lab's owner demanded, ready to pull off his champion.

"Naw. Let him kill that cowardly yellow bastard." Rufus turned and pushed his way through the silent crowd.

The yellow dog's rasping grew weaker, the Lab's jaw tightened on his hold. His owner stood with his hands folded over his chest and watched. The Lab looked up as if for the command.

"Kill him!"

The dog revived his vicious ways and began to shake his viselike hold on the cur. At last the victim's eyes went blank, and his body limp.

The crowd began to pay off their debts in low voices. The Lab lay down with the dog's throat still in his massive mouth. The cur's final death throes set in; his hind legs kicked in futile reaction. Zekial started for the horses. Plenty of money changed hands in dog fights and horse racing on the frontier.

He looked up and as she reined in the mare in the narrow alley, a look of shock on her face.

She motioned toward the street. "You's see that man rode by leading that black mule?"

"No." He glanced back to catch a glimpse. "Who is he?"

"That's McCord's man, Lighe Judson."

"You sure?"

"I knows him real good."

"Yes, you would. You stay here, I'll go see which way he went. He doesn't know me, I don't think." He carried his rifle in his right hand and he hurried forward.

"You be careful," she hissed after him.

Zekial went to the front of the building. From there he could study the two mules across the traffic-clogged street. A red and a black one. Alongside them stood a man under a black hat talking to someone. Nice looking, about thirty, black hair and clean-shaven. Well, he needed a shave, but obviously didn't wear a beard. Dressed in brown pants and a coat, he looked more like a businessman than a slave chaser. From now on, he would recognize the man.

From his spot beside the mercantile, he watched Judson questioning a man, who shook his head and then pointed to the saloon on their side of the street.

He'd seen enough. So, had the folks of Batesville. It wouldn't be ten minutes until someone would recall the black girl on the gray horse. He hurried down the alley, checked his cinch and swung into the saddle.

"Let's go." He glanced back over his shoulder, half expecting Judson to be standing there demanding her surrender. In a high trot, they went out the back way and headed downhill for the ferry to carry them over the broad White River.

One more river to cross.

X

GRISSUM PACED THE FLOOR. NO way he would get out of this damn log jail. When that boy got back from New Castle with no word of that preacher, his neck would be stretched on a hemp rope. Be a helluva note to be hung in this wild backwater where they didn't even have tombstones.

He glanced up at the sunlight coming in the top of the wall. Somehow, he needed to climb up there, make himself small as a wren and get out of this damned jail. If only Judson... Grissum shook his head. He'd never find him in time. The stupid butt got himself lost chasing a mule.

Grissum kept hoping that they'd make a mistake bringing him the sorry food they fed him, get complacent and let their guard down, so he could jump them. So far, one man, armed with a cocked rifle, stood back and watched while the other one gave him the food on a wooden slab.

He couldn't afford to upset his meal, if it wasn't going to get him out. The damn food was bad enough and would hardly sustain a piss ant.

"You can't go in there," the guard said out loud. Grissum turned on his heel to listen. His heart pounded with excitement.

"I only want to see if the man you have in there is the same man that killed my daddy."

The words brought a smile to Grissum's face.

At long last, Lighe Judson had arrived.

"Get back from the door!" the guard said, and the door flew open. His rifle stuck inside, the guard's knees buckled when Judson cold-cocked him over the head. Grissum tore his weapon away and nodded to his partner with a scowl.

"Where in the hell have you been?"

"I come quick as I heard you was in here. Something about a preacher?"

"Never mind that. Look around and be sure we can make a break for it."

The guard moaned and Grissum used the rifle butt to smash him on the head. He bent down and took the man's powder horn and his ammunition pouch.

Judson frowned at the looting. "Ain't no one in sight."

"They got mine." He tossed his head for the other man to get going. Outside, Grissum discovered his pack and official papers, but no rifle, no pistol, nor the rest of his things. He slipped on his pack and looked around. Anxious to be out of there, he rushed to the two mules at the hitch rail. In minutes, they were on the road and hurrying away without drawing any attention.

"That wench was in Batesville a day ago," Judson said, trotting his mule down the tracks that led north. "I missed them by minutes. They took the ferry. Then I learned you were in jail here. So, I came back and scouted out the whole thing."

"You sure it was her?" Grissum asked. "I seen her with a white girl, two days ago-yesterday, I think. I know that it was her and she seen me and then she run off in this wagon. But you say they took the ferry at Batesville?"

"The ferry man said a buck-skinner and a black girl answering her description went across the river on his boat just before I got there."

Hatless, McCord ran his fingers through his hair. He glanced back, grateful to be out of the jail and any minute expecting to see a posse come riding down on them. He listened for signs of pursuit, but the only sounds were of crows calling in the distance.

"Circle west. I still believe that slave was with someone's daughter. I'd recognize that white girl anywhere. If that wench ain't there, maybe we can learn where he took her."

"That's sure dangerous with you wanted for murder in this country," Judson said with a wary shake of his head.

"I know, but we could go off half-cocked instead of finding a good lead where they're headed."

"You're the boss." Judson didn't seem to enjoy the idea of hanging around.

Grissum headed his mule off into the timber. Obviously, the chasing around had tamed his mount considerably from the first day. It was great to be free at last and not under a death threat, but they still needed to learn all they could about this. Damn Broome and them dumb farmers anyway. They couldn't hold a good man for long. He looked back with a scowl, then booted his mule to catch up with Judson.

———

BOTH MEN LAY ON THEIR bellies in the woods across the field of rustling dry cornstalks from the smoke house. Grissum used a brass telescope to scan the woman and kids packing cloth wrapped pork into the low-walled log structure. He recognized among them the white girl who'd been with the black girl in the wagon, but to his disappointment no wench and no buck-skinner. He let the tip of his tongue wet his dry lips and watched the woman in charge through the glass. She would be a bed full. No man in sight.

"We need to go and question her." Propped on one elbow, he held himself up on his side. He closed the telescope, and then scratched his privates.

Judson was confused. "What we going up there for?"

"That's who I saw with our girl. They'll know where they're headed—if they really did leave, that is."

"You think they're still here?"

"I don't know, Judson. I don't know." His scratching did not abate the itch. He gave up and rose to his knees. "Let's get our mules and go see what she knows."

Judson didn't answer him on the way to their mounts. McCord stuck his foot in the stirrup and swung into the saddle. "He can't go far."

"Yeah, but he's sure clever."

"Got lucky." Grissum reined his mule around. "He just got lucky was all."

"Yeah. Well, I'll sure feel better when we get the hell out of this country." Judson dropped his head and shook it in deep concern.

"We will, as soon as we speak to her."

They rode on up into the dooryard. Betty Lou gave them a nod and used her hand to shade her eyes from the noontime sun.

"Ma'am." Grissum combed his wind-tossed hair back with his fingers.

The hard edge of caution steeled her voice. "Good day."

"I'm Grissum McCord. This is my deputy, Lighe Judson, and we're looking for a runaway slave." The children sucked in their breaths at the word slave. It was hard for him not to smile. The bitch had been there, sure enough.

"Not here." The woman shook her head once, still eyeing them with that cool reserve.

"She's been here?"

Not a flicker in those cold blue eyes "Not here."

"Where did they go?" It was all he could do not to get off his mule and thrash her with his whip. Snooty bitches like her needed their come-uppances, and he was just the man who could do it.

"You can see their tracks." She pointed to the north.

"Where they headed?"

"Mountains, I guess."

"Ma'am, to hide a slave thief is as bad as being one, and by the authority vested in me—"

"I know the law. There is no one here, sir. Now ride on."

"When I catch them—and mark my words, I will catch them—I may just come by and arrest you as an accomplice."

She began to laugh. Her mouth fell open and her laughter carried like a raucous crows' cawing. Shaking her head in disbelief, her breasts rose and fell with her amusement and mirth. At last she stopped and shook her head. "Mister, you won't ever return alive from that journey."

He checked the dancing mule up short. "What are you saying?"

"I'm saying, sir, that if you ever find Zekial Broome, he'll kill the both of you and leave you for the buzzards to pick your bones."

"Why, gawdamn your—" He swung the whip, but she avoided it easily as his mule spooked and shied away.

Judson hit him on the arm. "I hear dogs. Listen, Grissum,"

He blinked at his pale-faced assistant. "You what—"

"Bloodhounds. Hear them comin'?"

"I'll be back to teach your high-fluting ass a thing or two." Grissum shook the whip at her as Judson tore out across the cornstalk field on his mule. He turned his ear to the bawl-mouthed dogs on their backtrail. The damned posse was after them. No time for her. He lashed the mule into a hard run, busting through the brittle cornstalks after Judson and his mount.

XI

ZEKIAL STUDIED THE MURKY, RUSHING stream, its banks lined with the ghostly white trunks of towering bare sycamores. They were bigger around than his arms could reach. The smooth color of the tree bark matched the skiff of snow on the thick brown leaf-litter crunching under Red's hooves. Great streams of vapor issued from the horse's nostrils as Zeke held up and looked back at the bleak, wooded hills they'd come from.

Behind his mount, stood the bay mare and a large black mule, loaded down with their packs and bedding. At the back of the train, the black girl sat astride Eagle. She slouched in the saddle, huddled under a wool blanket against the cold. A blue calico rag covered her head.

"You sees anything back there?" Her horse snorted and bobbed. Her brown eyes darted around as if uncomfortable that he had even stopped. With an impatient frown, she jerked hard on the gray's bridle to make it be still.

"Like I told you yesterday, it ain't what I see, girl. It's what I don't see and feel in my bones that worries me more," he said. He made a swipe with the side of his hand across his whiskered mouth.

Nothing in sight, nothing moved. Still, somewhere, those four braves were on their back trail—somewhere in the folds and confines of the hills behind them.

He turned back to consider the task ahead. Deeply engrossed in his thoughts about the crossing, he absently finger-combed his hair that hung to his buckskin shirt collar. At last, he reset the wide-brimmed hat on his head, almost amused as his conception of what he must look like, more Injun, himself, than white man. He shifted the long rifle in his right arm.

The rushing stream before them needed to be forded. Wild animals had used this place, a few fresh elk and some deer imprints pocked the water's edge, but there were no signs of a horse or human prints on the sandy shore. No way to conceal their own tracks here either, but it would be too risky to take more time to try and find a more suitable ford in the swollen river. They simply didn't have the time to ride back and forth looking for a better place to enter the stream.

They needed to be on the other side and into the hills beyond, where they could choose a suitable place to defend themselves. If they were lucky, the churning water in midstream would not be over belly deep on the horses. The swirling dingy water held something unseen that made his empty stomach churn. They had ventured deep into Cherokee land. Everything west of the White River for a good week's ride behind them belonged to the displaced tribe. He'd purposely avoided any contact with the Indians, stopping only at one small trading post, where he'd bartered for some cornmeal.

Four warriors he knew of had been trailing them for the past two days. The afternoon before he had doubled back once and let them go ahead. The switch back gave him an opportunity to study them from afar as they followed their trail. One thing he'd learned about the small war party, they weren't armed with rifles. He considered, from their height, they must be Osage, not Cherokee. But who knew? They were red men—bloodthirsty bucks out on the prowl. Their obvious intent was to run the two of them down. His circling around in the mountains since sighting them had been evasive, but if they were any good at reading signs at all, they'd followed it like a highway. Hard for anyone to hide the prints of four head of stock.

He had not lived thirty-two years to become a scalp lock for a damn Osage, or any other buck for that matter. Too, there was the matter of her safety.

As he rubbed the side of his mouth where the facial hair itched he mentally gauged the small river and wondered if he always used the best judgment, like letting himself get so involved in things like her welfare. Grissum McCord and his man were somewhere on his back trail, too, but that was beside the point as the sharp north wind cut through his leather clothing. They needed to make camp—somewhere on the other side, so that anyone coming on their back trail had to make the ford, too. Cold as it was, the notion of wading across the stream might cool the blood-fever of the four Osage, though he doubted it would do much to deter them.

"It doesn't look deep," he said to her. For a long moment, so busy with his own considerations, he'd almost forgotten she was along and how much she dreaded these deeper crossings.

"You hang on to the saddle if he has to swim."

"I don't swim," she said in a small voice.

"I know that. You just hang on to that damn saddle. That one can swim." He frowned with impatience to impress her.

"I sure be hanging on."

"Good," he said and tossed the lead rope around the bay pack mare's neck. She would come after his horse Red, and the heavier laden mule would follow her to hell and gone. Days before, he had removed the small bell that she usually wore to keep the other animals around her. He kept thinking it would only invite detection and trouble.

At his insistence and clucking with his tongue to urge him on, Red started off the steep bank. Front hooves together, he finished his descent sliding down the clay bank, then re-found his footing on the gravel. Zeke glanced back; the mare had started off the bank. He could see on top the whites of Tilly's eyes as she crowded the gray in close behind the stalled black mule. A simple crossing, they'd made a dozen of them like it since leaving Choctaw Landing.

He urged the gelding with the heel of his high-top moccasins into the thin ice formed on the river's edge. It shattered under his hooves and floated away like shiny plates of glass. The current swirled around his horse's knees while the gelding scrambled some for his footing on the mossy rocks underneath. Zekial raised his own feet up to keep them dry and looked back as the pack mare started into the water, the mule stopped still considering the matter.

"Bust him good!"

He turned back to look at the far bank, a hundred-fifty-feet away. When the water reached his horse's belly, she whacked the mule, who give a loud grunt and then bolted off the bank into the stream with a splash. The river, by this time, had not only proved swifter, but deeper than Zekial had planned on. Realizing this would be no ordinary crossing caused a knot to form in the pit of his stomach.

"Oh, my Gawd!"

He looked over his shoulder to see her draw up her bare brown legs from the water. Red began to swim beneath him and Zekial's legs became wet despite his best effort to keep them up. He glanced back at the bay mare to see if she was having difficulty. To his dismay, she stumbled and floundered while he watched in concerned disbelief. Her head went underwater as she struggled for her footing.

"The mare!" Tilly screamed.

Wide-eyed, the mare fought the water. Her head went under again as if she'd broken something and her right leg wouldn't hold her up. The river took charge and swept her downstream. He helplessly watched her try to rise out of the water in a desperate drive screaming in pain.

Something needed to be done. With his legs in the cold water to help guide the animal, he jerked Red around in the stream. The red gelding breasted the force as he urged him back toward the black girl. He could see she was beside herself with what happened to the mare compounded by her own fear of the water. She clung to the saddle horn and shouted to him that the mare was under water. He could see all that and acknowledged her concern with a sharp nod. There were more important things to do than console her, at the moment.

"Here, take my rifle and powder." He handed them to her. "And then you get your ass up on that bank."

She strung the horn over her neck. "Which one?"

"The west one!" he pointed.

"What if—"

He slung his own pouch around her neck. He needed to keep his rifle, powder and caps dry at all costs. No time to argue with an upset female. More important, he could see the packs were not submerged as the now lifeless mare floated away downstream. It took so damn little to drown a horse. Something bad had happened to the bay mare, he didn't know what, but half their goods and supplies were in those packs going north up the river.

"Go!" Ignoring her screams, he lashed the gray horse on the butt. The mule was already climbing up the far bank. One thing had gone right, so far. Her gray charged through the water and he sent Red flying down the river. He couldn't afford to lose all his things in those packs.

His weaponry safe with her, he reined the sorrel after the mare. Red struck out in the river's force and began to swim until he drew close enough to the two bobbing panniers still strapped on the mare. Zekial prepared to leap from the saddle into the frigid water. He rose in the seat and dove for the packs hoping his weight didn't sink them. He landed on his goal and his fingers closed on the leather cover. The chilly liquid sought to quickly soak and weigh down his leather moccasins and pants. No time to lose, he trailed in the water behind the floating horse, drew his great knife and began slashing apart the tie down ropes.

The first pannier came free and he stuck his knife away. His feet shoved off the floating mare's body. The straps wrapped around his right arm, he swam for the far shore pulling his cargo through the water until his feet struck the hard bottom, and then he began to wade toward the bank. Slick rocks under his leather soles impeded his effort and the waist deep current threatened for a long moment to sweep him and his precious load away. At last, he won the tug of war. Dripping wet, he stumbled into the shallows with his pack in tow. Out of breath, he pulled the containers made of stiff hair-on buffalo hide to the shore.

"I got it," she said and took his burden from him. Both of her heels dug into the sandy ground, she strained to drag it up the slope away from the water's edge as he turned without a word and started back for the other one. His time left would be short. The cold would soon cramp his lower body. He still wanted his last pack but worried he would soon be swept away in the furious current.

"You sure going to freeze to death out there," she wailed after him.

Not answering her, he dove into the river and began swimming after the dead mare, already yards downstream. Sharp muscle cramps began to twinge the calves of his legs and his thighs stiffened as he swam after it. His legs grew too numb to even feel. At last, with long strokes of his aching arms, he reached the mare's side. He pulled himself up on the last pack and sought to catch some needed air in his desperate lungs.

In a head toss, he swept the wet hair aside from his face. With his knife out, he groped under the swift water with his blade as he and the corpse of the mare drifted downstream like some half-sunk out of control vessel. He finally cut enough of the restraints to release the second pannier. It floated free and he caught it before it was pulled away by the river's strength. No time to save the packsaddle, he had to get out of this icy water soon or die.

Each attempt he made to swim and tow the pack became an exerted effort. He wondered as he spat out a mouthful of fishy water what he could do to defend himself if the Osage caught him this exposed and vulnerable. A simple crossing had become, perhaps, the place of his death.

His legs turned to wooden stalks. He fought to stave off passing out, as his strength drained, and the river pulled him downstream. The water's promise of a long sleep almost bribed him into closing his eyes. He fought harder to carry himself and the parcel to the far shore. At long last, he reached waist deep water and, out of breath, began to lug his pack behind him.

When he finally looked up at the sheer bank that faced him either direction, he blinked his water-blurred eyes in disbelief. No way to get his load out of there. On top of the high cliff, her brown face paled with concern, she clung to a small tree and frantically pointed for him to go down stream. He shook his head in numb defeat and crestfallen began to slosh along the base of the high cut lugging the heavy load behind.

The water deepened as he waded. He glanced back but there was no way for him to go upstream. He was grateful anyway the buffalo pannier half-floated. The river's bottom quickly fell off and soon he was forced to swim some more pushing the buoyant pack ahead and thrashing his numb legs. He rode the current until he spotted a small side stream and beachhead coming in on his left. He used his last burst of energy to reach the shallows. At last, his feet were on the slick rocky bottom.

The force of the river threatened to sweep him away with it. He gritted his teeth to discover they were chattering while he fought to retain his gear. The pull of the pack proved too much for him to draw back as his slick soles found no footing.

"Zekial!" she cried out. "Don't you lose it now! You almost be here!"

Through slits of his eyelids, he glimpsed her jumping up and down on the bank. His short breath raged in his throat. He finally braked the force when his heels dug into some mud and he managed to pull the pack back from the clutches of the stream. The tremors of cold shaking him, he slogged from the river. At this point, the too-heavy weight of the pack had to be picked up and carried in his arms. The footing in the shallows proved nearly impossible. He reached the edge, out of strength, then he stumbled and fell on top of the pack.

"Here, wrap up in this blanket." She tucked it in around him. "I's going to start a fire."

He gasped for breath. A fire would only bring their enemies down on them. His body shook uncontrollably, confusing his thinking and numbing his senses.

"No fire." He used a lot of his strength to warn her. Exhausted, he dropped his head, closed his eyes and sprawled over the pack. His breath came in great rasping gasps that knifed his lungs. The stinking wet buffalo hide smell assailed his nostrils. Half aware, he slipped off the pack and spilled onto his butt.

"You can't sit here." She dragged him by the arm to the shore, then fought the pack up on dry ground before she rushed back to where he sat in a stupor, trying to remove his moccasins. Like a drunken man, he fumbled with the laces to his moccasin to no avail.

"You sure going to die with no fire." She struck his fingers aside impatiently, raised his foot up to her hip and began to unlace his moccasins.

"No, I won't. Get some blankets. I'll get out of these wet clothes. You can warm me." He tried to catch his breath, but there was not enough air in his gulping. "A fire will only lead them right to us."

"You sure be a stubborn man." She strained to pull off a soaked moccasin. When it finally came free, she stood above him and let the water drain from it.

"Stubborn is a damn sight better than dead." He sought more breath as he reached for the other lacing.

"You so cold now, you be lucky if you don't die." Kneeling before him she undid the laces and pulled it off while he undid the leather thongs that held his pants shut at the waist.

"Go get the blankets." He rose with an effort to skin the slick, wet, leather away from his butt.

"I'm going. I'm a going." She ran off in a flash of her skinny brown legs.

His britches off, he whipped the blanket around himself and tried to stop his shakes. Nothing eased them. His bare legs were too cold to feel anything, and his feet cramped despite his effort to push and twist them into a more comfortable position.

The sounds of popping made him look up. She was flagging out blankets and robes atop the bank. He struggled to his feet to climb up there. Standing on them helped the right foot's discomfort, but the left one acted as if it would curl up his toes. Unsteady as he went, he held the blanket half shut with one hand while the other one sought some support from the bushes.

"Get up here." Seeing his difficulty in walking, she rushed to slip under his arm and help him up the steep bank. With one arm locked around his waist to steady him, she gave a great effort to assist him in his climb.

"What you reckon happened to that mare?" she asked as they fought the steep grade until they finally were on top of it.

"I don't know—"

"You lie down here. I sure think a fire be better warming you than me, but you be the boss." She shook her head in dismay.

He dropped to his knees. Unrelenting, the wind seared the bare skin on his legs, feet and behind.

"Take off that wet shirt. I know it be your favorite beaded one, but it's soaked, too," she said.

The slick leather shirt clung to him as she helped him fight it off over his head. He settled down, disappointed at his loss of strength. She ushered him under the blankets and robes like an old mother hen.

At last beneath the covers, she heaped more covers on top of him. He began to shake like an earthquake had hold of his innards. His mind grew foggier.

"I go get them horses, rifle and stuff," she announced.

He managed a nod. Good, she'd thought of the rifle. They couldn't afford to lose it at any price. He hugged himself and clamped his teeth together to stop them from chattering, but that didn't do any good. Helpless as a baby, he'd become a shaking mass.

Tilly returned with the animals. Through his half-open eyes, he watched her unsaddle and unload them, then apply hobbles. Despite all the bedding piled on top of him, the trembling wouldn't stop. She put the rifle on the far side of them, then like a nimble cat, scurried underneath the cover to cuddle against him. In desperation to escape the agony of the chills, he closed his eyes and reached to hug her small form to him. Small, calloused hands furiously rubbed his numb skin.

"This sure ain't working."

He was too dumb struck to answer her. She shed her clothing and quickly moved her body against him, pressing her bare skin to his.

"My, but you be colder than ice—" She squirmed on top of him. Her nipples buried in his chest and her warm flat belly rested on his frozen numb privates. He fought it, but slumber quickly overwhelmed him. He wondered if he would slip from this world in her arms.

The world closed in and he crashed down into a deep sleep.

"Don't you die on me—you hear me!" she cried in the distance, but he knew her mouth was only inches away. "Oh, Gawd, please don't die out here!"

XII

HOW FAR COULD HE GO?" Grissum McCord stood on the deck of the keelboat Shirley, more concerned about the docking of the rickety skiff than the question he'd just asked no one in particular. He sniffed the cold air, sharp with the pungent odor of wood smoke, and shook his head.

Beside him, Judson scratched at his beard. "Them frontiersmen can go clear to the Pass-ific Ocean if they take a mind."

"Christ sakes, he ain't Lewis and Clark."

"What I heard folks say about him, he might be close to like them."

"Horseshit and whiskey talk is all you heard since Batesville about anything. If he ain't here, then we'll get us some horses and ride west. Somebody's seen those two, and they'll know right where they're headed."

He looked at the unchinked raw cabins sprawled about the river's edge. A poor enough looking settlement. Ricks of fresh-hewn timbers were stacked on the dock to sell to the keelboat captains.

"Ain't them army boys?" Judson pointed to a group of men in green uniforms milling about on the bank.

"Yeah. I wonder what the hell they're doing up here?" The damn military was supposed to be guarding the country west of the White River, keeping all the white settlers out. Everyone knew that was a big farce, though. Find the right officer to pay off, and anyone could go anywhere they wanted. Still... the soldiers could delay his plans to find and kill that bastard Broome and bring home that miserable black wench. The reward on her ass was a big sum of money, and to have her slip through his hands like she had was like letting a cold-blooded fortune go up in smoke.

Judson stood up a little straighter. "What are we going to do if they stop us?"

"You just let me handle the military."

"Yeah, but Boss—them guys can stop us."

"I know what they can do. I said, let me handle them."

"All right."

The skiff docked, and he sent Judson to collect their things from the deck. Guns, saddles, bedrolls and gear—they would need all of it out on the frontier. It was much nicer to track down a runaway in the civilized world. Out west there would be no roadhouses to stay in, or even any eating-places. They'd be lucky to see another white person for days. Damn redskins could be trouble, too. On top of that, this Zekial Broome—if that was even his name—was at home out there somewhere, just waiting for them. It would be a challenge to find his den. He'd do it, though. Then he'd laugh as he cut the bastard's throat and dragged that skinny, no-good girl back to Alabama.

An officer in gray and gold came down to the dock. Grissum didn't like the officious look on the man's pasty face. No matter. This territory was slave country, after all. He had every right of pursuit.

The officer blocked the end of the gangplank. "Sir, you are not planning to debark here, are you?"

Grissom stepped down on the log dock and puffed out his chest. "I'm here on official business. I'm after a runaway slave that's gone inland."

"I'm sorry, sir, but you must make a request to the authorities in St. Louis for such a search."

"St. Louis!" He snorted, looking down on the officer with disdain.

"Yes, sir, the Indian Agency office is located there."

"But the damn Indian lands are here. A man's valuable property has run off. And you, certainly, did nothing to bar her entry into the territory." He tossed his head toward the hardwood-coated hills behind them.

"Your name, sir?"

"I have papers." McCord reached inside his coat. This little twit in his spotless military uniform wasn't turning him back from his business.

Slave-chasing was a damned important part of commerce. The more of them that escaped, the more the others thought they could do the same thing. It always did good to drag one back, show how futile running really was to the rest of them. Why, he'd seen them look up from working cotton and shut their eyes at the sight of some well-whipped runaway brought right back where he belonged.

"I don't care about your papers unless they come from Thomas C. Murphy, the Indian agent in charge of this district."

"Mine, sir, are from the governor of Alabama."

"Sir, your name." An enlisted man in green had joined the officer on the dock and had a pencil and paper in his hand.

"Grissum McCord of Slottsville, Alabama."

"You spell that with two s's?"

This was becoming more than slightly tiresome. "Yeah."

"Is there anyone else in the party?"

"Yes, my deputy. Judson."

"And what is his full name?"

"Lighe Judson."

"Lighe?"

"Yeah—spell it L-i-g-h-e Judson. J-u-d-s-o-n."

"I will warn you now that I am under orders from my commander to place you under house arrest if you disembark here, Mr. McCord."

"And I will be forced to inform my Senator, the honorable Harvey Cornwall from the fine state of Alabama, if you do."

"My orders are—"

"Damn your orders, anyway. A valuable slave has run away into the Indian Nation and I intend to go in after her. By the authority vested in me by the state of Alabama, I will."

The lieutenant appeared unmoved. "You are welcome to stay here as a prisoner of the U.S. Army until a higher authority has told me different."

"What is your name?" This business was getting him nowhere. Once the army turned its back, he was going inland.

"Gerald Stines. First Lieutenant, B Company, U.S. Rifle Regiment."

"Who's your commander? I wish to speak to him!"

"That would be Captain Walker, sir, my company commander. He is not here. He is downstream at Batesville." Stines showed no sign of backing down. He made a small motion of his hand. Behind him, a handful of troopers unslung their rifles and fixed their bayonets.

"Forget it, but I promise you this, Lieutenant. I'll have your ass over this matter. This time next year, you'll be marching with your men as a private." McCord shook his head in disgust. He'd just get back on the Shirley, go on upriver to the next spot, and get off there. He turned on his heel and waved Judson and his pile of equipment back on the boat.

"Mr. McCord!"

"What?" He turned to look back.

"If you try to avoid my command and go elsewhere to disembark without proper authorization, I shall have the authority to shoot you and your party on sight."

"Soldier Boy, just get hold of your ass with both hands right now. Feel what it's like to have one, because when I get through with you, you won't anymore."

"You heard me, McCord. I have orders to shoot warned offenders. The same goes for Mr. Judson there, too."

Judson was less than enthusiastic about this latest turn of events. "What's he saying about shooting us?"

"Never mind. I need to talk to Captain Ogilvy about going to another port upstream." He glanced back to be sure Stines couldn't hear him.

There could not be that many soldiers stationed all along the river. Hell, not the entire U.S. Army—not that there was much of it to begin with. They weren't stopping him from pursuing that bitch and the buck-skinner who stole her.

Taking the steps two at a time, McCord went up to the deck over the freight cabin and met the gray-bearded captain of the vessel.

"So, you were turned back by Lieutenant Stines?" The older man smiled as if amused. "I meant to tell you not to debark if he was around. Usually he's gone out on patrol. Obviously, he wasn't today. Sorry about that."

"Where's the next spot I can get off without intervention?"

"Logan's Point. Another ten miles upstream." He tossed his head northward.

"Will there be horses for sale there?"

"Horses are scarce up and down this river." Ogilvy shrugged his shoulders as if he didn't know, then reset the brimmed cap on his head. "I thought your best chance to get mounts was here, but with Lord Wellington manning the post, I guess not."

"They ought to clear this land of the damned redskins and be done with it." Grissum studied the brown winter-gray hills that surrounded the river. The way the clouds were moving in, it would probably snow some more and slow down his pursuit.

"Getting rid of the redskins is an idea that I hail, sir, and it would bring me ten times the business."

"Look out there—them Injuns ain't doing shit with all this land, anyway. Why, some good slave-holding families move in here, they could have it all cleared, and crops planted in no time, making money for this nation of ours."

Ogilvy nodded in agreement. "McCord, you're speaking like a true American. Why, the freight business on this river would soar. I'd need more vessels."

"Logan's Point is the next place to get off, huh?"

"Yes. We'll be underway soon. Shouldn't take but a few hours to get there."

"What do you figure that damn Stines is heading that way, too?" Grissum frowned. The officer stood on the bank, speaking with several of his men and nodding toward the boat. After a moment, a trio of the green-coated riflemen straightened, saluted, and hustled up the riverbank and out of sight.

"Don't worry. On foot, they can't beat us to Logan's Point."

"Yeah, but when we get there, we've got to get horses and provisions." Even if the army did meet him upriver, three soldiers he could handle. He'd kill them, if necessary. Any more than that, though, and there would be trouble.

Horses—that would be his bigger problem. He'd be damned if he had to walk all over this part of the country looking for that damned bitch and her buckskin-clad frontiersman.

Grissum relaxed a little when the polemen began to walk up and down the rails, using their poles to propel the vessel and they were headed upriver. He buttoned up his woolen coat against the sharp wind and went back on the deck.

Judson joined him. "You figure he sent his men to stop us?"

"I think they're going to try."

"What'll we do?"

"If we don't get on our way quick enough—" Grissum stopped and lowered his voice. "We will simply kill them."

"Damn. Killing soldiers is serious business." Judson looked away at the bare trees lining the shore.

"How will they ever prove we killed them?"

"You're right, Boss, no one will know." He leaned on a crate of freight and spat tobacco onto the flooring. "But they'll sure suspect."

"No damn strutting army peacock is keeping me from finding that little hell-cat and dragging her ass back for five hundred bucks. Now let's get some blankets. I'm cold, standing out here." He rubbed his hands together against the icy wind and glanced back at the receding dock. He hated delays.

"Good idea. Say, you got any tobacco?"

"I don't chew. Don't need it. You chew up all yours?" Grissum frowned.

"I meant a cigar to smoke. Figured it would be warmer than chewing."

Grissum shook his head.

———

TWO HOURS LATER, LOGAN'S POINT came into view on the far riverbank, looking considerably less inhabited than the last landing. Grissum stood on the bow, all too ready to set foot on dry land and start up the chase again. He searched up and down the shoreline but found no sign of any soldiers. He hoped their luck held.

Grissum lugged a portion of their gear from the boat, followed by Judson. He paid a black porter to unload the rest. With all the equipment finally piled on the platform, they waved up at the captain and the Shirley shoved off, bound back downstream.

"We better find some horses." Grissum looked around. There was no one in sight, but signs of life abounded. A stream of black smoke billowed from a nearby chimney. The sound of crosscut saws echoed across the hills, along with the rhythmic thud of broadaxes. A few cur dogs barked at them from the relative safety of porches and woodlots, while scrawny chickens scratched in the dirt.

He stopped at the first cabin and rapped on the roughhewn board door. A buxom, red-faced woman under a shawl answered his knock. She was as wide as the entrance, and her breasts looked like great, ripe watermelons under the worn linsey cloth of her dress.

She squinted at him appraisingly. "Yeah, what do you need?"

Grissum removed his beaver hat and held it by the brim. "Ma'am, we need to buy a few horses. Could you direct us to a seller?"

The woman snorted. "I sure don't got any to sell. You'll be lucky to find one around here, let alone one to buy."

"Oh, surely someone must have some horses for sale."

"They won't part with 'em." She swallowed, looking hard at him.

"What price would they ask for them?"

"They won't sell them, Mister, I done told you. I can see one of us is stupid. Standing in the cold asking me foolish questions over and over. Good day to you, sir!"

With that, she shut the door in his face.

"She was one big ugly cow." Judson wrinkled his nose and shook his head. "What now? There ain't no horses for sale here and the damn army could be after us anytime."

"Shut your mouth!" McCord searched the hillside for sign of the closest woodcutters. Good chance one of them had a dray horse they could buy. "Get a few jugs of hooch from our things and come with me. With the right lubrication, by Gawd, we'll buy some of these precious ponies yet."

"Liquor does tend to loosen a man up in his dealings." Judson chuckled. He turned his collar up and hurried back to the dock for some whiskey.

At a half-run, Grissum started up the tracks where the logs had been snaked down the hillside, leaving ruts in the black-leaf mulch covering the ground. He spotted a bobtail dappled-gray horse dragging a large cut toward him, driven by a boy of perhaps twelve.

Grissum stopped him by rearing back on the rope lines. "Where's your father, son?"

"Up there, limbing that big downed white oak, sir." The youth clucked to the pony, who dug his toes in deep and soon had the log moving again.

That horse would do fine. Grissum drew a deep breath—he was out of shape, and climbing these slopes wasn't easy. His heart raced, and his lungs ached by the time he reached the top and found a man of perhaps thirty-five busting off limbs from a great downed oak.

"Sir, my name's McCord. I'm a lawman from Alabama." He stuck out his hand.

The man put down his axe and did the same. "Billy Dale Jerkins. Proud to meet you."

"Billy Dale, I seen that fine dappled horse that your boy uses. I was wondering if you ever considered selling him?"

"Naw, never did. He's sound. I sure hated it, but we lost his half-brother last year. He got too hot logging hitched with him. "

"Oh, you had another great horse like that and you lost him?" Grissum shook his head, trying to disguise his impatience with Judson for taking so long to get the damn liquor up there. "That's too bad."

"I brought them with me from east Tennessee when we came here a year-and-a-half ago." Jerkins looked past McCord. "We don't get many strangers round these parts. Is this man with you?"

Grissum turned and spotted Judson coming up behind him. "Ah, yes. Judson's my deputy. Meet Billy Dale here. I see you brought some libation for us." He turned back to the woodcutter. "Would you have a snort, sir?"

Jerkins gave him a broad smile. "Oh, yes, I would. Why I ain't had any whiskey in ten months."

"Well, you drink deep and be thinking of someone who might sell us some good horses. See, we're chasing down some criminals run off over into the Indian Nation."

"By damn, I don't know anyone around here that would sell you a horse. But I'll sure drink to your health." The man removed the stopper, laid the crock in the crook of his arm, raised the neck to his lips, then drank deeply. He gave a great 'ah' at the end, then re-corked the jug and handed it back. "Good whiskey. Whew, that was fine."

"Have another snort. You've been working hard."

Jerkins was more than agreeable to that. "Yes, I believe I will."

He grinned as the man downed another large swallow or two. "Anyone have a rideable mule?"

"Whew, good stuff." The local nodded. "Yes, but I'm near sure they wouldn't sell them."

"Who has one?"

"Rutherford has the best riding mule." Jerkins motioned with his head toward a far slope. "His place is down the other side of the ridge."

"How much does a team of oxen cost up here?"

"Maybe twenty bucks for a team." He shook his head as if he didn't understand McCord's point.

"I'll pay you fifty dollars for the gray. Then you can buy two teams of oxen and have money to spare. How's that?"

The man blinked in disbelief. "Fifty dollars?"

"Yes, fifty dollars." This was taking too damn long. No telling just how close those damn soldiers were by this time. Grissum glanced apprehensively toward the bottoms again but nothing moved there. He grinned. "We better have another drink on that, don't you think?"

"Sure, I'll have another drink." Glassy-eyed, Jerkins wavered slightly on his heels. "You'd really pay fifty dollars for old Dan?"

"I'll pay you right now and even give you the rest of that whiskey."

He jerked the jug from his mouth, batted his eyes, and dropped the whiskey down to his side. "You've got a deal, mister."

Grissum jerked his head toward his deputy. "Judson, go saddle that gray horse and bring up the rest of our gear."

"Yes, sir."

He turned back to Jerkins. "Who's this man with the mule again?"

"Rutherford?"

"That's the one." He was almost beside himself at the man's acceptance of his offer but restrained himself. Fifty bucks for a plug of a horse. Maybe the mule would be better, and he'd make Judson ride the bob-tailed horse. Their time drew short. They needed to get out of here.

"He's up the holler cutting some staves." The man made a wave to the right, off down the hill.

He pulled a pencil and check from the pocket of his jacket. Jerkins looked at him with confusion.

"What's that?"

"A draft on the First National Bank of Birmingham. Why, it's better than the U.S. Treasury itself, sir. The governor of Alabama himself sits on that bank board."

"Where can I cash it?" He scratched his head behind his ear.

"Anywhere." McCord signed his name with a flourish. "It's better than those yellow-back dollars the Feds are issuing, sir."

"I—well, I kind of like gold."

He pointed to the line on the paper under his name. "See right there?"

"Yeah."

"That means this is redeemable in gold bullion to the bearer. In Alabama, sir, we don't dabble in silver. We've got more gold than New York City in our state's bank vaults."

"I guess you being marshals and all, this is good for real money." The bumpkin stared at the check hard, still obviously unsure what to make of it. "Ya'll are marshals, ain't you?"

Grissum pulled himself up to his full height. "Do you need to see my papers authorizing me to recover these runaways and thieves?"

"Nope. No need. I believe you, sir. 'Sides, I couldn't read them if you showed me the words." Jerkins dropped his butt on a stump, then folded the check neatly and put it deep in his pocket. He raised the crock again in toast and took another drink.

"I hope you get them thieves, Mister, and hang 'em high. I hate a damn thief or cheat worse than anything else in this world."

"Amen, sir." Grissum pocketed the pencil. "Here comes my partner. I need to go find this Rutherford and see about his mule."

"Bet for fifty bucks, he sells him to you. Good luck." He waved the jug after him as McCord stalked off back down the hill to meet Judson. He pointed for the deputy to go up the canyon instead of all the way up the slope.

"How much did you pay for this horse?" Judson sneaked a peek at the former owner of the horse, seated on the stump with his crock balanced on his knee.

"Fifty dollars, drawn on the First National Bank of Alabama of Birmingham." Grissum looked over their gear and rifles piled every-which-way on top of his saddle. It all looked to be there—no time to make a mistake, they were fast burning bridges behind them.

"I didn't know you had an account there."

He chuckled. "I don't. When that firm collapsed last year, I managed to get hold of some of their finest gold drafts for my own purposes."

"Oh, I see." Judson laughed and went to whistling "Oh, Suzanna," off key. The only song he knew.

"I think I see the man up there making staves." Grissum huffed for his breath. He'd spotted a figure with an axe in his hand up on the hillside.

"Yep. And there's a blood-red mule up there, too. See him?"

"Yep." Grissum had seen the fine-looking mule as well, but he had greater concerns niggling at his brain—the feeling that trouble was near. He looked back down the canyon. They were fast running out of time. This transaction had to be swifter than the horse trade. "If this guy gives us any trouble, hit him over the head. We've wasted enough damn time haggling over livestock already."

"Sure."

They hurried down the hillside and crossed over the holler to the other side. The bearded chopper looked to be in his late forties. As they approached, the man dropped the axe and leaned on the handle. With a critical eye, he looked them over with some contempt. "You some kind of land agents come to tell me I can't stay here?"

"No, sir," McCord said. "We're lawmen from Alabama and need to buy a riding horse or mule."

"Not mine." The man shook his head and spit tobacco to the side. He wiped his mouth on the back of his hand.

"We have the authority to take that mule. We're in hot pursuit of two dangerous criminals. The law says we can use what we need in the pursuit, and you will be reimbursed by the proper authorities."

"You going to try and take him?" The man nodded in the direction of the rifle leaning against a tree about five steps away.

"I'm going to issue you a warrant on the state of Alabama for a hundred dollars for that mule. That's twice his value or more."

"I ain't going to Alie-bama to cash no Gawdamn worthless warrant."

Grissum was fast losing his patience. "It's legal tender in the United States. Because, sir, the great state of Alabama always pays its debts."

"Keep your tender to yourself. I'll keep my damn mule. I ain't selling him. He's the best damn mule I ever owned, and I don't want no worthless warrant on no Gawdamn Alie-bama!"

While they'd been talking, Judson slowly circled to the man's blindside. At

Grissum's nod, he struck the man over the head with a fresh stave from the pile. Rutherford—or whatever his name was—fell facedown like a poled steer.

"Get the mule saddled with my rig and make it quick. Them damn soldiers will be here any minute, I bet." Grissum stole a hard look back down through the trees.

"What you doing?"

"Writing him a warrant for his damn mule."

XIII

YOU NEED TO DRINK THIS." Tilly cradled his head on her legs. Careful not to spill it, she held the steaming liquid in the cup to his lips. Still shaking, he sat up in a daze and obeyed her. Scalding tea burned his lip and tongue. Cool air rushed over his skin and she adjusted the blanket over his bare shoulders.

"Your clothes ain't dry yet."

He nodded. "What's this you're giving me?" Zekial took another scorching gulp, then took the cup from her.

"Willow bark tea. It will help you." She steadied him as he cuddled the hot pottery cup in his hands. The heat of the liquid helped, but he figured nothing would ever again warm up his innards.

"I made a steam lodge for you."

"You built a fire?" Dammit, he'd told her not to do that.

"'How could I heat that tea? You was fixing to die. I had to do something."

"Lodge?"

"Yeah, you go over there. I bring the hot rocks, dump them in the water and that steam will warm you." She motioned to a small round-top structure close by. The dome shaped cone was covered with his hides. Impressed with all her efforts and how much trouble she had gone through to get all this done, he nodded his approval.

He checked the weak sun for the time of day, but an overcast sky obscured its location. Thick clouds sent light snow swirling about him. He rose to obey her, using the blanket for his robe. He walked over, ducked down and then crawled inside the small hut. The small shelter's dark interior warmed his bare skin. He tossed the blanket out to save it getting wet, then he sat on the fleshy side of a buffalo robe spread on the ground. Still chilled deep inside, he grasped his bare arms. When his eyes adjusted to the dim light, he noticed in the center sat a large kettle full of warm water.

"You watch out!" she shouted from outside and into the lodge she came with a head-sized rock slung in some green limbs and dumped it in the pot. Steam issued forth in a boiling fog and she immediately left, dropping the skin covering the doorway that shut out the light.

Several trips back and forth, she soon had the lodge heavy in vapors and he began to feel the pores in his skin open. As if awakened from a dream, he noticed that he no longer shook from being cold. He decided that he was warm.

"Whew." Tilly stuck her head inside. Her lower lip dropped open in a grin and showed her even white teeth and red tongue. "It sure be nice in here."

"Come join me." He waved her in. She deserved to share the small comfort.

"In a minute or so." Ducking outside the flap, she made two more trips to add more hot rocks. Then, naked, she slipped inside like a mountain lion. Her sleek brown skin glowed in the hazy darkness. He patted a place beside him for her to join him. She sat cross-legged at his elbow and breathed in the vapors with the rise and fall of her small, pear-shaped breasts and dollar-size black nipples.

"You think that fire's gonna bring them?" She refused to meet his gaze.

"I don't care. I'm proud to be warm again. You did good."

She bobbed her head in an understanding nod, but still never looked his way. "I was afraid you would die on me."

"We're about even, then."

"You saving me from that Grissum McCord was a bigger deal than this." She frowned like the two things were beyond comparison. She turned away, looking straight ahead, acting as if to look at him might break some rule.

He reached over, grasped her chin, and turned her face toward him. She closed her eyes and he bent closer until their mouths touched. For a long moment nothing happened, then her lips began to seek his—

He bolted upright. "What the hell was that?"

"That damn mule's braying about something!" She hopped to her feet and charged out of the lodge. Someone or something was coming up on their camp and that black mule was better than a watchdog about warning them.

Outside the lodge, the cold air rushed over Zekial's bare skin. He found his rifle. Kneeling beside a nearby tree, he caught sight of two Osage braves wading up to their waists in the swirling river.

Placing a cap on the nipple, he raised the rifle, aimed, and fired. The Indian on the right screamed and threw his hands up, hit hard in the chest. Without checking on the other one, Broome poured fresh powder down the barrel and rammed a patch in on top of it.

The second Osage charged him through the waist-deep black waters of the stream.

Tilly hugged a blanket around her form and she knelt beside him holding his powder horn and pouch. "He be coming, fast!"

Bullet rammed home, hammer cocked, and the nipple loaded, he drew a bead as the screaming warrior reached the shallow water on their side. The blast of Broome's rifle stopped him cold, and he fell backwards into the stream.

"Watch out, Zekial!"

He rose in time to use the gun barrel to break off the tomahawk attack of another brave attacking from a different direction. The Osage's forward motion tripped him up. He landed facedown.

Zekial smashed in the back of his head with the gun butt.

In the face of the results, down the shoreline fifty yards, the fourth brave in the party turned and started to re-cross the river to the far side. He waded frantically for midstream and swam for his life.

Broome's .50 caliber at last reloaded, he aimed and pulled the trigger.

The hammer clicked, but the rifle didn't fire.

Zekial replaced the cap, his hands beginning to shake from the cold. He drew a bead on the buck's naked back, but the swimming Osage was fast being taken downstream by the current and out of range of the rifle. Broome rose to his feet and raced bare-footed to the water's edge and drew a bead. The Indian took long, experienced stokes with his arms and disappeared in the turbulent waters as Broome fired again.

He could tell immediately that he'd missed—damn bad news for him and Tilly.

"You, all right?" She was beside him again, slipping the blanket over his shoulder. Dressed in her leather blouse, just one of the few pieces of clothing she owned, her brown legs glistening, she helped him back to the lodge.

"You did good." He swallowed with difficulty. Filled with disappointment, he shook his head as she took the long-gun and leaned it against the structure

"You better go in there and warm up. You be about to go back to shaking."

"I need to see about them—"

"They all be dead, except that one in the river, and he be likely to drown." She gave a headshake to dismiss his concern. "They ain't none of them others alive. I will check on them and finish them for you. Now you get inside."

Grateful for her push inside the lodge, he took his place seated on the robe in the still steamy interior. She brought two more hot rocks to hiss in the great kettle and then left him alone in the misty warm lodge, great beads of sweat seeping from his pores. He might never be warm enough ever again, not this warm. So good.

Weary from the exertion, he closed his eyes and drew deep on the steamy air, letting it fill his lungs. Finding a place for them to settle safely for the winter had, so far, proven hard.

———

LIGHT SNOW BLEW IN ON the early morning wind and filtered down from the leafless trees. There was no sun, its light choked off by the snow, mist, and gray, goose-downy clouds.

Zekial pulled on a pair of woolen linsey pants. They were the only other pair of britches he owned. Digging further down into the pannier he'd brought, he pulled out a leather shirt, a spare pair of moccasins, and a snowy elk-skin coat. Good thing he'd thought to bring another set of clothing.

He sat down by the fire and accepted steaming hot coffee in a tin cup.

They needed to hole up somewhere, but this wasn't a great place to do it. No beaver left in these hills—they'd been gone for years. Maybe he could secure some wolf hides and deerskins. A few elk remained, too, game enough for them to survive on through the winter.

Really, it shouldn't be so hard. The men he knew and worked with were all in the Rockies looking for beaver skins this time of year, dodging Blackfoot arrows and fighting worse conditions than those around here. They probably didn't have a woman with them, though. If they did, she was likely a squaw and accepted such things as his fight with the Osage last night as an everyday part of life.

No, he wouldn't put Tilly through the kind of hell they'd have in the high country. He'd do with less for a winter and survive. Besides, all those trappers blew their year's savings and fur pay on squaws and whiskey at each rendezvous in the spring. They always had to get supplies on credit to go back for more furs.

It wasn't so bad in this land. He would need to find pasture for his horses, somewhere with a cave nearby they could use to live in until spring. Probably have to root out an old bear from it. Damn, there must be ten thousand bears in this stretch of country. They hibernated this time of year. Any decent cave would have one or more bears sleeping it. No matter—he could clean one of them out. Finding a cave suitable for them might be the hardest proposition.

For breakfast, Tilly served deer steaks and corn bread. He used a little sorghum lick to dab the dodgers in. Grateful to be dry and dressed in fresh clothing again, he sat on the ground facing the fire and the radiant heat in his face. He savored the food, one bite at a time. She sat across but never looked up at him. Perhaps, when he looked away, she glanced in his direction, but otherwise her gaze was always down. He figured it was the way she'd been raised.

"You sleep good?" She paused, ready to refill his cup.

"I slept better."

"So, have I."

"You reckon we ought to sleep together?"

She bobbed her head. "If you be wanting me to—I will."

"No, not if I was wanting you to. Do you want to?"

"That be like we married?" She squinted her eyes and looked hard at him, as if taking the matter under consideration.

"That be like that." He waited for her reply.

"Can I think on it?"

"Sure." He finished off his coffee and handed her the cup.

"How long have I got?"

"As long as you need." He got up, dusted off his britches, and headed off toward the mounts. She needed time to think, and he had a myriad of things to do, for them to find safe-haven for the next few months.

He pondered the fact that they now only had three horses. Tilly could ride double with him on Red, and that would let the gray and the mule carry the packs. That would be the only way for them to take everything they needed.

As for the fourth Osage—the one he'd missed—he searched downstream for several miles and found nothing. No floating corpse washed up on the bank nor lodged in a brush jam. No obvious tracks on the banks on either side where he might have come out. Zeke could only hope the buck was in Indian heaven and not up north in some village stirring up more hotheads to come down and take revenge for their fallen brothers. If the Indian had lived—and it was a definite possibility that he had—they were in danger.

And what of the slaver, McCord? He was still out there somewhere, too. The Army was supposed to be guarding these parts, but he knew all too well that was the flimsiest of obstacles for an intelligent man bent on his mission. No, Zekial had shown him up and stayed just far enough ahead of him now for him to quit. Unless he missed his guess, this would be—as Tilly originally predicted—a duel to the death.

No doubt about it. They needed to move on.

He came back to the camp to find her staggering under the weight of one of the panniers, trying to carry it to the mule.

With a scowl, he took it away. "Leave them lay. I can carry them."

"Yeah, but I be the slave here."

"You ain't no slave. You run away from that." She hadn't been a slave since they'd left Choctaw Landing. She was crazy as a damn loon. He neither needed nor wanted a servant.

He hoisted the pack and the mule shied enough he had to give a knee boost to his load to catch the straps on the sawbucks.

"Whoa!"

In seconds, Tilly had the mule caught by the lead. With a great effort, Zekial managed to hook the pack over the cross bucks.

"Thanks."

She placed a hand on his chest. "Wait."

"What now?"

"You want me to be your woman?" Her eyes grew dark as pools of brown ink. She gazed up at him for an answer.

"Yes."

"You can have me, you know that?"

"I know that." He went after the other pannier.

She trooped along beside him. "I been worrying that maybe I was too ugly."

"You ain't ugly. You're nice looking." He hefted the buffalo robe case and straightened, the muscles in his lower back protesting the weight.

"I thought maybe you only liked women with big—ah—breasts, huh?"

He tried to get by her with his arms full. "Nothing wrong with yours. You've got pretty breasts."

"Oh, I'm sorry. Get around, Jake." She pulled the mule around so he could load the second pannier.

Out of breath from holding the load so long, Broome bent over and used his knees for support. It was getting them nowhere, all this talking. What the hell did she want from him?

"Tonight, then." She moved over to catch the gray, then Red, returning with them a moment later.

"You sure that's what you want to do?" He cinched up the chestnut gelding. Finished, he dropped the stirrup and turned to look her in the face.

"I be real sure, Zekial. You'll see." She winked wickedly at him and smiled enough to show her even white teeth and red tongue.

———

THEY PUSHED SOUTHWARD MOST OF the day. He spotted some buffalo grazing in a grassy meadow and noted their location near some prominent hills. Higher mountains rose on the horizon, and they headed toward them. He wanted to find the headwaters of this tributary of the White River they'd been following. Somewhere in the south where the streams came from rose the Boston Mountains. He planned for them to winter there if he could find a suitable cave and pasture for the mounts.

"Boston Mountains?" Tilly repeated as he explained his thoughts to her.

Broome nodded. "They're south of us. I was there once before. There ain't many go there. We can be alone."

"You been thinking on this business for a long time?"

"Going to the mountains?" He guided Red around a great fallen walnut tree, the twisted roots towering over their heads even on horseback.

"No, no. This business of you and me." She took a firmer hold around his stomach, then righted herself on the saddle behind him, pressing her body against his back.

"I studied on it long enough."

"You could have had me, anyway. You know that?"

"I didn't want that."

"Why not? Most white men would have. You didn't have to go ask me like I was some high-class white woman."

"You're a person, ain't you?" He shifted the rifle and dried his sweaty palm on his pants leg.

"No. I be black."

"You ain't been that since we left Choctaw Landing." He shook his head and wished the growing discomfort in his belly would go away. He didn't like this kind of talk.

"Sure, you says I ain't a slave, but you's don't own me."

"No one owns you now." He rose in the stirrups and peered down the open, grassy park ahead. Maybe they should graze their stock for a few hours. "Do you smell anything on the wind?"

"No, why?

"Good. I haven't seen a sign of anyone since we set out this morning. We may let the horses graze here for a while. Lots of tall bluestem grass." He reined Red in and studied the mountain to the west, then down the river bottom they'd followed. No sign of anything threatening. The south wind had swung around in their faces and warmed the air.

"Fine with me." She took a deep breath, stretched, then eased herself off the horse. Gathering her blanket around her against the cold, she took the lead ropes.

Zeke dismounted and moved to loosen the cinches. "We better get some more blankets out."

"No, right now you better listen to me."

He turned.

She wore a pained expression on her face, tears matting her thick lashes and running down her cheeks. "You be a good man, Zekial Broome. You done this poor black girl a big favor, but I ain't what you think I is." She shook her head in disappointment.

"What's that?" He took her in his arms and raised her defiant chin upward with his hand until he could look into her wide brown eyes.

"Oh, don't you see? I don't be no virgin."

"Neither am I." Then he kissed her.

XIV

DO YOU SMELL WOOD SMOKE?" Judson sat up straight in the saddle as he pushed the gray horse up beside McCord's mule.

"I sure hope so. I could eat a damn raw bear." Grissum booted the mule forward and studied the column of smoke trailing off in the wind. Someone had a good-sized fire built in the tree line across the snowy creek bottom. Judson and McCord urged their mounts down to the stream to investigate.

A voice suddenly echoed across the hillside around them. "Hold it right there! Who are ya?"

"Alabama lawmen! Ease your hammer back!" McCord reined the mule up and spotted a man dressed all in leather standing with his rifle at the ready just beyond the blazing fire.

The white-bearded man kept the rifle aimed at them. "State your business."

"McCord's my name. This is my deputy, Judson."

"By damn, get down, then. Can't be too careful. This country is eat up with damn crazy breeds and murdering bushwhackers." The man lowered the rifle and put it aside, but in handy reach.

Relieved, Judson and McCord pushed their mounts to ford the small creek, mounted the opposite bank, and reined up next to the fire.

"I can see you've been fortunate at hunting." Grissum nodded to a trio of brown turkey carcasses roasting on a spit. Judson peered at them, too, then took the reins of the mule from his boss.

"Aye, I planned to cook them and have me some bird to eat on my way."

"Oh, you're on the move?" Squatting in the snow, Grissum held his bare hands to the heat. The man in leather tossed some more dry wood on the blaze and the smoke made Grissum's eyes water.

"Whew, this weather is sure cold." Judson returned from tying up their mounts to join them by the fire. He wrung his red hands together and stomped his feet to get warm.

"Being as you're lawmen, I aim to share these birds with you." The stranger scooted in closer, inspected his cooking, and then he quarter turned the spit to cook them more. "Who are you after?"

"A black wench of eighteen and a man called Zekial Broome. You ever heard tell of this Broome?"

"Naw, can't say I ever knowed anyone called Broome. What did he do?"

Judson chuckled. "Busted McCord here over the head for one thing."

'He did, huh?" The man laughed at the notion.

"Besides attacking an officer of the court, he aided and abetted a runaway slave's escape," Grissum snarled. "In Alabama, that's a felony. He interfered in the legal process and then fled prosecution, too."

"What's this Broome look like?" The man poked the fire's red coals with a stick, trying to mound them under the birds. "In case I cut his sign."

"Tall, my height. Barrel chested, yellow hair and blue eyes." The heat from the fire warmed Grissum's coat front. Thank God the damn snow had stopped. "Never caught your name."

"Whistling Dick Hogan."

"You live around here, Hogan?"

"Naw, I live wherever I want to."

Judson laughed at the man's answer. His hilarity drew a scowl from Grissum, who hated laughter at times when it wasn't funny.

McCord turned back to Hogan. "You know this country well?"

"Well enough to find me way back, I guess."

"You wouldn't hire out as our guide, would you?"

Hogan wrinkled his lip under the white mustache in distaste. "Where you want to be guided?"

"I need to find this Broome and that slave girl."

"You got any notions where they went?"

Judson rubbed his hands again. "We thought they went up the White River. They were on horseback and we took the boat to get ahead of them."

Grissum cut the younger man off with a look. "We'd hoped we could learn something about where they went when we left the boat, but there were no traces, and nobody had seen them. I'm certain they've tried to find refuge in some civilized place, and since there were so few in the territory, we should be able to locate them fairly quickly."

"Some white folks over on Osage Creek and at Carrolton. Then there's some more settlers further west at Boonesboro. The government's got a fort down on the Arkansas River." Hogan scratched his snowy sideburns and dropped his gaze as if trying to squeeze out of his mind some more places white folks had squatted on the Indian lands.

"Could you show us these places?" Grissum pressed. "For a fee, of course."

"Ain't much to it. I can put you on a trail to Carrolton, and from there they can send you to Boonesboro and then they can point you to this Fort Smith on the Arkansas."

"That's about all there is out here?" Maybe he really had overestimated the chances of finding Broome and the girl out here in the wilds.

Hogan shrugged. "Most of it."

That wasn't very reassuring. Grissum sighed. "Come morning then, you can show us how to get to this closest place?"

"I can do that easy. Carrolton is what they call it. You go right by the Shawnee village on the way."

"I've heard of them. They dangerous?"

"No, not any more. They're looking for a home, camped down there on a stream. They been pushed around, and most of the tough ones are dead. But be aware, remember them's savages and not white men and you'll make it fine."

Judson stirred. "So where are you going?"

"Hell, like I said—anywhere I want to." Hogan grinned, showing a mouthful of broken and missing teeth.

"Of course."

This old man was a rare find, one of those drifting frontiersmen that spent their time living off the land and avoiding contact with others. He'd given them their first real knowledge of the land since they'd stepped off the Shirley three days before.

Grissum settled his butt on a deadfall and sent Judson off to find some more firewood. If the places in this part of the territory were that few and far between, they should have this Broome treed and that girl back in their custody in a week or so. And this time, he'd teach the little bitch never to run away again.

Drops of grease from the turkey carcasses fell and spat in the hot fire. The aroma made his stomach churn. After three days of hardtack and raw bacon, this would be a meal fit for a king. Hogan handed each of them a browned bird on a stick. Judson, straddling a log, put his before him on the old, bleached wood and licked his lips. Grissum found a slab of bark to lay his food on, then placed it in his lap. He could already taste the rich bird's meat as he sawed off a sliver with his knife.

Judson ripped a hunk of meat off a drumstick with his teeth. "You ever been to the Pass-ific Ocean?"

Hogan nodded. "Three times."

"How far is it?"

"Two, three thousand miles or more. I never measured much like that. It's a helluva long ways, though."

"You ever going back?"

"Depends."

"Depends?"

"Yeah. It depends how fast folks get to showing up in this country. You get a bunch of females in here stinking up this place, I'll move on."

"You don't like women?" Grissum paused from taking his next bite of turkey.

"I like Injun women. They know their place. But all a white woman knows how to do is nag. Wanting churches built and whiskey stills torn down. They ain't worth it. If I go to seeing many of them calico dresses in this country, I'll skedaddle for damn sure."

This tickled Judson again. He laughed. "So, you never had a white woman for a wife?"

"Once."

"She die?"

"Yeah."

"Childbirth?"

"No, a shovel."

"A shovel killed her?" Judson's mouth, full of half-eaten turkey, fell open.

Hogan was unapologetic. "Yeah, I hit her over the head with it. She wouldn't shut up about me taking a few drinks with some friends at a gathering."

"The law do anything to you about it?"

"I reckon they would if they ever found her body. They might even have issued a warrant. I buried her and then rode my horse back and forth over the ground. Then I lit a shuck out of them Carolinas. Ain't been back since. Furthermore, I ain't going back."

"Hell no, and another thing, you live where you want to live." Grissum chuckled to himself at the man's philosophy. Why, he'd done the same thing with toadstool poison to his lazy wife. He licked the turkey grease from his fingers—food fit for a king. They'd sure been lucky finding this old coot.

"That's exactly right." Hogan peeled off another sliver of meat from his bird's breast with his large skinning knife. "And ain't nothing a woman can provide that's better than that."

———

THE NEXT MORNING, THE OLD man shot three fat fox squirrels out of the treetops, hitting each through the head with his rifle. The show of marksmanship impressed Grissum McCord even more. After eating them fried for breakfast, they mounted up. The wind had swung around to the south and Hogan forecasted warmer weather as they rode up on the road he'd promised to show them.

"This road goes all the way to Boonesboro. Mind yourself going by that Shawnee camp, but they really ain't half bad. You could trade with them for some food. Deer jerky and the likes to tide you over. I don't figure they'll have much more than that to sell you at Carrolton, being a new town and all."

Grissum pushed his mule in close to Hogan's shaggy white horse and stuck out a hand. "Sir, you ever come to Slottsville, Alabama, you come look me up. I shall treat you to the finest food there is."

Hogan shook it. "I ever go there, I will, sir. You boys keep your hair. Them Osage are bad to sneak down and jump a man when he ain't looking."

"Many of them out there?"

"Aw, mostly they come down in raiding parties from up in Missouri and fight with the damn Cherokees. They kill some whites here and there, too, if they jump them unawares."

"We intend to keep our scalps."

With a mock salute, the old man reined his horse around and headed south, back in the direction they came from.

———

LATE IN THE AFTERNOON CROSSING a stream bottom, Grissum shot and downed a small deer. They let their mounts graze the head-high cane while they cleaned their kill in a spring-fed stream.

"A fresh liver at last." Judson washed the brown leaves off the organ with his bloody hands. "This will give me back my strength, for sure."

"Heart, tongue and kidneys are what makes a man's rod stiff." Grissum chuckled and set aside the deer's parts on a flat rock. He flung his hands half-dry before using his pant legs to finish the job. They'd feast on venison this night. Maybe, Dame Luck smiled on them at last. "Judson, you go gather some firewood. I'll get that frying pan from my horse. We're only a short while from eating like kings."

The deputy wiped his hands on his pants. "Don't forget the salt."

"Ah, yes, that's the only thing the turkey lacked last night."

"I'd sure eat another, salt or no salt."

"You'll think you've died and went to heaven when we've got the backstrap from this deer all cooked."

"Cook the liver first?"

"Liver first." Grissum jerked his head back toward the trees. "Now you go get some dang wood."

"I'm going, I'm going."

Grissum sighed. This frontier business wasn't at all like moving around after runaways in civilized country like Tennessee or Kentucky. There were road-houses to stay and eat in every night. Plenty of drink and plenty of husky maidens willing to share a bed—a real bed—with a man for a few pennies.

Out here in the wilderness, though, there was none of that. Nothing but a few fleeting wild animals it usually took him three or four shots to hit—if he was lucky enough to hit them at all—and a few old hermits like Hogan living on the edge of civilization between Injuns and whites.

He sighed, studying the clearing sky. The warmer temperature felt so much better than the deep cold of the past days. The snow had been melting all day, making a mushy mess underfoot, but it wouldn't be so bad to sleep if they could make a mattress of boughs to keep their blankets out of the mud.

Mattresses. Blankets. Maidens. Damn it all.

Movement in the distance caught his eye and stilled his hand, quelling his sharp appetite. Four riders, winding their way through the gray-black timber—and they didn't look like whites.

Where the hell was Judson when he needed him?

He rushed to his mule. With feverish hands, he unlimbered and loaded his rifle, then checked the two single-shot pistols in his waist sash. At last he could see Judson coming at a run with an armload of firewood, looking over his shoulder like a dog was chasing him.

"Injuns are coming!" The man's eyes were big as saucers and his breath came in great gulps. Under his black beard, his face had turned stone white.

"Throw down that damn wood and get your rifle. I can see what they are!" He rested his barrel over the back of the mule and took aim.

XV

HER NIMBLE FINGERS UNDID THE ties at his waist. Out of breath from their kissing, wild anticipation filled Broome, nonetheless. His hands tenderly molded her firm breasts and she gasped at his touch. Under the pile of robes and blankets on the grassy hillside, the glare of the midday light bore witness to their coupling. They sought each other's lips until the sunbeams no longer shone behind his tightly compressed eyelids. He used the tip of his thumb to tease her right nipple erect. Hungry to taste her, his mouth covered it and he sought to consume her with fervor. She moaned in pleasure and hugged him to her chest, smothering him.

Wild with their desire to become one, she tore his pants down from his hips. Pushing them past his knees, she moved beneath him, spreading her slender legs and raising her knees.

Dazzled by the overwhelming need to take her, his heart stopped for a long second when her long, calloused fingers clutched his shaft. He ached to crash into her but restrained himself as much as possible in this downhill race. He let her set the pace as he poised himself, stiff-armed, above her. Breathless, he bent over and kissed her tenderly as he explored the velvet tightness of her womanhood encircling him.

"You do it now!" She arched her back and cried out with pleasure as he worked into a steady rhythm. "Do it harder. Oh, please!"

She clutched his shoulders to draw him down to her wanton mouth. Her bare heels drummed on the back of his calves. Could he satisfy her? For a moment, she went limp, but when he paused and looked down at her with concern, her brown eyes danced with pleasure.

"Don't stop!" Her hard-muscled legs wrapped tight around him, holding him inside her and moving him in and out with her fierce motions. Pelvis to pelvis, they ground out their delirious needs. Her muscles squeezed his swollen appendage tighter and tighter. Time floated by while their energy soared again and again. Then, deep in the depths of his manhood, the rush began to build. He rose on his knees and straightened his back, grasping her legs to hold her against him and drove himself deeper inside. The blankets fell from his shoulders. Holding her hard against him, he sought the final moments deep inside her.

Exhausted, they lay in each other's arms, a few covers on top of them to hold in their body heat. Their animals grazed nearby, the sharp chomping of their teeth cutting the brown grass as they snatched their midday meal. Too weak to move from their bed, his hands explored her sleek muscular body as he kneaded her hard butt, then allowed his fingertips to trace up the velvet smooth skin inside of her legs.

She shivered beneath him. "Where we going to live?"

"In a cave in a canyon."

"My, my. When you do something, you sure do it right." She reached over and playfully tousled his hair.

He rested on his elbows beside her. "What's that?"

"Well, I says to myself, back in Choctaw Landing, when you gets on that Grissum McCord on account of me, you sure be a good-looking hunk of a man. But I figured he would kill you and whip me some more."

"What then?" He plucked a long stem of grass to chew on while he studied her smooth, youthful face.

"Well, then we took off and on that first night why, you never said for me to take my clothes off or get under the covers with you. I wondered some about that." Tilly shook her head and stole a glance at him, grinning. Then, embarrassed, she looked away. "I figure you don't like me 'cuz I ain't got big tits."

"Nothing wrong with yours."

"I'm glad they suit you. I never experienced anything like what we did here today with anyone but you." She closed her eyes hard.

He stared at her with a frown. "You going to cry?"

"Maybe." She sniffled. "I's wake up in the mornings thinking I be dreaming. I's never done figured anyone would be so nice to me."

Broome grinned, and pulled her back to him. "Maybe you won't think that when I get through with you today."

"Oh, yes, I will." She forced a wide smile and spread her knees apart to admit him. "My, my, my. We sure don't be finding that cave today, is we?"

"Who cares?"

"Sure don't be me." She pulled his face down to her mouth again and ended the conversation.

———

IN LATE AFTERNOON, A RED sundown cast the round-topped hills in a rich, scarlet light. Zekial hobbled the horses and set off on a wide swing of the meadow while Tilly built a cooking fire. With a parting kiss, he promised her meat for the skillet when he returned.

There were no human tracks along the stream as it gurgled over the rocks and spread into a pool before spilling over another little riffle beyond. Carrying his rifle in his right hand as he dogtrotted, he covered a lot of country and found no evidence of people anywhere in the area. Satisfied as to their safety for the moment, he turned his search to game. This land abounded with it.

Topping a small rise beyond the creek, he spotted six antlerless deer grazing in a wide clearing. Curious at his intrusion, they stiffened and raised their heads to sniff the air. The leader, a large doe, stomped her front leg at him. He eased forward, watching them twitch their great white tails at his approach. With the rifle at his shoulder, he sighted in on the second one from the right—a beautiful fat doe no more than two years old—and squeezed the trigger. The rifle's wreath of black smoke drifted away from around the muzzle. Hit hard, his target bolted a few yards and stumbled facedown as the others tore away.

Promise kept. They had food for supper.

With his large knife, Broome slashed open the deer's throat to bleed it out. While he waited for the red fluid to drain into the dark soil between the patches of snow, he reloaded his rifle and listened intently for movement. Had his shot alerted anyone nearby? His caution was a necessary evil for survival. After a long listen, he decided that there was nothing he could detect, except some noisy crows heading for their roost. With the skill of a man accustomed to butchering in the field, he bent over, swiftly gutted the animal, and saved the vital organs. Kneeling, he shouldered the limp carcass, then picked up his rifle for the hike back to camp.

XVI

THEM INJUNS WANT TO FIGHT?" Judson drew a bead on the four riders milling about on the far side of the snowy meadow. Gathered in a cluster, the Indians seemed to be holding a pow-wow on horseback. To McCord, it grew increasingly obvious they were talking over some damn serious business—no doubt, his and Judson's lives hung in the balance.

Finally, an Indian wearing a beaded shirt and stovepipe hat with a large eagle feather stuck in the band punched his horse away from the others and rode toward them holding up his right arm in a peace sign.

"What the hell does he want?" Judson's hand shook on the forestock of his heavy long gun.

"I think he wants to talk."

"About what?"

"Gawdamned if I know. Hush up and listen."

Twenty yards away, the man reined up his brown horse. "White man, what do you want here?"

McCord eyed the rider warily, uncertain as to how to proceed. "We're lawmen from Alabama. We're looking for a white man and a black girl."

"No see white man with black squaw."

"Well, he came this way. Maybe you missed him?'

"Where you think he go?"

"The white settlements to the west." He tossed his head in that direction.

Judson couldn't seem to keep his mouth shut as he kept his rifle on the other three in the distance. "You think he's the head chief?"

"Now, how the hell would I know that?" Grissum swore, then turned back to the wrinkle-faced man on the horse.

"You the big chief here?"

"My name is Butler."

"Mine's McCord. This is Lighe Judson, my deputy."

Judson laughed, a high-pitched, hysterical little giggle that gave Grissum second thoughts about the man's stability under stress. "How did he get a name like Butler?"

Butler scowled at them. "A Gawdamn missionary gave me that name."

"Listen, Chief, we don't want your land, your women, or your money. We came here to arrest an outlaw and take back a runaway slave, and that's all we aim to do. We get them, and then we'll be out of this land forever. I promise you."

"You pay, then, to cross our land."

"How much?"

"Fifty dollars."

"Fine. We'll be glad to pay you fifty dollars to cross this land of yours."

Butler pointed at them with forked fingers. "Fifty dollars... each."

"I have here a warrant from the governor of Alabama. I shall issue you a check in the amount of one hundred dollars." Grissum waved the checkbook at him.

"Not no damn paper money!" Butler waved his free hand to dismiss the offer. "Gold is only thing we take."

Grissum waved the pad of blank checks again. "This is as good as gold."

"No paper. White man wipe his ass on paper."

"All right. Gold, then." Grissum ground his teeth together. The notion of giving a hundred dollars to some redskin bandits for their passage chapped his ass. Nothing else to do at his point, though, except fight them. And while he'd love nothing less than to shoot these red bastards down and gut them for their disrespect, these odds weren't to his liking.

He stuffed the pad of checks back in his pocket and reached for the purse strung around his neck. Pulling a drawstring sack from underneath his shirt, Grissum opened it and counted out five gold double-eagle coins. It took a couple of long breaths to control his rising temper and still his shaking hands. With deliberate movements, he replaced the purse around his neck and buttoned up his shirt. Rifle in hand again, he stood and walked slowly out from behind the mule.

Grissum stopped a few feet from the Indian leader's horse. The animal bobbed his head and fought the leather rein. It gagged on the tight loop around his lower jaw. "How will other Indians know I've paid you for safe crossing?"

Butler held out his hand, something in it. "This card has my sign. Show it to my people, and they will let you pass."

Grissum studied the worn and bent playing card—the king of spades. He had the sneaking suspicion it was all horseshit, but you didn't live as long as he had in this business playing a lousy pair against four of a kind.

He held up his fist with the coins and dropped them one at a time into the chief's brown palm.

Butler smiled a crooked smile. "You don't stay too long in this country."

"We damn sure won't." Grissum watched the man ride back toward his companions. There were war whoops all around when Butler showed them the handful of gold. His breathing didn't return to normal until they rode off, pushing their horses up the mountain through the timber to the west. Obviously, they were off to have a great drunk on the money they'd just extorted from him—something else Broome and that damn slave would pay for now.

Judson leaned on his rifle as if exhausted. "How many times we going to have to pay them bastards?"

"I ain't no damn fortune teller, Judson. How the hell should I know?" He glared at the younger man. "I do know this, they better watch their red asses. If I ever get a chance, they'll damn sure be dead Injuns."

"What kind of Injuns was they?"

"Damn it, I don't know. What kind did they look like to you?"

Judson looked at the ground. "Hell! All I did was ask."

"And I'm tired of being asked. Let's start a fire and cook this damn deer."

"Yeah, I'm hungry. Them wasn't Shawnees, was they?"

"I don't know!"

"All right, all right."

McCord studied the darkening mountainside. Shadows of evening engulfed the bare timber. Stars had begun to appear overhead and he wondered when the moon would come up. It was at a quarter size and would be late to rise that night.

The Indians had gone, but for how long? Something about the whole deal that made the skin on the back of his neck itch. They'd not seen the last of those scruffy Injuns. Of that, he was sure.

———

THE LIVER THEY COOKED WAS flavored with bitter bile and wadded up in Grissum's mouth. He finally spat his mouthful out on the ground.

Judson smacked his lips. "You sick?"

"Liver didn't taste right."

"Tasted good to me."

"I must have got a bad piece." Grissum rose to his feet and stretched. A knot in his stomach threatened to double him over. His skin crawled with some unknown premonition.

"You all right?" Judson refilled his wooden bowl with more meat from the pan.

"I'm fine."

"Paying them Injuns really upset you that much?"

"I wish I knew—" He scrubbed the side of his bearded face, stared off in the darkness at the outline of the brooding hills against the skyline.

"Wish you knew what?"

Grissum didn't bother to answer the man. He had a strong urge to kick the shit out of him, but he smothered that notion.

"You ain't eating anything else?" Judson nagged.

"No." Grissum shook his head. He'd plumb lost his appetite. "We need to cut us some cane to make a platform to sleep on tonight, so our blankets don't get all wet on this mushy ground."

"Good idea."

"That horse and mule hobbled good?"

"Same as always."

"I sure don't want them to wander off nowhere."

Judson bobbed his head, his mouth so full his cheeks stuck out like a squirrel's. "They're hobbled like always."

"Good. Let's go cut some cane."

"Can I finish eating first?"

Grissum McCord crossed the ground to Judson in three steps, stopping just short of where he sat. The seething rage marring McCord's ugly face answered the question.

———

THE LIMBER BAMBOO STALKS PROVED to be satisfactory when laid in a large pile to spread their bedding upon, keeping it from soaking up the mud and water on the ground. Before he turned in, Grissum went out under the stars and checked on their animals one last time. They were asleep on their feet and the mule snorted when awoke.

"Good boy." He rubbed the animal's snout to sooth him, then went back to join Judson on the bamboo mattress. To save weight on the mounts, they shared the same quilts. He turned his side of the covers back and the cane sank under his weight. He lay awake for a long while and watched the stars, lying with his back to the snoring Judson. It was an hour or more before sleep finally came.

Grissum dreamt about Butler, the Indian with the stovepipe hat and the king of spades as his calling card. The old chief made his way catlike through the night, tomahawk in hand and that silly hat cocked to one side of his head. Starlight glinted off his bare legs and he cast strange shadows on the tree trunks as he stole his way silently through the woods. Out of nowhere, Butler rushed across the open ground, jumped on Grissum's mule and gave a blood-chilling scream to drive the gray before him.

Grissum rolled out of bed, grasped his rifle and knelt listening to the sickening sounds of drumming hooves heading off into the night. The war cries of the retreating riders were no dream. Reality struck him like a hard slap in the face. His breath came in great gulps that knifed his lungs and his exhalations made clouds of vapor. The truth gripped his heart.

It was no dream.

Judson's head appeared from under the quilts, black hair going in every which direction. "What is it?"

"Them red bastards done stole our stock, Gawdammit!"

XVII

HOW MANY BEARS YOU RECKON there be in that cave?" Tilly slipped off the rump of the big sorrel to the soft ground below. Together, they studied the large opening in the limestone cliffs above.

"One bear to each hole." Broome kicked his right foot over the saddle's fork and landed on his feet with his rifle in hand. "Leastways, that's how it usually goes."

She gathered the leads of the sorrel, mule, and gray. "You be careful, you hear me? I don't want you all eat up by no bear."

"No bear's going to eat me. Besides, these are black bears, not grizzlies."

"I ain't never seen no grizzly around here and I don't want to. I ain't going to mess with none of them."

"Ah, Tilly. Where's your adventuresome spirit?"

She looked at him with dread in her pretty brown eyes. "It sure ain't up there in that cave. I be plenty happy camping out here and letting that bear keep his old hole."

"Not when it rains and you're all wet. Then you would say, 'I sure wish I had me a dry cave.'"

"Go get that dumb bear out, if he be in there. I don't want to watch you do it. I's take care of these horses. You go ahead."

He nodded, winking at her, and set to climbing the pile of jumbled rocks facing the lower bluff. It sure was fun to have her along. It had been a long time since he'd taken up with a real woman.

First time he'd had a woman of his own, he'd been all of sixteen, working as a pole-boy on a keelboat running supplies up the Missouri River. He'd first met her at Choteau's trading post where the Kaw River joined the Missouri, a girl from the Fox tribe, close to his own age. Later, on his way upstream to the army post, he couldn't forget her. When they landed, he quit Herman Stiles' crew amid much ribbing from the older men about what he intended to do. He returned overland to the Choteau and found his "Song in the Willows"—her name in her native language.

They lived in a small lodge by themselves. He hunted. Willow made him clothes from deer and elk hides. He could still recall the intimate tenderness of their time spent together. All through the summer, they lived as man and wife. Then one day, as the first frost turned the hardwoods to gold and red, he returned from a daylong hunt to find her gone. He searched high and low for her without success. The whole tribe was gone. Finally, Zeke went to the post to ask the main trader what he knew about their disappearance.

Choteau was apologetic. "She's gone with her own people, my friend. Her parents were angry she chose a white man. They took her with them on the fall hunt for the buffalo and promised her to an older buck in their camp."

He recalled blinking in disbelief, shaking with anger.

"But she was my wife!"

"Ah, Cherie, you'll have many Indian wives in your lifetime. Do not despair. Indian wives are like the passenger pigeons, there will always be plenty of them."

Broome spent two long years looking for her in Indian camps on the edge of the prairie to no avail. She had vanished from the face of the earth. Whiskey became his new bride and he rutted with fat, ugly whores in St. Louis when he passed through. The pretty young ones only reminded him of Willow.

The next year, he joined a fur company and chased the elusive beaver across the icy Rocky Mountain streams and went to Rendezvous at the end of the season. He threw axes in contests, shot in competitions, and drank bad whiskey until daybreak with the best and worst mountain men in the world.

He awoke one morning on the Wind River, hung over after a fierce night of celebration. In the chill of dawn, something came over him that changed the way he would live. He'd had enough drinking and whoring. Enough acting the part of a fool. He decided to grow up.

So, he saddled his horse and rode away without saying good-bye, nor giving salute to his friends who were still lying about in their liquor-induced haze. Never again would he play the role of a foolish drunk.

His eyes drifted off the ledge just outside the cave entrance, bringing him back around. Tilly stood out in the open down below near the horses. Her white palm flashed in the noonday sunlight, and he returned the wave.

Satisfied that she was all right, he raised his eyes to the horizon and searched the tall, hardwood-clad mountain to the south for any sign of life. The winter sun warmed him, and the breeze dried the sweat from his brow. Things had been quiet for them for several days now. While there had been no sign of anything threatening, growing complacent could invite disaster—hence the need for a place to hole up in.

He turned back to the hole in the rock face, checked his rifle, and edged forward into the yawning opening. There was a large open portion around the entrance filled with sunlight. It would make a great front room for their new home, with an unobstructed view of the surrounding area. He sniffed. A bruin was easy enough to detect by odor alone, and the faint fecal scent in the air was enough to confirm this cave contained at least one resident.

Obviously, the animal—or animals—would be sleeping deeper inside, well out of sight. This far south, most bears slept for short spells as food got scarce. As a result, their sleep was light. He searched about the floor for a stick or something with which to fashion a torch. Finding nothing, he set down his rifle and went outside. Edging his way around the bluff, he found a dead cedar tree and used both hands to tear off a branch about the size of his arm. Back in the cavern, he sank to his knees and pulled out his kit. Using his flint and steel, he started a fire in some tinder, always remembering to keep an eye on the dark tunnel leading into the bowels of the mountain.

Soon the small fire licked into the base of his branch. With the flaming torch in his left hand and his rifle in his right, he began his careful examination of the cavern's interior.

The orange light from his torch reflected off the gouged walls as his moccasins padded softly across the gritty floor. Forced to climb up on a small wall, he rose up, again grateful the cave was still tall enough to stand in. The opening's bright hole grew smaller each time he glanced back. By torchlight, he peered with care into every nook and cranny. There were more than a few short side-tracks that dead-ended after a few feet, and several longer offshoots that appeared to have simply collapsed long before. A slight breeze fluttered the flame of his torch. That was a good sign. It meant there was fresh air circulating inside the cavern, likely from at least one other entrance. With ventilation, he needn't worry about poisonous gas as long as the good air fed the flames—when the flames went out, the smart man fled.

He held the light as high as possible to see what was ahead. The roof dropped lower, and he was forced to get on his knees. The odor of bear grew stronger in his nostrils. He'd hoped to find the bruin in the taller portion of the cave, but no such luck. At this point he had no other options, but to continue forward.

He crawled on his hands and knees in the tight confines of the cavern, still holding the torch. Finally, he tossed it in front, pulled up his rifle and then repeated the movements until he had progressed deep inside the cave without any sign of a resident.

His light threatened to go out. He was forced to stop and hold it pointing downward so the flames could ignite more material. At this rate he'd be out of room to hold it soon, and out of light completely not long after.

Raucous and angry, a low growl suddenly echoed off the age-smoothed walls around him.

Caught by surprise, Zekial jerked his head up to find the source of the sound and struck the roof of the cave. Lights exploded behind his eyes, and the blow addled him so that when he brought the rifle up, his fingers closed on the trigger in panic. The accidental shot deafened him. From out of the darkness, a massive, clawing beast piled on top of him.

The fecal stench of bear fur made him gag. Pinned under the animal's weight, he couldn't move, couldn't hardly breathe. He fought to reach the knife sheathed at the small of his back but couldn't shift far enough either way to reach it. The beast roared and clawed, snapping its teeth as it shredded his shirt and the skin of his upper chest and left arm.

When he began to wonder if he could last much longer, a warm stream of liquid began to spread across his chest and stomach. He was being pissed on. With one final series of stomps up the length of his body, the animal moved off him at last.

Out of breath, Zekial lay on his back, wondering what was broken. No time for that. He rolled over, found most of himself still together, and with the rifle barrel in hand, checked for his powder horn and purse. All there. He should not have survived that, unless he somehow wounded the brute with his first shot.

He scrambled to his knees and rushed through the darkness after the beast, pulling the rifle after him. From outside came a scream, echoing faintly through the cave opening.

Zekial raced to the ledge, his heart pounding in his chest. He blinked his eyes in the bright light of day and looked down upon the sight of Tilly with an axe in her hands, standing over a giant mound of still black fur.

"Damn you! You done gone and killed my man!" She raised the axe, ready for another blow.

He cupped his hands to his mouth and whistled.

She dropped the weapon and looked up at him, her eyes wide as saucers. "Oh, praise be the Lord!"

Careful not to lose his footing and take the faster way down, he descended the rock face to the bottom, where she waited for him with tears streaming down her cheeks. As soon as his feet touched the grass Tilly wrapped herself around him, grasping him tightly in her arms and burying her face in his chest.

"Oh God, I just knew he done kilt you."

"You're going to get all nasty hugging me."

"You do stink." She stepped back and wrinkled her nose. "My, he done tore up your good beaded shirt and what else. How come you so wet?" She made a face of disapproval, then helped him out of it.

"You ever been pissed on by a bear?" She shook her head. "Well, I have."

"And here I be worrying myself that you be dead, and you only pissed on?" They both laughed.

His scratches proved superficial, but she doctored them with care, nonetheless. They spent the rest of the afternoon setting up their housekeeping in the cave, dressing the bear and fleshing its hide.

The next day, their newfound home gave them shelter from the cold rain.

Streams of water ran off the face of the entrance while her small fire in the center of the big room provided ready warmth. He stared out at the gray sodden world and drank a cup of fresh coffee.

She sat down beside him. "This sure be all right."

"The cave is nice."

"Beats being out in that ol' rain." She hugged him around the waist and then she pressed her hip to his. He looked down at her and winked.

"We need to start getting some hides together, so we can trade for some things we'll need."

"What we going to need?"

"Coffee, meal, gunpowder, caps, leather to mend the saddles and ropes...." He listed more items off the top of his head. He didn't mention it out loud, but he also wanted some store-bought material for a new dress for her, and maybe some new pots. All women liked pots. Indian women up and left their husbands for traders with pots. Trinkets and beads were good trade items for sexual favors, but he knew the best thing to offer a mature squaw was a new skillet or Dutch oven.

"We sure going to have to kill a lot of them to ever get that many hides."

"We'll be busy."

"When we going to start?" She moved in front of him and pressed her pelvis against him suggestively.

He grinned crookedly. "Well, no need in worrying about going out in the rain today."

"Good thang." She pulled his face down to hers.

The sweetness of her mouth sent his mind spinning, and he reached down to sweep her up into his arms. Her long fingers framed his face while her hot tongue sought his own.

No furs today.

XVIII

GRISSUM KNELT ON ONE KNEE in the grass and studied the tracks in the soft ground. The long, narrow prints among the hoofprints had been made by his mule. He searched the timbered hillsides for some sign of them but found nothing. All they had were the tracks to follow and he had no idea how far they would go. He and Judson needed to overtake and ambush them before they reached their village. Four bucks they could probably handle, especially if they managed to take them by surprise. But against an entire camp of the red devils, they stood no chance at all.

They needed to move faster.

With some effort, he pushed himself back to his feet. Judson, carrying a pack across his back and bags in both hands, huffed his way up the creek bottom.

"Whew!" Judson dropped his cargo to the ground, rested his hands upon his knees and panted for breath. "I want to kill them bastards."

McCord kept his eyes on the path ahead. "So, do I. But first, we need to overtake them."

"But they've got our horses. How're we ever going to do that?"

"Don't worry, they'll stop soon and camp. That's when we'll get them."

The deputy jerked his chin toward the sky. "Clouds moving in. Gonna rain."

"More reason to hurry. Rain could wash out their tracks."

"I figured Injuns would hide their tracks better than this."

"How can they hide tracks? A horse puts his foot down, he leaves a track."

"I guess so...."

"Come on, we're going to catch them."

A moan escaped Judson's lips as he bent after his pack. Grissum ignored it and set out again with long strides, following the tracks.

He glanced toward a small stream off to his left. The Indians seemed to be moving toward the headwaters. By his calculations, the thieves had left the crude road to Carrolton some five miles back and they were now moving southwestward into the mountains.

At the next stream crossing, they were forced to strip down and wade across. Redressing on the far bank, Grissum shared no words with his assistant. The anger within his chest over the Indians' thievery weighed on him like a great stone burdening his every step. He stomped off again while Judson was still putting his boots back on. At a half-trot, he continued following the tracks. Even the sour odor of fresh horse apples scattered across the ground failed to ease his mounting impatience.

By mid-afternoon, the clouds had grown much darker. Fat drops of rain struck the brim of his beaver hat. Consumed with a new fury to capture the thieves, he began to run, drawing on his inner reserves. His leg muscles complained as their trail twisted upward through the timber. The rain soaked him and his clothing, but he never stopped his push except to wrap his rifle's hammer in some oilcloth to keep it dry. Once he looked back to see his bumbling deputy following along behind, shuffling through the growing storm.

By the time he reached the top of the mountain and stopped in the pass to wipe his eyes, he was chilled to the bone. He tested the air with his nose. A whiff of wood smoke brought a smile to his face as he tested the air.

"Thank you, Lord." He drew deep on the wet, cold air, savoring the feeling. "You have delivered my enemies to me. Now, like the children of Israel, I shall slay them for you."

Judson staggered up the hill, huffing like a locomotive.

"I found them."

"What?" The younger man perked up. "Where?"

"Just over this hill. They have a camp."

"How many of them?" Judson dumped his pack unceremoniously on the ground and dropped to his knees. Another wave of wind and rain swept over them, slashing at their clothes.

"Four, I guess."

"What we going to do now?"

"Wait until dark. Then we'll sneak up and kill them."

"Wait, how we gonna do that? Our guns are wet—"

"With our bare hands."

Judson raised his head and looked at him in disbelief from under the dripping brim of his hat. "You ever killed anyone with your bare hands?"

Grissum nodded grimly. "Plenty. We use our knifes and hatchets, then we can use our hands on the last ones."

Judson shook his head. "I never killed no one in my entire life."

"It's time you killed a few Injuns."

"I guess."

He didn't like the deputy's uncertain tone of voice. "Think how they made us chase them all this way and the time we've done lost. Think about every step you made today on account of them."

"I'm thinking it's made me tired as hell." Judson sagged down into the mud in the lee of a large tree. "Can we start a fire?"

"A fire? Have you lost your damn mind? They might smell it."

"I might freeze to death, too. I'm wet, cold, hungry, and tired. I don't even care about them damn horses anymore."

"Quit your damn whining. You remind me of my dead wife. We've got to wait until dark. Then we can sneak down there and get them back."

———

CHILLED TO THE BONE HIMSELF, Grissum sat wrapped in his sodden blankets in the darkness and watched down the mountainside as the flicker of the Indians' campfire went down.

He crawled back over the divide and shook Judson awake.

"Time to go."

"Jesus, I'm cold. You think they've got a fire?"

"Yeah, they got one. We'll be dry in a little while. Keep low and quiet. Stay close to me."

As miserable as it was, they couldn't have asked for better conditions for their mission. A cold wind moaned through the spectral treetops above, and the patter of the rain masked his footsteps across the soft leaf mulch.

Grissum slipped down the hillside, tree to tree. The distance to the camp proved farther than he'd thought, and they had to cross several freshets of run-off that ran halfway up their calves. Cold water squished inside his boots. Hatchet in his right hand, skinning knife ready in his sheath, McCord's grip on the axe handle tightened as he stood with his shoulder to a great white oak and peered at the orange flames of the huge log they burned for heat.

How good that radiant warmth would feel. He closed his eyes to the notion. With a deep exhale, he noted, despite his clumsy slipping around, Judson had managed to catch up. No sign of anyone moving in the camp. Their two lean-tos were set up to catch the fire's heat and shed some water. Across the way, a rope was strung between two trees. The faces of the sleeping horses and his mule shone in the firelight.

"You take the far lean-to," he whispered. "Use the pistol I gave you on the one on the right, then bury your hatchet in the other one."

"What if it misfires?"

"Kill him with your bare hands. Just make sure you kill the first one."

In the dim light, Judson shook his head. McCord wondered if the man had the guts to do it or not. Their lives depended on it. Four dead Injuns. He needed them all dead.

With care, Grissum crept closer, waving Judson around to the far side. When Judson crept to the edge of the other shelter, he nodded to him and drew back his hatchet. When Grissum looked inside, there were two figures under blankets on the ground in the firelight. With all his might, he delivered the hatchet into the first figure. His first victim began to shout; he whipped out his knife for the second one. Then with both hands on the handle in the screaming confusion, Grissum sprang on the other form fighting the covers to get free. He bore the large knife down with all his weight into the wide-eyed Indian's chest. The buck beside him wailed in pain as he fought to remove the deeply embedded ax from his chest. Grissum's blade went to the hilt in his second victim and the buck squirmed under Grissum's weight. He knew this one was done for. Raising up, he struck the hatchet-fighting Indian hard enough in the face that the blow silenced the man.

Grissum struggled to his feet and across the fire's light he could see Judson on the ground, an Indian about to club him with a shaft of wood. He drew the single shot pistol from his sash and cocked the hammer. The shot shattered the night and a circle of black smoke around the muzzle shone in the fire's light. His bullet struck the buck in the shoulder and he dropped the stick.

Grissum rushed around the fire, leaped on top of the downed brave before he could rise. In the ensuing scramble, his powerful hands closed on the red man's throat. He began to shake the man's head back and forth while he throttled the life from him with his thumbs. His victim's eyes widened, the last of his strength slacked as he tied to pry Grissum's fingers free. With his teeth gritted so tight they ached, McCord sought to choke the last drop of life from the heathen bastard. Even when the buck's neck muscles went limp, he continued to clutch his throat, crushing the windpipe flat, then shook him for any sign of life.

"He's dead," Judson said, out of breath.

Grissum looked around. The man wasn't there. "Where's Butler?"

"He got away. The bullet in my pistol was no good. I shot at him first, but I could tell it didn't have no power. Must have got wet."

"We didn't need for him to get away."

"I shot him."

"I know." Grissum spilled on his butt. Heat from the fire danced on his face as he tried to rethink the entire attack. Butler had escaped. The other three were "good Injuns." They had their horses back and some more. Still they'd missed killing the most important one.

"Gawdamnit! I shot him!" Judson shouted.

Grissum blinked at his partner. First time, he'd ever killed or tried to kill. He nodded an acknowledgement.

"Go get some sleep. I'll stand guard," he said.

"I can—"

"Get some sleep. It'll be a long ride back."

"I'll sleep over here. Them guys ain't dead over there. I can hear them."

"Go—never mind, I'll do it. Stay here."

Stiff and his clothes sodden, Grissum crossed the camp to the other lean-to. Twice he checked on the tall shadows and reflections of the fire. Nothing. He found a long-bladed knife in a sheath on the first Indian who lay on his back mumbling about something, the bloody hatchet still buried in his rib cage. Grissum, with a foot on his chest, jerked the ax free. The young man's eyes widened. Grissum reached down, grasped a handful of hair and slashed open the Indian's throat from ear to ear.

Without hesitation, he leaned over and did the same to the second one. Then he removed his great knife from the Indian's chest and wiped the blade clean on his wet pants as the last throes of death made his victim's feet jerk. He went back across the camp and sat down on the ground, ignoring the rain and let the fire warm his face and front.

Three dead bucks out of four wasn't bad.

———

CLOUDS PARTED IN THE MORNING. Their clothes had dried out some from the fire's heat. After a few hours' sleep for himself, Grissum awoke to a cold wind that swept the mountain. Tramping around the camp, he found no sign of Butler. He was ready to go back to the Carrolton Road. They had four more horses, some extra blankets and hides to sell, a few knifes, bows and arrows. In the lot, he found a gold locket with a drawing of a handsome man inside it. "Priscilla Horner" was inscribed inside the case.

"You figure they killed her?" Judson asked, looking over his shoulder.

"Probably did. How else would some bare ass bucks like them get such a thing? Way I see it we done society a big favor killing them three. Been a bigger one if we'd got that Butler."

"He going to stay on our trail?"

"If he can find it. You must have shot him some. That should slow him down." He stretched his frame, and then checked on his knife in the sheath.

"Their saddles ain't as good as the ones we left back there."

"We'll ride back and get ours. Come on, hurry up. The quicker we get to this Carrolton, the sooner that we can catch that damn Broome."

"Yeah, I almost forgot what we came for."

"Well I damn sure ain't." Grissum narrowed his eyes and studied the far line of gray hills. His memory was better than that. He owed that Broome for the headache he gave him. The top of his scalp was still tender from the knots he put on it and where that bastard, Broome, had busted the mug over his head. He'd not be forgetting him soon.

XIX

ZEKIAL WATCHED WARILY AS THE line of Indians on horseback rode up the valley. Uncertain of their destination, he turned the gray horse around and urged her up the flat toward his camp. There must have been sixty Indians headed in his direction, men, women with travois and children even. That usually meant they were friendly, but he wanted to warn her before they arrived and to gather his stock. Horse stealing was a game with most Indians.

"What's wrong?" she asked, getting up from fleshing a deer hide.

"A whole tribe is coming up the creek." He dismounted and handed her the reins, seeing the other two nearby. The mule brayed, and he went to quiet him. He spoke softly to reassure him, then patted him on the neck.

"What do they want?" she asked, joining him and standing on her toes to crane her head for sight of them.

"Maybe nothing. They have women and children with them." With the mule settled, he walked into the open. Three bucks broke away from the column and came toward them. The looks on their faces unfriendly, they came up the meadow riding toe to toe.

"What tribe they be from?"

"Plains Indians. Look like Comanche or Kiowa. They have some good horses."

"Oh, they for sure be coming now."

"You go to the cave." He put his arm in front of her at the sight of the three men's approach on horseback.

One wore a bull buffalo headdress, the others simple eagle feathers. The older man under the fur cap came forward with his hand raised in peace.

"Go on!" Zekial said under his breath to her.

"I stay here."

"I ain't got time to argue."

"I stay here with you."

"White man!" the chief called out.

"Yes," Zekial said and stepped forward. He wanted to dry his hand holding the rifle on something. Watchful as he went forward, he noted the other two held back their colorful prancing paint ponies and allowed the leader to come forward to meet him. He stopped about thirty feet short of the older brave, set the rifle down and held it by the barrel.

"You live here?"

"Yes, my woman and I live here."

"This is sacred land. We come here in peace."

"I saw no marks of such a place," Zekial said. Nothing in the area denoted the sanctity. He had seen such places elsewhere and respected them.

"Since before my father's time, we have come to this valley. There is salt under the bluff." He gave a head toss to the east. "All tribes come here in peace to mine it."

"I will honor such peace. I only wish to winter here."

"Good." The man turned and waved the other two to come forward.

They rode up and he spoke to them in guttural words. They gave hard looks at Zekial and her, and then they spoke more with the elder man. From the conversation Zekial could hear, despite the lack of understanding of their language, he decided the older man held the rein on them in some leadership form.

"Who they be?" she whispered from behind him.

"Comanche, I think."

She made a frown. "They sure be a long way from home."

"Yes, a long way." He never took his eyes from them.

"My name is Bull-Who-Screams," the older one said and dismounted. On the ground, it was obvious his right leg was stiff from some old accident or wound. "This is Takes Horse and Sleeping Wolf."

"Zekial Broome's my name," he said with a nod.

"Let us smoke to our peace, Broome," the older man said and drew a long pipe from his things on the saddle.

"What he wants to do?" she hissed behind him.

"Sign a peace treaty," he said over his shoulder.

"Good, if'n they going to keep it."

The three Comanche took a seat on the grass. The afternoon sun shone and out of the wind in the canyon the warmth made it pleasant. Zekial handed her the rifle to hold and joined them, seating himself cross-legged and facing the three bucks.

Bull made a big deal of presenting the pipe to the four directions and mumbled about it, occasionally issuing a loud word in his language to punctuate the blessing. To Zekial, the whole matter was authentic enough and he waited.

"Your squaw is a buffalo woman?" the one called Sleeping Wolf asked in a sharp way that sounded more like he knew the answer and was only commenting.

"She is that."

"She is the prettiest one I ever see."

"She is pretty."

"Maybe Wolf would give you ten ponies for her?" the one called Takes Horse said and elbowed his friend.

"She is not for sale."

"We did not come to trade for his woman," Bull said as if displeased with their conversation. The other two pressed their copper lips together and nodded solemnly, but their brown eyes danced with mischief. Bull struck flint and steel to ignite a small tuft of grass he'd taken from his medicine pouch. When traces of a fire appeared, he transferred it to the pipe's bowl.

In a moment, he issued small puffs of smoke with a look of satisfaction on his broad face. Then he handed it to Horse who drew on it in quick pulls. Issuing a stream of smoke from his mouth, he handed it to Wolf who did likewise, then the pipe came to Zekial, who nodded to the threesome before he drew on the mouth piece. He recalled the last Indian pipe he smoked. This tobacco mixture tasted as bad. The whang of it bit his tongue and he fought the powerful urge to cough.

With a nod, he blew out the mouthful and then handed the pipe back to Bull. "Will you stay long in this land?"

"No, we will only be here a few days, then we must return to our people. Many new tribes have moved into the lands to the west." Bull shook his head as if confused by what they had seen. "They are tribes we have not known before. White men, too, are coming to this land."

"The Indians are Cherokees," Zekial said, indicating to the west.

"Ah, yes, but they have been here. Some of them have been here for many years. These are new tribes that come now, too."

"I have not been in the west for three years," Zekial admitted.

"You will be surprised. Many tribes who speak different tongues. Tell me, since you are white, do white men have two and three babies each year from their wives?"

Zekial shook his head. "No, but there are many of them."

"One white man said if they walked by here, four in a row." Bull held up four fingers. "They would never stop passing, there are so many."

Zekial agreed with a nod. "There are many."

"Come, ride with us to the salt bluff," Bull invited.

"I would like to see it."

They rose to their feet. Wolf dusted off the seat of his breechclout and looked hard at the gray horse.

"You are a rich man," he said. "A fine Buffalo woman for a wife and such good horses."

"Yes, I am," Zekial agreed. He was not pleased with the looks his new wife drew. Perhaps because she was black and good-looking, she had caught their attention. Horses, he knew, were fair game, but their interest in Tilly upset him more than he wanted to admit even to himself.

"What we going to do?" she asked.

"Saddle a horse, we are going to the salt mine."

"Huh?"

"That's what they're here for."

"Salt mine, you's got to be kidding?"

"No, they've come a long way for this."

The sorrel saddled, she rode him and Zekial rode the gray.

The procession of happy children made themselves busy chasing squirrels that dared to dash down from one great tree, then scurried up another. A barrage of rocks and sticks sent the bushy tails far up into the high empty branches to peer down, shake their tails and chatter at the children as if commenting on their lack of skills.

"Why them women all cut their hair so short and look so bad?" She pushed in close to his horse.

"They aren't supposed to appeal to another man when they married."

"See that girl over there? Now, she is pretty. But the rest of them look real bad off to me."

"They are obeying tradition." He found the girl riding the short-legged pony that she meant. Her raven black hair braided, the beaded yellow buckskin blouse filled out by her budding form. He spotted another girl, the same age, her belly swollen with child, her hair severely cut with jagged edges and wearing an old shapeless wash-worn skirt and blouse. She led a horse pulling a heavily loaded travois and walked with some effort.

They crossed the small stream and took the right fork of the canyon. Ahead, above the tall sycamore and walnuts, limestone bluffs rose much like the one that housed their cave, but even taller. Zekial had never investigated them.

Bull dismounted and waved for him to join them.

"What I do?" she asked him under her breath.

"Talk to the women." He pushed the gray through the party to join the men.

"I don't know no Comanche."

"Learn some."

He dismounted. A youth took his reins and looked at him hard as if he wanted to know what white men were made of. He could see that Tilly had dismounted and was holding up a baby. Good, she would fit in.

"The ancient ones were here," Bull said as they started up the footpath that led to the left-hand edge of the great overhang. The trail was steep and well worn. Once under the ledge they were forced to duck and almost go on their knees, but quickly the rim rock roof grew taller. He tossed a glance at the camp a hundred and fifty feet under them as the women began to set up shelters and build fires.

Room-sized rocks that had fallen from above were spotted along the great open wedge under the bluff. Bull took Broome back along the wall and then pointed to a small vein a finger thick. The chief wet his finger, touched the pale rose colored layer, and then tasted it.

Zekial did the same. When he put his fingertip to his mouth, his saliva told him it was salt. He could see the crude efforts done in times past by others to chip the rock strata away to reach this precious line of mineral.

"How much will you need?" he asked the chief, curious about the amount of work they would have to expend to get it out.

"Many buckets."

"I will honor the peace of this place," he said, ready to leave.

"You are a strange white man. This woman you call yours is not your slave?"

"No, she is my wife."

"Are you not afraid that she will have buffalo calves instead of sons for you?"

"No." He shook his head, amused at the man's concern.

"White men have such black women as Comanche have Apache women as their slaves."

"She is not a slave," he repeated.

"I can see that."

"A few days ago, there were some Osage north of here. They attacked my camp. One rode away. I think he might return one day."

Bull narrowed his brown eyes, considering his words. "Why do you tell me?"

"If he returns with a war party, they may find your camp 'fore they find mine."

"This has always been a place of peace."

"Do the Osage know that?"

"I have never known them to come here."

"Good enough," Zekial said and nodded to the other two bucks.

He'd warned them, now he had work to do. His hide pile was growing. Two gray wolves had made a mistake the day before and paused to look back at him. One bullet took both of them down, and they added to his stack in the cave.

"You seen enough babies?" he asked her, leading his horse up to where she knelt and teased a cradleboard-confined youngster.

"Oh, yeah. Did you see that salt mine up there?"

"It's up there."

"I sure never think salt be in these mountains, did you?"

"No," He looked back. The mineral's existence proved a big surprise to him, and the Comanches coming hundreds of miles for it was equally interesting. Obviously, it was an old tradition and they expected to cross the paths of few enemies coming and going, for they brought women and children along with them. But who else would mine the salt? Not the men, for certain. He smiled to himself as he boosted Tilly up on the sorrel. They had to have the squaws along. They would be the ones to work the vein.

XX

"**T**HIS MUST BE SHAWNEE TOWN.**" Judson swiveled around in the saddle as they rode up the creek. A dozen screaming bare-butted Indian kids ran along the stream and hurled small crooked spears at something in the stream. The splash of cold water made them lean back, but only for an instance before they rushed in to recover their weapons and did it again, following some unknown prey.

"What are they after?" Judson asked.

"How the hell should I know? For Christ sake, go ask them," Grissum said.

Grissum booted his mule on as he shied away sideways from the noisy children. Made to go ahead, the mule tucked in his tail and shot past them. McCord sawed the beast down with the reins in a short distance.

"Whoa, damn you." He swore, taking in the camp around them. Smoke from a hundred fires hung in the valley, stinging his eyes. Several Indian women walked in the opposite direction carrying armloads of wood or baskets of corn. Some were nice-looking, and he tried to recall his last encounter with a woman. Too long, if the stiffening in his pants was anything to go by.

"These Shawnees?" Judson asked.

"I guess." He reined up the mule, then dismounted at the crude log store.

"What are we going after?"

"You hold the horses and stay out here with them. I'm going inside and learn all I can. Broome may have been by here."

"Yeah," Judson grinned at his discovery of two girls in their late teens going by. Their dark eyes flirted with him.

"We're here on business!" McCord spoke sharp enough at Judson that his assistant bolted to attention in the saddle and turned to face the store.

"Yes, sir."

"Keep your wits about you." He tried to look stern enough at the man to enforce his concerns.

"I will."

"Howdy." A bearded white man appeared from behind the counter as McCord entered. A small whale oil lamp hanging overhead shed a circle of light on the worktop.

"Hello." Grissum ran his hand over his bristled mouth and wondered what he could ask for that they needed.

"Heading west?"

"Not if I can help it. I'm a deputy for the justice system, state of Alabama, and I'm looking for a man calls himself Broome. He has a fugitive black wench with him. Has he passed through here in the last few days?"

"No. A man named Samuels came through with his wagons and family. Headed for Carrolton. He had three slaves. Two bucks and a mammy."

"No, this man is dressed in buckskin. Has a red and a gray horse." Grissum studied the storekeeper. Tall, lean, his beard trimmed, and his hair cut close and combed into place, he looked respectably out of place for this raw store. Grissum guessed him to be in his forties.

"Sounds familiar, but lots of folks pass through here all the time these days."

"This your reservation? You the agent?"

"No, I'm the trader is all."

"I've got some extra horses. Since good ones are so short in this region, I thought you might wish to buy them."

"I could look at them."

"They're out at the hitch rail. You ever hear of an Injun called Butler?" He paused, wondering if the chief came from this village.

"He's an outlaw, runs with three other braves just like him. Why, did you run into them?"

"Butler got a price on his head?" Grissum's interest was instantaneous.

"Yes, down at Russellville on the Arkansas River they'd pay fifty dollars for his head. Did you kill him?"

"No, but I tried. In fact, I've got his horses and things out there."

"Lieberman is my name." He extended his hand.

"Grissum McCord is mine, sir. Come out and see these horses." He released the man's firm handshake. A terrible weight had been lifted from his shoulders. He followed Lieberman outside. They were all outlaws and wanted men—good news. No one would mind buying their horses and gear. For once, things had a way of working his way.

"This is Mr. Lieberman. My assistant, Lighe Judson."

"How do, sir." The merchant walked around the horses, looking them over.

"That white one is a good one," Judson said.

"He should be. He was stolen from a man up here in Missouri last summer."

Judson shot a questioning glance at Grissum who dismissed him with a small headshake. He was more concerned if the others were that recognizable. Be damned, if he'd give up the animals without a reward.

"I can collect twenty dollars for the return of the white one," Lieberman looked at McCord.

"We risked our lives getting them horses back. If he ain't worth fifty, I'll just keep him."

"Mighty high."

"Horses and mules cost over a hundred a piece over on the White River and they're scarce." Grissum tried to bridle his rising anger at the man's cheap offer.

"Money's scarce in these parts, Mister."

"Someone will pay that for him or I'll use him."

"I'd pay forty." Lieberman shook his head. "Probably be stuck with him at that price."

"Them other two? I'll keep the sorrel horse to ride ourselves."

"Twenty a piece. About all I can go."

"Give me a hundred and I'll let you have them."

Lieberman shook his head and folded his hands on his chest. "Too high."

"A hundred and you can have the three head."

A crowd of Indians began to gather to watch the trading. Dressed in an assortment of hand-me-down-clothing and mixed leather, they acted like judges. Occasionally saying something in Shawnee, they elbowed each other as the two men bantered back and forth. The merchant's offer rose from eighty to eighty-five for the lot and met the stone-faced approving nods of the onlookers.

"They're worth a hundred dollars and not a dime less," Grissum said and threw down his right arm as if in the final stages of the deal.

"Maybe you can sell them in Carrolton for that. I'd give eighty-seven dollars and not a penny more."

McCord wet his lips, the sharpness of his facial hair burning the edge of his mouth. At eighty-seven dollars, he'd only be out thirteen dollars of what that dirty thieving Butler had escaped with.

"Sold." He went to take the leads from Judson.

"This man is a lawman," Lieberman announced to the stone-faced Shawnees standing around in the afternoon sun. "He's looking for a man in buckskin called Broome who has a black girl with him. Anyone know of such a pair?"

Lieberman held out his hands for a reply. The slow headshakes were enough for Grissum, they had not seen them either. Or else, they weren't telling him. He worried that he had gone too far, or Broome had gone south and followed the Arkansas west. No, all he could learn earlier downstream from folks who had seen them pass by said they had headed in this direction. Maybe they'd learn more ahead at Carrolton. He hoped so. Some of the Indians led the horses away for the man, and the storekeeper went inside to get the money to pay him.

Lieberman returned, dropping coins into McCord's eager open palm. The gold coins in his purse, Grissum took the lead on his mule, Judson came after him on the bobtail gray and led the sorrel horse with their bedding and things tied on the Indian saddle.

Judson's dry whistle of "Oh, Susannah" carried across the brown grass meadows. Meadowlarks chirped at them and a red-tail hawk screamed to his mate circling low for prey.

"Did you find out how far it is to Carrolton?" Judson asked.

"No need to even ask, it's right down this road. We'll get there when we get there," he said over his shoulder.

"Let's camp down in that grove," McCord said after riding a while, pointing toward the cluster of cedars and trees on the creek.

"Still early," Judson said looking at the sun.

"Maybe, but it's been a hard ride already."

"I only thought—"

"Camp down there."

Judson knew not to argue from the edge in McCord's voice. He followed his boss down the slope toward a copse of trees.

"Unload our things," McCord directed. "Start a fire. I'm going over the hill to look for some game."

He sent the mule up the hillside. The steep climb forced the animal to cat hop under his weight. Out of wind they reached the top. He put his heels to the mule and started off the other side. In the valley below, he spotted a dozen or more black stick figures and quickly dismounted. Wild turkeys. He needed to sneak up close to get one of them.

With the mule tied, he checked his rifle, and then steadily moved down hill, tree by tree. He could hear their clucking and the sound of two of them fighting. The slap of their wings and sharp cries were territorial as he eased himself off the mountain. Then as one great bronze breast stepped out between two white oaks, he took aim and fired. An acrid stench of gun smoke burned his nose. The other birds broke to the air in a thundering of wings. They would eat turkey for supper.

Triumphantly, he crossed the field, took hold of the turkey, and slung the large bird over his shoulder. He headed up the hill to where he'd left the mule. A deer, two days before, now a turkey, he was getting good at this hunting business.

XXI

WE'VE GOTTA GO TO FORT Smith soon." Zekial announced as they sat on the floor of the cave eating elk steaks. Heat from the fire warmed them. The outside temperatures had plummeted with darker gray skies.

Tilly looked at him, then covered her mouth and rushed to the cave entrance. He set down his plate and rushed to help support her while she vomited. How had the notion of Fort Smith made her so sick? He considered how helpless he seemed holding her by the hips to steady her as she coughed and spat up phlegm.

"What made you sick so fast?"

She straightened and stood unsteadily on her bare feet, smiling cryptically. "You ain't figured it out?"

"No."

"Well, we going to have us a baby is all."

"You and me?" He blinked. Hard.

"Ain't going to be no one else's."

He hugged her, smiling. Not that the thought had occurred to him, really, what with the reason they were together and living in a cave always on his mind, but a child with her, that did make him happy. He began to swing her around in a circle until she begged to be put down. They were going to have a baby. He could hardly believe it. Would it be a son? He had lots of places and things to show a son.

"When's it coming?"

"Next fall, I'd say."

"That long?"

"Be soon enough, I figure." She remained standing and looked whimsically out the cave entrance as if in deep thought.

"I do need to go to Fort Smith then and get a broadaxe. A baby sure needs a fitting home. We're going to build a cabin."

"Here?"

"Somewhere close."

She shrugged. "I likes this old cave."

"Hey, you better eat." He picked up his plate and looked at her for an answer.

"Maybe later."

He cut up his elk meat. "You and me. We can have that baby all right up here?"

"They just come out, ones I seen."

"I got to catch it?"

"Yes, siree, you sure do got to catch it." She laughed at him and shook her head. "Someday I sure do have to thank that slaver for him finding you for me, huh?" She rushed over and hugged his head to her lower body.

"McCord. Grissum McCord," he said.

He wrapped his arms around her and put his cheek to her muscled stomach under the gathered skirt and rocked her back and forth on her feet. Tilly was a good wife for him.

"He ain't never going to find us here?" she asked in a small voice.

"He won't ever, I promise."

He stood up and began to kiss her but paused and looking into her eyes. "We going to hurt—the baby—if we do it?"

"Lord, no," she said with a serious headshake and pulled his face back down to hers. No trapping or hunting this morning, he lamented to himself as he hugged her tight and sought the fire of her mouth.

———

THEY LEFT FOR FORT SMITH after the next rainy spell. The weather pattern stretched into three to four days per spell, and each day after the passage of a cold spell, it warmed again. He chose the first one past the rain, hoping for two days to ride down there without getting soaked.

Cold air had pushed in the night before. The horses' breath came out in great clouds of steam as they stomped around ready to be on their way. His new wool blanket-coat she'd made him turned the cold. Her gray wolfskin coat did the same for her as she rushed about. He pulled down the wide brim on his beaver hat and climbed on the gray. She rode the sorrel with all their bedding, trade furs and camp goods piled on the pack mule as they headed down the silver-frosted valley to the southwest.

He looked back at the cave on the side of the towering bluff and nodded. Their new house would soon begin to take shape. In the spring they would need to make a corn crop in this valley, too. How many years had it been since he had fought at farming, as a boy in Virginia. He had not forgotten all he knew about such a vocation. Seed corn—they'd need some to plant—and some cotton, too, for cloth. It would grow in these mountains, but he couldn't plant it too early. Cotton was a tender plant. Squirrel's ears—oak leaves needed to be that large when he planted corn. Yes, he recalled his grandfather's words.

"What you thinking about?" she asked.

"Crops and time. About that baby in you and what we're going to do up here."

"Ever since I told you about it, you sure been excited."

"Never had a child of my own before." Full of pride, he swung the gray mare around and let Tilly go first down the bank with him, grateful that the stream crossing here would be shallow.

"You done told me you lived with Injun women."

"I never had a child."

"Hmm, you never knowed you had one coming was all." She raised her legs up and then gave him a sly grin as Red splashed across the ford.

"Maybe." He turned to listen to a crow cawing on the wing. He searched the ashen colored tree trunks that timbered the slopes.

Something was wrong. He could feel it. He ran his palm over his whiskered mouth and tried to fathom what it was that upset him. Those crow calls were not the right pitch. He twisted in the saddle and tried to see a sign of anything wrong. Then he noticed something that moved.

"Run!" he shouted to her as she and Red reached the far bank.

"What's wrong—"

The Osage war cries shattered the canyon silence. Their blood curdling screams made the hair raise on his neck. How many of them, he wasn't sure, even one on the water in a canoe. The swish of arrows sliced the air.

He set heels to the gray, but the sharp deep thud of an arrow struck his left shoulder and the mare screamed. He fought the pistol out of his waistband and shot the first buck in the face who emerged from out of nowhere under the creek bank. Then he stuck the handgun under his thigh, feeling the heavy weight of the bobbing arrow lodged in his shoulder, and twisted in the saddle with his rifle.

At point-blank range he shot another warpaint-faced buck charging at him with his tomahawk raised to throw. Then he drove both heels into the gray and headed after her. No time to reload, he tried to slide his pistol into his sash, but missed, the gun falling to the ground. He shouted for her to let go of the mule's lead and ride for it. He looked back. The Osage in the canoe had gone back for their horses. Three or four other men watched them from the far side of the creek. They had a decent lead on their attackers.

"Run, Tilly!" he shouted, wishing she was on the gray.

"But you hit!"

"Don't worry about me. We got to get away!"

A concerned look on her dark face, she went to whipping Red to hurry. He glanced back. Osage were still milling around, undecided on their next step. He hoped they did that all day and turned his attention to the timber and limbs that he must dodge.

They crossed over the mountaintop and came sliding downhill off the other side. Osage whoops still followed them somewhere from over his pained shoulder. Their shrill cries cut through the air like blades. He pointed downstream to her when they reached the creek bottom. The pain in his back seared him like a red-hot iron. He rode up beside her.

"Break it off or pull it out," he said to her when they reined up their hard-breathing horses.

"You needs a doctor."

"Damnit. Break it off, we can fix it later."

She rose in the saddle to obey him and reached over. In a jerk that almost blacked him out, she brought the arrow out and showed him the feathered shaft. He knew it hadn't been in deep, but it burned like fire.

"Good, let's go!" he said with impatience. No time for sympathy, they had to escape the Osage. Warm blood ran down his back and glued his shirt to the skin as it dried. He pushed the gray after her.

By noontime, he knew they needed to rest the animals. In a wide valley surrounded by conical mountains, he stopped at a stream. She rushed to help him from the horse. He tried to focus on the range they had come from. Were the Osage still coming?

"I'm fine," he said with a thick tongue. "Water the horses."

His knees buckled, and she caught him, lowering him face-down in the damp sour-smelling grass. Despite the bright sun overhead, his world went dark.

———

HE AWOKE AND SMELLED THE musk of their bodies. He frowned. He didn't dare to raise his head and cause himself more pain than the fire that already consumed his shoulder and upper back. Slow-like his senses returned and he discovered he was lying on one of their blankets.

"Hey, he's coming around, gal," some man said. "Hard to kill a blame mountain man with one arrow."

"That you, Whistling Dick?" He recalled the older man's tone of voice.

"It damn sure ain't his brother. You get strong enough to sit up and drink some, I have a jug of corn squeezings that might oil your pain a might."

On her knees, Tilly struggled to help him up. Forced to grit his teeth, at last, he managed to sit up. His efforts put him in a deep sweat that quickly chilled when the fresh wind swept his face. She arranged the blanket on his shoulders.

"Had you a run in with the Osage, the little woman told me." Dick handed him the small crock jug.

"I guess I got careless in my old age. Weren't any sign of them around for the last few weeks."

"Kind of figured that I'd find you somewhere. Didn't think about you being all shot full of arrows."

"One." He lifted the jug to his lips and took a deep swig. The stuff was pure fire and burned his mouth and throat sliding down. Maybe it would ease his hurting.

"One's enough to slow any man down. She got it dug out."

Zekial nodded, then wiped his mouth on the back of his hand. He set the jug down between them. "It wasn't in deep. What have you been doing?" he asked the mountain man.

"Killing a few bears. They've got a grease factory going over at Batesville, you know that?"

"We know, we were through there."

"You know a man called Grissum McCord and his partner Lighe Judson?" Dick asked, ready to sample some of the lightning.

"Where was he?" Tilly looked wide-eyed with concern at the man, and then at Zekial.

"I saw them somewhere near the mouth of the Buffalo and the White River, say three weeks ago. They showed up one night in my camp." He threw back his head, took a deep drink, and then made a loud "ah." "He was asking about a pair just like you two. Asked if I knew a man named Broome." He smiled. "I said, I didn't one bit." He set the jug down again.

"Much obliged for that. Zekial reached with his good arm for the jug. It had helped ease the pain. "Where do you reckon they are now?"

"They're coming from Shawnee Town to Carrolton, then to Boonesboro and last Fort Smith, I reckon."

"We better not go there then." She squatted beside him.

"Grissum McCord isn't stopping me from doing anything," he said to her, but he took some more of the medicine.

"He ain't, huh? Well, them Osage nearly did it today. They done nearly stopped you from living," she said.

"I'm, still, here aren't I?" He looked at her, displeased with her words.

She nodded and pursed her lips. Obviously, that was all she intended to say on the matter. But he could see from the look on her dark face that she hadn't said everything she wanted to. He wished he could humor her more than that but couldn't think of a thing to say. After a moment, he turned back to listen to Dick.

"I made me a little scout while you were out. I don't figure them Osage bucks ever came off those mountains. They wanted you, but not that bad," Dick offered, taking the jug from him.

She glanced back to the north. "I sure hope you be right."

"They've lost four bucks now," Zekial said. "Maybe they had enough."

"They better get busy making some more at that rate." Dick replied, laughing.

Zekial looked back to where the red sunset touched the tops of the winter-bare mountains. The sharpness in his shoulder abated some with the raw whiskey. He hoped that was what those sneaky Osage did—went home and made more of their own and left them alone. The news of McCord on their trail was even more unsettling than the future threat of the Indians. Somehow, he always managed to out figure or outrun Indians, but the two slavers coming after them had him more concerned for her safety than anything else.

XXII

SO, THIS IS THE PLACE?"

They came over the pass and looked at the valley filled with smoke from land clearing. Wind, cold enough to make them huddle under blankets, swept over them. A pungent bitterness from the fires stung their noses.

"Have I ever been here before?" Grissum asked disgustedly.

"I don't reckon you have. I sure ain't and can't say I want to come back here again, either. You reckon that Broome is here?"

"I knew that, I'd be president," Grissum said and slapped his mule with the reins, making him tuck his tail in and trot. Judson could ask the dumbest questions of any man alive. It was past being anything but distressing to them not finding that bastard nor any sign of him or her since they left the White River.

He wondered if that trail tramp, Whistling Dick Hogan, had lied to them. No, he decided. They'd come from Shawnee Town to this settlement, and there was one more named Boonesboro, then the river fort still beyond that. Maybe the rascal Broome had gone to the Pacific like Judson once said. They'd track him to there, too.

Judson began whistling again. Same damn tune, too. Grissum could see a rough log cabin and set the short-coupled mule for it. A chorus of hounds came

around the corner of the structure and bawled at him. A tall, rawboned woman
came out on the porch, smoking a long-stemmed pipe. She blew a thin stream
of smoke from her mouth and grinned openly at Grissum.

"Howdy, strangers. Light and rest them critters. They look plumb tuckered
out." She pointed at their mounts with the pipe stem. "Shut up, dogs!" They
didn't listen to her and went on yapping. She gave them a scowl of disgust then
turned back to Grissum. "Come in here and tell me what's going on. Been a
while since I heard any news." She sucked on the pipe some more and waited.

Grissum guessed her age to be about thirty. The gray hair at her temples
stood straight out like it resisted her combing it back with her darker hair that
was wound up in a bun on the back of her head. She had a wide nose and large
lips, not a pretty woman, but sure open enough with strangers.

"Loosen the cinches, we may be here awhile," Grissum said to Judson, not
taking his eyes off her.

"Come on in," she offered again. She turned on her heel and went inside the
cabin as the men dismounted.

The smell of food made Grissum's mouth water when he entered the room.
He looked around the small cabin. Roughly chinked with red clay, there were
still places where narrow shafts of sunlight filtered into the room from leaks. A
spinning wheel took up part of the room by the hearth. A great bed made from
cedar posts sat in the other corner and a rough table and benches filled the rest.
The main light came in the open doorway despite the coolness of the day.

"Your menfolk gone?" he asked.

She nodded. "He went to kill a bear early this morning. Won't be back till
tomorrow anyway."

Grissum rubbed his palms on his pants and considered her.

"You want to eat or go to bed?" she asked with a knowing grin that showed
the two missing teeth.

"I can always eat," he said, feeling himself getting worked up.

"Less you want him looking in on us, go close the door then."

"You got any corn out there to feed them critters?" he asked.

"I'd sell you some." Unbuttoning her dress, she turned away from him.

"I'll buy it."

"Figured you would." She grinned at him and opened the dress. Her large breasts came free of the material and swung free. "You looked like a man of means when you rode up. Tell him it's in the barn loft."

Grissum shook his head at the sight of her breasts and then strode to the door. His empty stomach churned at the notion of having her in bed.

"Get some corn out of the loft for the animals and don't disturb us." He shut the door and let out a war cry.

Already in the bed, she pulled up the covers to her chin. He fumbled with taking off his boots. A cold shiver ran up his spine as he shoved down his britches and the cool air found his skin.

"My name's Margaret Pauls." She held up the blankets for him to join her, showing off her voluptuous curves in the dim light of the lantern.

His mind swirled with desire. "Um—Grissum McCord."

"Good name."

He crawled between her parted legs. His heart stopped when her icy callused hand grasped hold of his member. In an instant, he was pleasure bound and quickly forgot about Judson's incisive whistling, that buckskin bastard Broome, the black wench or anything else as she bucked away beneath him.

She shouted like a wild Indian at him for more the whole time.

———

AS NIGHT FELL, MCCORD AND Judson sat at the table and ate some of her turnip-venison stew. The green tops and white roots were diced up with lots of deer meat. A stick-to-a-man's-ribs kind of meal.

"Have you seen a man in buckskin and a black wench ride through here lately?" McCord asked between gulps.

She shook her head, leaned on her elbows and watched them eat. "I seen lots of settlers moving in. Here, and down on the Osage River both."

"This good land?" Grissum asked.

"It's free. Ain't free land always good?"

"I guess."

"The damn planters took our land in Tennessee. Screwed us out of it. So, by Gawd, we came here. Guess they'll do the same thing here eventually, screw us out of this. Legal mumbo jumbo like they did Daniel Boone in Kentucky."

"The next town is Boonesboro?" Grissum tossed his head, reminded of where they must go next.

She nodded, then struggled to her feet and went to the hearth. "Getting too damn dark in here. I'm lighting more candles."

"Fine," he said as she set the straw on fire, guarding the flame with her other hand. The second candle sputtered. She blew out the straw. At last she settled back on the chair. "As you were saying?"

"Boonesboro? Must be close to a hundred miles across to there."

"Daniel Boone lives there?" Judson asked.

"Naw, he's put his spurs down in Missouri somewhere, an old man, now. I guess he was there one time or else someone from Kentuck' liked that name."

"But you haven't seen no sign of this Broome and a black girl?" Grissum asked, confused that such a damn nosey woman as she hadn't even heard about Broome or his passage.

"Seen a few slaves. They all belonged to folks moving in."

"Your man coming back tonight?" Judson looked up from his eating.

"Doubt it. He went to get a big bear. Took the ox to bring him back on the sled." She curled her thick upper lip and laughed. "You scared to sleep with me for fear he'll catch you?"

Judson swallowed. "Naw, l ain't scared of much since I came on this trip."

"How come is that?" She turned her attention to him.

"Injuns. Some Chief Butler-"

"They attacked us down below the Buffalo," Grissum spoke up.

"It was hand to hand combat and we killed three of them," Judson added.

"How many got away?"

"The worst one, Butler, but Judson shot him. So, he might have crawled off and died."

She nodded. "You two must be double tough sumbitches. They mention Butler around here and folks go to bolting their doors."

"What kind of Injun is he?" Judson asked.

"Mean bastard. I don't know what tribe. They say he went to white school back east and learned English, then run off and become a damn outlaw. Him and his cutthroats were here last spring. Everyone slept with their rifles for a month."

"He's probably dead by now," Grissum offered.

She nodded, scratching under her left breast. "He's a mean one. Hope you killed him. This country ought to give you a damned medal."

"You heard about the exodus, huh?" Grissum asked.

'What's that mean?"

"They got soldiers going to move you east of the White River. This is all Cherokee land."

"That so?"

"Hell, we came face to face with some soldiers just to get up here," Judson said.

"They better bring a big-ass army to move all these folks. They ain't going to move either. Most of them lost their land, like we did, to them planters and banks. They better send a damned tough bunch up here to root us out of these hills."

"They will, when the time comes." Grissum stretched his arms over his head and yawned.

"Hard again?"

He nodded.

"Just as well go to bed then." She blew out the candles.

"I'll go outside," Judson said, sounding uncertain.

"No need. The bed's big enough for all three of us. Besides he won't last very long." She laughed richly as the two men looked at each other, then shed their clothes in the orange light from the hearth's flames.

———

SHE ROSE IN THE WEE hours and Grissum watched her through slitted eyes. Her strong musk still clung to the body-warm bed covers. First, she squatted down like Eve and built up the fire, and then stood with her back to him. She stretched her arms over her head and made a loud yawn. With her naked form outlined by the blazing light, she hugged herself and rocked on her bare feet. Satisfied with her fire making, she began to dress slowly in front of the fireplace light. The orange-yellow light danced on her large, firm breasts until at last she tucked them in the dress and buttoned up the front. She knew he was watching her. He knew women well enough to know when one was showing off.

She slipped out the door with a pail on her arm, closing it behind her. Grissum got out of bed and hurriedly dressed, curious what she was doing. He'd let

Judson sleep. With some effort, he pulled on his boots. He stuck his pistol and knife in his belt, left his rifle and slipped out the door into the crisp pre-dawn.

A million stars shone overhead. He searched around the dark yard. She didn't have a cow to milk. Where did she get her water? He cornered the barn as she screamed. The sound came from a deep holler behind the pens. He hurried across the thick frost underfoot and leaped over a rail fence. In a rush he went downhill, uncertain as his soles slipped on the glass-slick clay. He caught a hickory sapling on the steep part to steady himself. She kept screaming.

He hurried down the pathway, which led to some spring in the holler. Ahead, he caught flashes of her struggling with someone. A damn Injun was attacking her. He stopped and peered in the night. Too dark to aim his pistol.

"Turn loose of her you sonuvabitch!" With unsure footing, he rushed down the steep track.

Out of nowhere two pairs of strong arms grasped his biceps and despite all his strength he could not shake them. One of the Indians' breath stunk like a bear. Grissum shoved the buck on his right down hard enough he lost his footing and then all three of them went tumbling down the hill. It gave Grissum a chance to pull out his pistol and fire it point-blank in the other attacker's face.

The stench of smoke burned his eyes and nose as he began to beat the second one on the head with the gun butt. The one he shot staggered around screaming about his eyes. Grissum fought for his footing on the sheer hillside. Blinded by his anger, he pounded the other Indian on the head, smashing and slashing like a wild man. The Indian threw up his hands to protect himself.

Finger bones cracked under the wild, angry slashing attack by McCord. His one-time attacker fell on the ground and begged for him to stop. Begging sounds the same in any language. Filled with rage, Grissum continued his blind rampage.

At last, out of breath, Grissum's lungs ached deep inside. In the dim light, the woman, her dress torn open, wiped her bleeding mouth on the back of her hand. She was half standing with her back against a large outcropping of rock.

"You all right?"

"I think so."

"Who the hell was it?" he asked with ragged breath.

"Butler. You didn't kill him good enough."

"Where did he go?"

"Maybe up there to kill your friend in bed." She raised her gaze toward the hillside behind him

"Gawdamn him! No!" Grissum tore up the mountain. "That bastard!"

His soles slick on the thick frost, he lunged up the pathway, his lungs hurting worse by the minute. He scrambled, tearing out saplings to propel himself upward. Still under the brink of the canyon, a turkey gobbled—no turkey. A death chant. Then the muffled sound of a rifle shot. He was too late.

The figure of the Indian backed out the door of the cabin. The barrel of the long gun in his hands smoked from being fired. Butler turned, grinned at Grissum and ran to his horse. Unable to reload, Butler mounted the horse on the run and Grissum reached for him a second too late. The Indian and pony thundered away.

"You-no-good-bastard—" Grissum fell to his knees with hands splayed out on the cold ground to support his heaving body. He tried to recover his wind. Still out of breath, at last, he rose and staggered for the front door. The woman stood fanning out the fire in the bed covers with a broom.

"Judson?" he gasped trying to see him.

She jerked the bedding off and balled the blankets up to put out the fire. Grissum could see the pale white body lying still on the mattress. Judson looked stiff as a board. His bare skin shone bluish under the streak of black that ran from his throat to his privates. He never had a chance—Butler had shot him in his sleep. The bloody mess that once was Judson's face glistened in dim firelight, a blackened, crimson, unrecognizable mess.

Grissum dropped his butt on the bench and began to cry. Lighe Judson was dead. Killed by a bloodthirsty Indian outlaw, while he was enforcing the laws of the state of Alabama.

"We going to bury him?" Margaret asked, covering the corpse up.

"Yeah." McCord sat there and didn't want to ever move again.

XXIII

THE BANDAGE SHE'D WRAPPED AROUND his chest constricted Zekial when he reined-in Red. The road to Fort Smith loomed before them on the wooded peninsula across the snaky-muddy Arkansas River. They rode down the sandy bank from the Van Buren settlement of cabins and shacks to the ferry. The water level was way down. They crossed a wide sandy portion of the riverbed to reach the barge strung on rope cables.

"Morning," the ferry operator said. A whiskered man in rough clothing and a shapeless, peaked felt hat, he looked the three of them over trying to figure out what to charge.

"How much to cross?" Dick asked and dismounted.

"Five horses, two men and a nigger wench. Let me see. That comes to seventy cents."

"Half a dollar is too much," Dick said, looking to Zekial for his opinion.

"Sounds plenty to me," Zekial agreed, musing to himself how Dick handled the likes of the ferry man.

"I've got my costs—"

"You're taking us over for fifty cents," Dick said sharply. "I could hire someone to kill you and take it across ourselves for less."

"Listen here—" The man's face reddened under his straggly beard.

"No, you listen, partner. You want our fifty cents, or are you going to feed the damn catfish?"

"Get on board," the man grumbled.

The mule made a fuss about boarding, but Zekial had his lead and Dick busted him hard on the butt, so he clambered aboard with the horses. The complaining ferryman began to work the reel handle that pulled them across.

Water slapped at the sides of the barge and the cool wind swept down the river from the north. The ridge of mountains stood behind the Van Buren hillside that towered above the river crossing. Zekial stood and watched the far shore.

———

OFF THE FERRY, THEY HEADED up the wagon tracks, passing a squad of soldiers chopping firewood. A mound of fresh-split wood filled a two-wheeled cart. A team of oxen stood placid under the yoke, chewing their cud and waiting for the command to move out.

The wagon tracks grew muddier, forcing them to crowd the tall green cane at the edge of the right of way to prevent bogging down their horses. At last, they rode up on higher ground and the mud became less of a problem. Cleared fields and rail fences closed off the brown, stripped cornfields. A small patch of cotton showed traces of the white lint clinging to the frosted dead plants.

Smoke swirled from rock chimneys. The whacking of axes sounded. Zekial smiled at the crow of roosters. They spooked five thin sows out of one mudhole in the road. The slab-sided sisters caked in dark dirt eyed them suspiciously from a distance, ready to run further at the first move toward them.

At last, the threesome reached the cluster of log stores and taverns that served as the town. The military base known as Fort Smith was further down on the riverbank. The wide street in front of the buildings was a complete quagmire and log walks were caked with mud. Both men dismounted on the driest piece they could find that joined the log walkways.

"Take the horses out in the country and let them graze," Zekial said to her. Then under his breath, his voice low, he warned her. "Keep an eye about you. McCord may already be here."

She nodded her understanding and pulled on the many reins to get her wards to go with her. He stood holding his rifle and watched her ride north. She shouldn't have to go too far to find graze; horses were in short supply here and there was lots of grass. He'd only seen a few oxen on farms since he spotted the army's team.

Dick motioned toward the tavern. "Let's wet our whistle. We can find out if they've seen McCord, too."

"'Good idea." Zekial led the way into the grog shop.

A red-faced man greeted them from behind a raw board bar. "Howdy. What'll it be, gents?"

Dick cocked an eyebrow. "Whiskey?"

"Got some corn squeezings."

"We'll try some."

Zekial carefully eyed the crowd. No sign of the big man in the unbathed scruffy lot drinking and loafing on the benches. He returned their hard looks before he turned back to Dick.

A potbellied Indian squaw came over and bumped her hip against Dick's, then laughed. Her actions drew a few hee-haws from other customers.

"Get him, Ruby!" some old boy shouted. A round of laughter rippled through the dark smoky room.

She looked up at him with glassy eyes. "Buy me whiskey."

"Hell, girl, you're drunker than Hooter's goat right now," Dick spoke above the room's racket.

"Me got big pussy."

Her words drew more encouragement and agreement over her statement from the boys. They all leaned forward to watch the show and see what she'd do next to the mountain man.

"I bet you do," Dick said and nodded at her.

"You want some?" she asked. Her head swung loose on her shoulders and rocked from side to side.

Dick laughed. "Girl, I'd have to be a hell of a lot drunker than I am right now to want you."

"You get horny, you find Ruby, huh?" She poked him in the stomach.

"I will, sure enough," He held up his tin cup for more of the smooth corn liquor.

She turned to Zekial. "You horny?"

"No, ma'am." He grinned at her, then turned back to the bar.

"Gawdamn." She swore and staggered back to the boys along the wall. "No one wants pussy anymore."

Her words drew more hoots and laughter.

"You ain't seen a big man from Alabama in town?" Zeke asked the barkeep. "McCord's his name."

"McCord?" The man mulled over the word before he poured Zekial's cup full. "Don't ring a bell. What's he do?"

"Slave chaser."

"Nope, there was a pair came through here last week looking for some bucks run off down at the Russellville settlement. One of them was named Naples. He won't get them back though. Them bucks get down with some of them Injun tribes, they won't give them up."

"Thanks." If McCord wasn't there yet, they could get their supplies and head back to the mountains.

Dick finished off his second cup. "You ready to go get your needs?"

"I'd like to get back before it rains again," Zekial said with a bob of his head. "You coming back with us?"

"No, I may slip upstream to Fort Gibson, though. See what the army's doing over there."

"We're on an east fork of Lee's Creek."

"I'll bet I can find you. Ready to go get them supplies?"

———

THE GRAND STORE BORE A hand-painted, crooked board sign tacked over the canvas door that Zekial parted. The interior was barely illuminated by translucent skin-covered windows and two whale oil lamps. A small man with a bushy mustache welcomed them. "My name's Alpha Reinhardt."

"Zekial Broome. That's Dick Hogan."

"Glad to meet'cha fellows. You got any skins to sell?"

"Some prime wolf skins. Deer skins, too. How much are they worth to ya?"

"A good wolf is worth maybe three dollars. A deer in good shape a dollar." He nodded. "I'll go get the lot."

"I'll stay here," Dick said. "I want to look over the gee-gaws he's got."

"Be right back." Zekial headed out the front door. Outside, he took the path between the store and the next structure to head north. The north wind swept his face. He set out in a long jog to find Tilly and the horses. Soon he found her tracks that ran alongside a neat rail fence. Ahead were the horses, heads down grazing. A smile crossed his face.

"Tilly!" he called.

No answer. He looked around, squinting against the bright midday sun, a knot forming in his stomach. The animals acted undisturbed, but she was nowhere to be found.

He knelt and read the signs. Her bare footprints stood out in the damp soil. His eyes watered from the sharp wind while he studied the barren woods beyond the clearing. Something was bad wrong. Tilly would never leave the horses unless she had a good reason.

XXIV

A SHARP NORTH WIND SWEPT brown leaves around them as they toiled in the hard dirt. Hard red clay and rocks gave little each time Grissum swung the pick. His shoulders ached, and his arms burned from the stretching as he rested on the side of the knee-deep grave and Margaret scooped out the latest pickings.

"Going to have to do for him," Grissum said with a shake of his head. Bone tired and they hadn't gone two inches deeper in the past hour.

She agreed and caught her breath. They both climbed out on their knees. Dog weary, they straightened. Grissum looked down the valley at the post oaks on the far slope still tight with their brown leaves. Tall bare sycamores were stark white along the creek banks. Somewhere out there, that damn Butler probably spied on them and laughed at his efforts to bury Judson. He paused and drew a deep breath. "Let's go get him."

In the cabin, he shouldered the blanket wrapped stiff body and she led the way. He carried Judson like a log balanced across his shoulders. Grissum walked slow, watching his footing on the rock-strewn yard. He didn't need to twist his sore ankle again.

Hesitating at the edge of the hole, Grissum slid down the slope he'd left at the end of it. The body hopped about on his shoulders, nearly knocking him down. With a grunt, McCord shrugged, and the corpse tumbled to the ground.

At last, Judson rested on his back and Grissum climbed out of the grave.

"Should you pray?"

"Too late. I figure Judson made his own deal with the man."

"I understand." The wind whipped the skirt of her dress around her legs. She wore a red sweater and hugged her arms close to her body to hold in the heat.

He nodded and took up the wooden shovel, piercing the mounds of earth by the hole. The dirt fell into the grave with thuds. He hurried to cover the blanket wrapped figure that once whistled "Oh, Suzanna" all day.

At last, he patted down the red mound and raised himself upright. She nodded in approval. A worried look in her eyes, she chewed on her full lower lip. He drew air into his starved lungs and stared at her. Icy sweat dripped from his face.

"What you going to do now?"

"Get drunk!" Like a one-handed spear, he stuck the shovel in the mound. Grateful that task was over, he considered what he should do next besides drink himself senseless. Somehow, Judson's death had drained all the drive from him.

She nodded her approval. "Can't argue with that."

"I got some whiskey in my saddlebags."

"Good." She stared up at the cabin as if she dreaded the trek back uphill. Then with a sigh, she led the way.

———

MARGARET WENT TO SPREAD THE word among her neighbors that the outlaw Butler was about and had killed a man. Seated at her table, whiskey numb, and alone, McCord stared out the open front door and wished he were home in Alabama. He considered all that had happened since he left home, capturing that runaway wench in Kentucky, having her stolen, and now, he'd even lost Judson. He shook his head and rapped the tin cup on the tabletop. His belly on fire, he tried to think of how to trap Butler.

Despite a pistol wound, that damn Indian had come back to haunt him. When they met again, McCord would use a hatchet on him. Yes, dammit. Next time, Butler would have to come back from the dead in small pieces.

He poured himself some more whiskey. The thirst to get real drunk had evaporated. He was all fired to find Judson's killer and take revenge for his friend's death.

Sounds came from outside all of a sudden, carrying above the howling wind—a sled runner squeaking on the rocks, someone's voice goading an ox. Rising, Grissum stepped out on the porch, expecting Margaret's man had returned. He studied the red longhorned ox hunched under a load as he came uphill. The furry, crow-black mound on the rig behind him looked as big as a black bear, and the ox was having a hard time dragging it up the hill to the cabin.

The medium-built man with the steer didn't look at all surprised to see him standing on his porch.

"Margaret here?"

Grissum shook his head. "Gone to warn the neighbors."

"Jacob Pauls is my name. What's happened?"

"Butler attacked her down by the spring about daylight. I went to help her and maimed two of them red devils. While we were fighting them, Butler ran up here and shot my assistant in bed."

"His grave?" He jerked his head toward the fresh grave.

"Yeah."

Turning, Jacob shaded his eyes with his hand to see down the valley. "Looks like she's bringing some of them back."

"Sure does." Grissum dropped off the porch to watch the line of men driving two half-naked Indians in front of them

Margaret cupped her hands to shout over the sound of the wind. "They got two of them devils."

By God, they had. One had a nasty gash across his scalp and dried blood on his face—that must be the one he'd clobbered down the hill. The other man sported a gunshot wound in his shoulder.

A burley, handsome man stuck out his hand to McCord. "I'm Captain Fancher. We caught these two hiding down on the creek."

"Grissum McCord. No sign of Butler?"

"No one's seen him. He's a ghost."

"Damn live one." Grissum shook his head in disgust. Butler weren't no ha'int. "What do you aim to do with these two wags?"

"After Margaret told us about how you saved her life, we figured you'd like to help us hang them."

He glared at the two downcast bucks. "Captain, I'll jerk the rope."

"Take them down on the creek, boys," the captain ordered. "We'll use that big walnut down there."

"You want to come along, Jacob?" Grissum asked.

The five men who'd come with Fancher crowded around the sled to gawk at the massive bear. Impressed, they began taking bets as to its weight and size.

Jacob nodded. "I think the bear can wait a while."

————

I N THE GRASSY CREEK BOTTOM, someone tossed a homemade rope over a stout limb. A noose was fitted on the first Indian's neck. Three men, including Grissum, took hold of the rope.

"You got anything to say?" Captain Fancher asked the condemned.

The man never batted an eye.

"Go!" Fancher directed with a slice of his hand.

Grissum put his shoulder into the rope and, aided by the others, jerked the buck into the air. The Indian swung, kicking and gasping. A fecal smell of his released bowels stunk the air while the men tied off the rope. They watched him turn blue. His feet trod slower and slower until he finally hung limp.

"You shoot me!" the second Indian begged on his knees. "Shoot me!"

"Drag him over," Grissum waved to the men holding his arms. "You red bastard, we ain't giving you but one chance. Where's Butler? We get him, you go free."

"Head water—King Ri-ver—"

Grissum looked to the captain. "You know where that is?"

"Where up there?"

"Got a cave up there."

Grissum jerked him up by the sore arm on the wounded side and got in his face. "You're lying!"

"No lie. Butler—he there."

"Good." Grissum put the noose on the man's neck.

"You say, go free if I tell where find Butler!"

"Yeah, but we don't know you ain't lying."

"No lie. No hang me."

"If we find him, we'll even say we're sorry." Grissum jerked him to his feet and nodded to the men on the rope. Then held up his hand for them to wait another moment. "What's your name?"

"Blue Fox. Why you ask?"

"So, I can say I'm sorry, Blue Fox, when I kill that Gawdamn Butler up there. Hang him high, boys."

Blue Fox screamed as they jerked him off his feet. He tried to walk in the air. Urine soon ran down his pants leg and dripped off his dusty feet. His struggles subsided like a candle burning its last, until there was nothing but the wind to sway the two corpses.

Grissum dusted off his hands in disgust. "I've got a jug of whiskey. Up at Jacob's house."

The grim-faced men, unaccustomed to such violent deaths, nodded and they walked up the hill in silence.

"Whiskey's what we need," Fancher agreed.

"You ain't seen a buck-skinner with a black bitch, have you?" Grissum asked.

The other man frowned. "No."

"He stole a slave from me in Choctaw Landing and headed this way."

"Oh."

"Do you and a couple tough men want to go find this Butler in the morning?"

"I guess."

"We can ride my horses."

"Good." Fancher looking relieved. "I'll be ready at dawn."

―――

GRISSUM'S JUG WAS PASSED AROUND until empty. Jacob went and found another. The men sprawled out in the sun on the ground, drank from the neck of the crock and talked softly.

"I need two men to ride up with Grissum McCord here and me to this place where Butler is hiding on the King's River," Fancher said.

Men searched each other's faces. No hands went up. They acted uneasy and doubtful.

Grissum spoke up. "Someone can use my man's rifle. It's a percussion model."

A freckle-faced boy in his late teens stepped forward. "I guess I'll go."

Fancher nodded. "That's Ab Mercer. He's a good man."

"Count me in." A thin-faced man in his thirties stepped forward.

"That's Talbot Higgins."

"I have horses for us to ride," Grissum said.

"I'd go," a short man said standing up. "But my Jenny is puny, and I need to get back to her."

"Hope she gets better, Lem," the captain said to the man. A chorus of other men's wishes were added for her recovery. Grissum decided they probably had the best men from the farmers to accompany them. Jacob, the bear hunter, might make a good one to go, but he never offered. No way to know what the man thought. He'd not acted surprised that Judson was in his bed when he was shot. Still, a man who hunted bear alone was no one to upset.

Captain Fancher rose to leave and he shook Grissum's hand. Their plans set, the three men agreed to be there before sunup to make the trip. The midday sun warmed them out of the wind and the other men either shook McCord's hand or thanked him. He noticed how warily they glanced at the strung-up outlaws as they passed them, then quickly looked ahead as they filed homeward.

———

GRISSUM HELPED JACOB AND MARGARET slaughter the bear. Margaret rendered the fat in a large cast iron pot. They cut up the carcass, rubbed salt in the meat, and then hung the parts in the smoke house to cure. That completed, he washed his hand in a pail and tried to get the flecks of rough salt out of the raw spots.

"We'll have tenderloin tonight," Margaret announced. Grissum hoped she had plans to cook lots of it. Like most rural folks, they never stopped for a noonday meal. Two meals sufficed them, and they didn't lose an hour of daylight.

Weary from all the work, he dropped his butt on the porch. He realized neither her husband nor Margaret had said much while they'd butchered the carcass. As a matter of fact, the whole butchering process had been a mute experience for him.

He wiped his tough palm over his lips and tried to figure out what was wrong. He shrugged and looked again down the long valley. The two corpses still hung there. To make it perfect, he wanted two more down there on the same limb—Butler's and Broome's.

He frowned when she came out and sat close to him to smoke her pipe. He had enough troubles, he didn't need her man getting jealous.

She read his mind. "Jacob being back don't change nothing."

"Why not?" He looked displeased at her intentions.

She searched around for her man, and then settled down, satisfied he was out of earshot. "We ain't really man and wife."

"You ain't?"

"Can't be." She shook her head and looked down at her bare feet. "Jacob's my half-brother. Indians killed our father and my mother in Tennessee. We were thrown together, so we said we were married, but we could never be married. We never—you understand?"

Grissum nodded, suppressing a grin. Stranger things had happened on the frontier. Back home, he knew a full brother and sister who'd birthed a whole house full of idiot kids, eyes so close together, they looked like they only had one. Every one of them appeared so dumbstruck, he wanted to hit all of them in the head whenever he rode by their place and they lined the road to wave at him. What a mess.

"He's gone for a while. You want to come inside?" She put her hand on his leg and rubbed it with her strong fingers.

"Sure." He smiled and then rose with some effort. The digging and butchering had tolled on his muscles, which made him sore all over. The butchering had found every cut in his hands, too, so it hurt to brace himself that way, too.

Tomorrow he'd go find Judson's killer. The fresh grave reminded him of his responsibility and culpability. What was that whore's name back in Choctaw Landing? On the way back, he'd need to stop and tell her Judson had died.

He shook his head to dismiss the emptiness of his loss. With a sigh, he followed Margaret inside. Arms over his head, he stretched and watched her undress beside the bed.

She looked up and paused in her unbuttoning. "Close the door. That way he won't come in on us."

"Sure." He shut it.

XXV

DICK!" ZEKIAL REINED UP IN front of the store. Tilly was gone, and he was beside himself with concern. Nothing needed to happen to his woman. Hogan's wide-brimmed hat appeared in the doorway. "What's wrong?"

"Someone's taken Tilly. Come help me sort out the tracks." He booted the red horse up close and gave him the reins to his bay.

Hogan ran out the door and vaulted up on his saddle. "Who did it?"

"What's wrong?" The storekeeper came outside to see what was wrong.

"Someone stole his woman." Dick wheeled his horse hard, and punched his spurs, starting off after Broome at a run. He rode up close behind his friend and trotting his animal. "No sign of her?"

"No sign. I figured you could see something in the mud that I missed."

"She run off?"

"She's pregnant with our child. No, she didn't run away."

The pack animals tugged on their leads as they approached. Impatient he glanced back. Dick moved in and waved his arms to make them go. They reigned in to a stop at the place where he'd found the horses grazing. Dick dismounted and began to circle the area in a widening ring while Zekial rolled his chapped lower lip under his sharp upper teeth.

"Two men in moccasins took her."

"White or red?"

"Can't tell. They weren't big men." Dick leaned over and studied the ground.

"Where did they go?"

"West."

Zekial knew one thing. It wasn't Grissum McCord. He had big feet. "Let's get these animals undone and go after them."

———

A DEEP-ROOTED NAUSEA SET in as he followed Dick through the tall cane breaks. Irritated at the horses, he realized that she'd been the one to handle or drive them in the past weeks. He'd forgotten how stubborn they could be.

They reached a wide beach with several canoes sitting on the high ground above the river. Dick rode to the water's edge and came back. He studied the far side. Smoke rose in the sycamores from cooking fires across the Arkansas. "They took her by canoe from right here."

"Wonder where they took her?" Zekial asked, filled with a new urgency. Water didn't leave any tracks.

'We can cross over in one of these canoes."

"We need to cache our things and horses first." Zekial strained his eyes to see across the muddy river.

"Looks like an Injun camp over there."

He agreed, from what he could make out. Lodges and shelters cloistered across the stream. Enough wood smoke that it was obvious there were people over there. Damn, they had to find her.

The sharp wind swept his face. He rode back into the head high cane breaks to search for a place to leave their horses and halfway hide their possessions.

He turned the horses out, the gray mare hobbled so they'd stay close. Their things hidden in the cane, they hurried back to the river.

"Strange, they didn't touch a thing but her."

Zekial had noted that, as well. Grateful he had Dick and his tracking skills to assist him, they shoved the best-looking canoe into the water and used the hand carved paddles to send them flying over the strong current and across the river. On the far bank, Zekial leaped out with his rifle in hand. He dragged the bow up onto the sandbar.

"You go that way." Dick leapt out and headed north. "They left tracks if they came over here."

Zekial hurried down the sticky clay shoreline. At the second canoe, barely beached, he spotted her familiar splayed toe tracks.

"Hey! Here they are." He waved Dick back, feeling satisfied that they weren't far behind the kidnappers.

Dick came on the run with his rifle in his right hand. He agreed they were the right tracks and they both looked at the village spread down the bank above them. A few onlookers had come to stare at them. Many were small children dressed only in thin shirts that didn't reach their waists. Girls and boys were obvious from their exposed genitals.

"You see two men with a black girl?" Dick asked the oldest one when the two of them reached the top of the bank.

The youth's nod settled Zekial some. Still filled with gut wrenching concern, he stood on his toes and tried to see up river.

"Who was it?" Dick asked carefully.

"One called Gut Line, the other Black Heron. Don't know black girl's name in the wolf-skin hood," the boy said.

"That's Tilly," Broome said.

"Which way did they go?" Dick asked.

"Have horses. Ride south."

"Three horses?"

The boy shook his head. He held up two dirt stained fingers to show the number they rode out on.

"Show me their tracks," Dick said and then turned to Zekial. "You better go back and get the saddle horses and our things. They've taken it on the run with her. I'll follow the tracks on foot until you catch up."

"Good enough."

Zekial set out in a run for the canoe. He found, with only one man rowing, the current proved powerful. Paddle in hand, he wondered about swimming the stock across the river. The water was deep enough under the muddy waves that slapped the side that they would have to swim to ever cross it. On the far side at last, he rushed to locate the horses.

Out of wind, he found the grazing horses and with fumbling fingers saddled the three, then repacked the mule and Dick's pack animal. It would be a long crossing and he dreaded the prospects. No time to wait, he swung up on Red and led the resistant line through the cane breaks until they emerged at the riverbank.

He'd have to drive them across. Otherwise, the stubborn mule would stay on this bank. He herded the gray mare in the water. She paused to drop her head and drink. The others followed to get their fill. When she raised her head and looked at the far bank, he began to shout and pound his leg to get them started into the river.

He hurried Red up and down the boggy shallows behind them, hoping there was no quicksand. Shouting and yelling at the horses to get them into the water. At last, the gray took the lead. In the river, she leaped high in the water, when the bottom gave out. Her shrill squeal made him sick. But on the second leap, she began to swim in the swift current and her head pointed across the stream. The mule joined her route, his packs bobbing on both sides. Dick's two began to tread water after them.

He put heels to Red with a great "Yee Haw!" When the sorrel horse began to swim, Zekial held the rifle up in one hand and clung to the horn, using his feet to kick. His arms ached, and the frigid water sought his leg muscles. His leather pants grew heavier.

Ahead, the gray climbed out and shook. He staggered up from the shallows and noticed the entire Indian village had come out to see what sort of damn fool swam five horses across the river on the coldest day of the year. He swung his wet cramping leg over Red and went to gathering leads. No time for drying out. Dick was already somewhere ahead on their back trail.

"Crazy white man!" a gray-haired Indian said out loud to a pregnant squaw standing beside him.

Several more nodded. One teenage girl pointed at him and giggled. Zekial barely noticed them as he set Red into a lope and his string came on the double. Crazy or not, he had a woman to find.

In an hour, he caught up with Hogan loping along with his rifle in hand.

Dick took his bay horse's reins. "Have any trouble?"

He shook his head. "They far ahead?"

"No, we should catch them by dark."

"Good, on the move they can't hurt her much," Broome said.

"We have to be careful when we get close," Dick said, standing in the stirrups. "They might try to kill her."

Zekial nodded and then whipped Red into a lope.

They rode through the tall-brown bluestem, following a dim wagon trail that headed for the mountains which rose in the southern sky, a place where Zekial had never been. Their barefoot horse tracks plain in the soft ground, he finally let Red drop into a walk and get his breath. The mule snorted, sounding grateful for the reprieve.

"I think we're close." Dick reined in beside him.

"Whatever you think." He rose in his saddle and tried to see across the sea of windswept tall brown stalks. A half-mile ahead, something bobbed in the seed-tops and it resembled someone on horseback.

"What should we do?" Zekial asked.

"Leave the pack stock here and give them a rush."

"Good enough. We'll let the horses breathe a little, then do it."

Zekial stepped off Red and caught the gray. His left shoulder ached, and the bandage had gotten wet from the river crossing. He decided, in a race, the mare could catch any horse. Besides, she hadn't been carrying anything but the saddle all day.

"She fast?" Dick asked.

"Very."

"She looks it. You ready?"

Zekial nodded and mounted her. They left the mule, Red, and Dick's pack-horse to graze. On the start, they rode nose-to-nose as their two ponies parted the grassy sea. Seed heads pounded their legs while the fresh wind swept their faces.

In his right hand, Broome held the rifle. Leaned forward, he urged the mare to greater speed. She swept away from Dick's bay, the steady stride of her powerful legs drumming the ground, and quickly outdistanced the other horse.

The riders ahead began to whip their ponies, looking back in fear, but it was too late. The gray quickly closed the quarter mile distance. He swung his rifle and batted the back rider off his mount with the rifle barrel.

The rider rolled off his mount on the other side and disappeared in the thick grass while his empty saddle bounced away on his spooked horse.

The hard-eyed buck riding behind her looked back. Zekial's heart sunk as he watched him draw his knife as if he would slit her throat. He urged the gray on and the mare gave a burst of speed. The rider with Tilly in front started to reach around her with his knife. The gray closed the gap. Desperate not to hit her, Zekial could only hope his desperate ploy worked.

He cocked the hammer, pushing the gray up close enough, stuck the muzzle at the renegade's head and fired upward. The gray shied at the shot and went tearing off to the side. Acrid smoke blinded Zekial as he tried to see the results. He sawed on the reins one-handed and looked back to try and see if it had worked, or if Tilly lay on the ground, her throat slit.

XXVI

IN THE CHILLY PREDAWN DARKNESS, they saddled the horses. Mc-Cord was grateful for the three of them to go with him after Butler. He took his mule to ride. The boy picked the bobtail, Fancher the bay, and Mercer the Indian pony. Margaret gave Grissum a poke of cooked bear meat and corn cakes for them to eat.

He gave Judson's rifle, pouch and powder horn to the boy. The faint perfume of the Choctaw Landing whore still clung to the leather as he handed it all over.

"Shoots straight enough," Grissum advised the boy. In some awe, young Mercer nodded gratefully and held the rifle in both hands. "You shot one before?" he asked, wondering if the teen could even use the gun.

"Not one this fine."

"Aim and squeeze, right?"

"Yes, sir." The boy sorted out the bobtail horse's head from the others.

"Captain, you go first. You and Higgins got powder and lead?" Grissum asked concerned. No sense starting out after a killer like Butler with unarmed men.

"Yes." The captain mounted in the dim light of the candle reflector. The boy followed him on the high-stepping bobtail. Higgins, who had said little the whole time, swung up and nodded to him and Margaret as he rode out of the pen.

"You be careful." Urgency colored her voice.

"I'll try." He looked after the dim outlines of the riders in the starlight. His mind was already on the day ahead.

"You be back?" She clutched his gun arm to her bosom.

"May have to go to Boonesboro first."

"You know where I'm at?"

"I know." Then he nodded his head and hoisted his rifle. Mounting the mule, he gave her a nod and a smile. He slapped the mule on the butt with the stock. It tucked tail and set out after the others in a stiff jog.

Fancher led them down on the dry Osage Creek and up the steep far mountain. The way was hardly more than a game trail. The man referred to the way as the mail road, but to Grissum's mind, there seemed little that resembled a road. It was a packhorse path under good conditions. Grissum didn't care, he had to go this way to Boonesboro anyway, and the chance that they could catch Butler in his lair made him all the more anxious to hurry.

By late afternoon, they were headed up the King's River valley. Twelve-foot high cane choked the river bottom, but Fancher found a pathway. Grissum had to admit to himself that he respected the man, an obvious leader. He knew the land and had trekked over most of it. Though he offered no idea about the possible location of Butler's hideout, in late afternoon, Fancher halted them and called for a conference.

"We don't have much daylight left. We could stumble on his place any time. If we camp, he might smell our fire and flee."

"Or sneak up and cut our throats," McCord said.

"Right. I say we go ahead on foot and see if we can locate it."

"You're the leader," Grissum said and the others nodded in solemn agreement. "Let's hobble the horses."

The men stripped off their saddles and stashed them. They made hobbles of soft rope for their horses. That completed, Grissum handed out some cold greasy bear meat and dodgers to each man.

"You ever been this far up before?" he asked the captain.

The man shook his head. "I've been on the east side that leads to the Buffalo, but never on this side of the mountains."

"No idea where he's at?"

"I think there are caves up in these bluffs ahead. Lazy Injun ain't going to build him a cabin if he can find a free cave." Fancher smiled at him.

Grissum nodded. Good thinking. He hadn't been putting his mind to this task. Fancher appeared competent enough but looking in caves for a killer like Butler was like going into a bear's den. A man wanted to be sure he had every advantage. McCord drew some saliva in his mouth. Her dry cakes had taken it away. Fancher told him to bring up the rear, in case Butler circled them.

A thick curtain of cane swallowed them as they hurried single file up the narrow path. The skin on the back of Grissum's neck itched as he trotted in the back. Frequently he looked back as the curtain of leaves and stems closed in for any sign of the tricky killer.

The sun had almost set when they reached the bluffs.

Fancher squatted down. "Someone's coming from up there."

Grissum kept low and advanced until he was close to the person. An Indian woman walking as if she'd left the cave directly behind her. He watched the squaw coming down the slope. Obviously, she must be coming down for water. They needed to separate her from Butler, if she was even with him.

"She'd damn sure know if he was home," Grissum whispered.

"Yes, if she's his. And, if she'll talk."

"Leave that to me." Grissum figured Fancher had no stomach for forcing her to talk.

"We'll wait here and cover the cave."

Grissum nodded and studied the woman's direction. He moved cat-like through the thick cover, satisfied he could move in when she dipped the water if he hurried. In the thick of the bamboo, he couldn't see the bluff or the cave. The light was dropping fast.

He paused and listened. She wasn't far ahead. Like a deer he burst through the thicket and she bolted wide-eyed to her feet. He caught her arm and slung her down before she could run. She squirmed like a wild hog under his weight as he undid his thin-bladed knife.

The tip of the blade at her throat silenced her grunting. She stopped struggling. A plains Indian girl in her mid-teens, Butler, no doubt, had kidnapped her from some village for his own purposes. No place for her to run but the endless trails in the cane. This was her prison.

"You speak English?" he hissed in her ear.

She nodded. Her brown eyes wide as she held her breath, waiting for his next demand.

"Is Butler in that cave?"

"Yes."

"You want to live?"

She nodded, pinned under his weight.

"Then you call him out here like you broke your leg." He rose up and forced her to her feet by the arm.

"He kill me." She shook her head in sheer terror that he would even ask her to do such a thing. "No, he kill me."

"I'll kill you if you don't. Besides, if I get him, you can run off to your own people, okay?"

"How you get him?"

"Four guns. Now hurry, we got to do this before the last of the daylight is gone." He pushed her roughly ahead until the cane thinned.

"Start screaming now. 'My leg, my leg', right there. One funny move and I'll shoot you with my pistol."

She nodded, and he pushed her down.

"Oh! Oh, my leg!" she shouted from the ground holding her thigh as he hovered in the stems. The light was fast fading on the bluff's face.

"Louder!" he hissed.

"Oh, Butler. My leg is broke!"

A dark figure loomed in the opening of the cave and rushed down the steep slope. Rifles spoke in the night. the blaze of their barrels' orange-red smoke blasts. Butler clutched his chest and sprawled onto his back.

Grissum rushed past the girl and up the hillside to where Butler lay groaning on the ground. He cocked the pistol and pressed it between the man's eyes before he could fend it off. He turned his head aside and pulled the trigger. The bullet cut short Butler's last scream. The outlaw's body flopped in death's throes. Grissum, drenched in sweat, stepped back, to catch his breath. He stowed the smoking pistol in his waistband with his blood-spattered hand.

"Abe, go find a light in the cave," Fancher ordered.

The youth scurried up the hillside to obey.

Higgins stood leaning on his rifle. He spat tobacco to the side and nodded his approval over the man's demise.

The squaw came forward, cautious like, shaking her head and holding her arms to her body. She peered down and shook her head.

"Him dead?" she asked.

"So is his spirit," Grissum said and nudged his body with his toe to show her. "You got food for us? We're hungry."

"Fat possum and a coon." She stared at the dead outlaw.

"That'll do for starters." Grissum gave a head toss for her to go fix it. "Here, Higgins, get his other arm. I want to see him laid out."

Fancher carried their rifles. Abe showed up with a torch and lighted the way. The last orange of sunset went down on the western range when he and the farmer drug the fabled outlaw back into his den.

Judson had been avenged.

Now back to Broome.

XXVII

TELL ME YOU'RE ALL RIGHT." Zekial was out of breath. He hugged Tilly's body tight to his chest, so small his arms swallowed her as she sobbed in his shirt. He held her at arm's length, so he could inspect her. Her eyes watered with tears. He could see nothing else wrong.

"I told 'em you'd get 'em," she cried. "I be fine. Nothing the matter with me."

"Why are you crying then?"

"I be so glad to sees you." She dove in and hugged him hard. "How you ever find me?"

"Dick tracked them down. Which one did I shoot?"

"Blue Heron, they call him."

"Gut Line must have got away," he said in disgust.

"I don't care." She shook her head. Standing, she ran after the gray mare.

"I sure think she be fast as lightning," Tilly said as she led her back. Proudly, she patted her muzzle.

He rose up on his toes. Dick was coming through the waves of cured bluestem with their other stock.

"What we do next?" Tilly asked.

"Sell some furs at Fort Smith and get home. How did they kidnap you?"

"I was minding my own business when them two rode up. One, the one got away, says, 'Black girl, you a slave?' I say 'No, I'm a man's wife.' They go to laughing at me. That dead one over there, he say, 'You be my woman, now!' They be drinking lots. I run. Next thing I know. he got me, and they took me across that river and loaded me on that pony. Nothing I could do."

"You did fine." He stopped and caught her arm. His head turned, he looked hard at her stomach. "That baby all right?"

She beamed at him. "He be fine."

"Good."

———

AFTER THEY COMPLETED THEIR TRADING in Fort Smith, Hogan headed for Fort Gibson and they went back to the east fork of Lee's Creek. The last day of their return trip, they rode in a cold drizzle that froze on the trees in the higher elevations.

Grateful to be back in their cave, Broome sharpened his new broadaxe. The real work was about to begin for Zekial. Strange, but for once, he didn't even dread it. Maybe he had settled at last. He planned to slash clear several acres in the bottom and fence them with rails for corn, a garden and some cotton. The cabin would come later.

He walked to the cave entrance and listened to the wolves howling in hot pursuit of something, a deer most likely. Good to be back in his own domain. She soon came for him and took him to their blankets. He was not hard to coax.

———

DEEP SNOW FOLLOWED THE RAINS, and they were cavebound for a while. His stock grazed in the cane thickets down below, though, and managed to find enough food to keep them happy.

He rose the next morning, ready to bag a wolf hide. The man in Fort Smith paid two dollars each for prime pelts, and a snow was great for tracking.

"You be careful," she warned, then slipped some corn cakes into his pocket.

"Yes, ma'am." He paused and looked into her eyes.

She shook her head and shoved him toward the opening. "You go kill me a fancy wolf skin today."

"I'll do it."

In an hour, he found the site of the pack's bloody kill of the night before on the mountain bench high above his cave in a grove of great white oaks. Red snow on the patch marked the area. Few traces of the unfortunate victim remained, a large hipbone and hair, enough to tell it was a deer. The rest of the kill had been consumed or carried off by the pack. Their tracks went east.

The way to track wolves was to find a fresh set of prints in the snow and walk them down. Avoiding any actual eye contact, he kept walking up their back trail. He did that until, in a few hours, the curiosity of the pack members made them raise up and peek at this insistent follower. They become bolder as the sun rose higher. Obviously upset by his continuing to track them, they stopped more frequently to study this creature that could follow them, and they could not understand his uncanny ability to dog them.

His rifle ready, he carried it loosely in his right hand. When the time was right he would have one shot to drop the best one. In his side vision he had seen a dark-coated male, his fur an ebony black. That was his goal. Sleek and fat, the main male would be his target when the time was right.

He checked the sun—almost an hour until noon. Ahead around some cedars, the gray faces of the disturbed wolves looked back at him. Obviously, they wanted to lie down and sleep, but his continued presence forced them to move again. They were becoming bolder.

A female curled her lip back and growled at him, then ducked for cover. The big male was less obvious, as they ran uphill in the stark timber. A flurry of snow set up in their wake. The male ran in close to the lead, red tongue out, moving with ease.

He set out up the steeper grade, knowing they would double back. To his right he caught a flash of gray. They had already come back to check him out. Among the thick trunks of the maples that clustered the north slope, curious faces appeared close enough to shoot.

The big male advanced from behind a tree, fifty yards uphill. In his monarchy, all submitted to him. The wolf tested the air with his nose and his small eyes filled with anger at Zekial's intrusion. He allowed no other male to offer any resistance to him. It was submit or die. Still, caution made him wary of this strange visitor.

He jerked at the click of the hammer. Still trying to make out his latest competitor, the male raised his head higher. The flash and smoke came too fast. The .50 caliber lead ball tore through his small brain before he could move sideways. His life ended without a whimper.

Zekial reloaded as the gunsmoke drifted away. A second male rushed out, sniffed with respect at the still leader. Then, caught up in the excitement over the fact the king could no longer snap at him, he tried to mount the dead leader and began to hump him.

A mistake for number two. The iron sights captured the big male's chest as he tried with zeal to find a place to copulate with the limp corpse. The rifle roared in Zekial's hands and a halo of gun smoke surrounded the muzzle of the gun. The wolf rolled end over end, rose to his feet, blood rushing from his mouth. With death in his eyes, his muscles stiffened. He shook all over, and then fell on the snow in death's arms, kicking his feet to escape the pain.

Broome reloaded the rifle as the others raced away in the cold sunshine. He could count on four dollars anyway for the two prime hides. The pack's yelping rang out over the snowy mountains and re-echoed. Obviously disoriented without the main males, there would be much fighting ahead to choose another leader.

Zekial reloaded his rifle and then drew out his skinning knife. Both wolves weighed well over a hundred and fifty pounds apiece, so he needed to skin them and carry the hides home.

XXVIII

YOU LIKE IT BEST WITH me on top or you on top?" Margaret sat astride him on the bed. With the blanket wrapped around her, all he could see was the deep navel in the roll of her belly.

"I like it both ways." Grissum grinned up at her. She was a big, strapping woman with nothing pretty about her, but he couldn't overcome his fascination with her. She sure knew how to take him to the moon.

She bounced her butt to get his attention. "You leaving today?"

"I need to go on to Boonesboro and see what I can learn. That damn girl he took is worth five hundred dollars."

She whistled.

"Yeah, lots and lots of money. That's why I want her back."

"You could stay another day. Jacob's gone hunting. We could play."

"He go hunting a lot?"

"In the winter he does. I told him he should find him a widow woman to bed. But he don't ever say much about it, just shakes his head."

"He ever had a woman?"

"Yeah, a couple of times." She sounded troubled. She rose and stepped off the bed, gathering the quilt as she went.

"She live around here?"

"Yeah, she does. But we swore off doing that." She rewrapped herself in the quilt and didn't look at him.

"Oh." Awkward silence fell between them. "I better get up and get going. This snow is going to be bad enough to travel in. It hardly ever snows down in Alabama. Don't get this cold neither." He shook his head at the prospect of having to wallow around in it.

"It may turn warm in a few days. You can't tell about this weather."

"I'll just take that mule. I'll pay you for caring for them horses till I get back."

"I may use that bob-tailed horse to skid some logs in with when Jacob gets back, if it's all right?"

"Fine, he's a good logging horse. They were using him for that when I bought him." He quickly dressed before the hearth. She stood around wrapped in the quilt, then followed him out in the cold while he saddled the mule.

Barefoot and standing there holding his rifle with only a thin blanket on her shoulders, he wanted to shiver for her. The mule saddled, he strapped on his saddlebags, took the rifle from her and kissed her on the lips. He couldn't recall ever kissing a woman of his goodbye before. Maybe he didn't because the others had tobacco juice all over their mouth.

"Take care of yourself, Grissum McCord."

"You do the same, Margaret. I'll be back before you know it and have that damn girl with me, you can bet on that."

He slapped the mule with the reins and left out for Boonesboro. At the foot of the hill, he looked back. She waved, redid the blanket so he caught a flash of her breasts and belly before she tucked it out of sight.

He'd have to come back.

———

THE FIRST NIGHT, HE FOUND a bluff to den under. He had not passed a single rider all day on the trail. For supper, he ate some cold bear meat and corn cakes she sent along. The small fire hardly warmed him. Dry wood was a short commodity under the blanket of snow. His backside half frozen, he shivered and regretted the loss of Judson as he warmed his numb fingers over the flames. Bad as he hated his whistling, he could use some "Oh, Susannah" to make him feel better. He had been a damn fool to run off and leave a big heater of a woman and her bed in the midst of this cold snap.

He rolled up in the blankets and tried to sleep on the hard rock of the bluff. This place was dry, and the fire did give him some heat on one side. He lay awake for a long time. Somewhere off in the night a mountain lion screamed, then the wolves added their voices to the starry darkness. Finally, he fell asleep.

———

AT DAWN, HE SADDLED THE mule and rode west. Mid-morning, he spotted a white man coming with a pack train. Two slaves walked beside the line of horses, switching the slow ones. The lead black carried a rifle.

Grissum reined in his mule. "Morning."

"Morning." The white man raised his hand in a signal and halted the train. He turned in the saddle. "You two check all them cinches."

"Yes, sah," the rifle bearer said, then he leaned it carefully against a tree.

The man turned back. A full trimmed beard, his coat looked of fine, heavy, gray, woolen cloth and his britches were the same. An expensive beaver hat shaped in a plantation owner's style with the wide-brim rolled up at the edges shaded his face. The man looked him over. "Going west, huh?"

"Yes, I'm after a big man in buckskin and a black wench. Grissum McCord is my name." He straightened in the saddle and drew the mule up.

"Baxter James." He didn't offer to shake Grissum's hand. "Ain't seen the likes."

"How far you come?"

"We were at Fort Smith a week ago."

"No sign of him there?"

The man shook his head. "She a runaway?"

"He stole her."

"Then he's up on the Green River." The man laughed haughtily and shook his head. "You'll never find that mountain man, if one of them took her."

"Green River? Where's that?"

"A thousand miles or so, that way." He tossed his head over his left shoulder.

"Didn't aim to go that far."

"Then you'll never find him."

"You been to this Boonesboro?"

"Yes, two days ago, but I wasn't there long."

"Never saw nor heard no talk of this fellow, Broome?"

The man shook his head. "You a bounty hunter, huh?"

"Duly deputized."

"You may as well give up on finding those two. They could be clear to the Palouse country."

Grissum frowned. "Where?"

"Indian tribe up on the Columbia River."

"You been to all those places?" Grissum could hardly fathom anyone having been thousands of miles. Hundreds of miles wore him out. It was even worse going by himself.

"Yes, and you better keep your wits about you going across there to Boonesboro. There are several bands of young Osage bucks out on the war-path this winter."

"In the winter?" He could hardly believe a damn Indian got out of his tepee in weather like this.

"They sure are. They've already struck some isolated settlers' places."

"I'll ride lightly then. Much obliged for the information." Grissum could see no purpose in talking all day to this rich man. His pompous attitude made him angry. He reminded him of the kind of man he brought slaves back to, then they didn't want to pay him his full bill.

"Good day, sir," James said and waved his arm for the train to move out.

Pondering James' words, Grissum decided he must make the attempt to check out both places, and then, he planned to return to see Margaret. The thoughts of her back there waiting for him niggled him all the time. James' pack string and the two barefoot blacks went by him, and he sent the mule up their sloppy tracks in the melting snow.

By late afternoon, he found a tavern and store, no more than a crude cabin with a lean-to. He bought half a bushel of wormy shucked corn from the squeaky-voiced proprietor, then went outside and fed the mule about half of it. He put the rest in a poke to feed him later and left the mule tied at the rack, chomping in peace.

"You got some whiskey, now?" A terrible thirst had gathered in his dry throat and mouth. Grissum held out his tin cup for the man to fill and the man produced a crock jug stoppered with a red corncob. It thumped like a watermelon when he popped the cob out and the man poured the cup half full.

"Strong stuff there, stranger," the man warned him. "Me name's Archie. Archie Quire."

"Grissum McCord." He wiped his mouth on the back of his hand. The saliva already flowing for him to savor the lightning, he raised the cup and sipped. Hot as fire and good. He nodded his approval. "Ain't half bad."

"I know, I made it myself," Archie bragged. "Ain't got no damn federal stamp on it either. I can drink untaxed whiskey a damn sight better than I can the taxed kind."

"I don't reckon they'll be coming up here to check on you right away neither." Grissum raised his cup for the next sip.

"They do, we're leaving, ain't we, girl?" he asked the dark-headed teenager with a broom stirring up dust sweeping the dirt floor.

She looked up and her crossed eyes made Grissum sick.

"We sure as hell ain't a paying them for no damn stamps," she drawled and went back to sweeping which made Grissum grateful. To look on someone that cross-eyed for very long was bad luck, maybe even contagious, he'd been told.

"Good girl." The old man motioned to her. "My Pearlie can cook, sew and got her ma's wide hips. Not have no trouble birthing a passel of kids for a man."

"Aw, Paw, quit trying to marry me off. That man has probably done got him a wife some wheres." She shook her head in dismay.

Grissum nodded sharply and took another gulp of the liquor. It hurt him to even look at her. Shame too, because she had a nice figure and the old man was right, wide enough hips for having babies, even the bosom to feed them, too.

He ate supper with Quire seated at the table by the fireplace. Pearlie served them venison stew. By then, Grissum was mellow enough on the moonshine that her eye condition didn't bother him as bad. He ate his stew out of a turtle shell bowl and the warmth of the fire made him feel drowsy. Four men came into the store, eyed him and then crowded up to the makeshift bar for drinks. Locals, they all knew Quire when he hurried over to serve them. A younger one in the crowd followed Pearlie around the store with his hat in his hand.

"Good food," Grissum said. She nodded her thanks. "I'm going to put my mule in the pen and I'll sleep out in the barn," he announced.

"Be fine, there's hay out there. I'll have breakfast early," she said as he paid her ten cents.

"Good, I'll want some before I ride on." He said goodnight to everyone and they nodded to him.

The fresh-faced boy stood back and swallowed every chance he got. Grissum decided that boy's bobbing Adam's apple would be worn out before the night was over with him hovering over Pearlie. Outside, the cold wind struck Grissum square in the face and sobered him in a hurry.

Full of doubt about leaving the warmth of the store, he hurried over the frozen snow for the shed. It would be another night to shiver himself to sleep.

His mule still chomped on the corn he gave him. Grissum left him tied, munching on the dry feed in the manger. He rolled up in the musty smelling hay pile and shut his eyes. Sleep wouldn't be long.

He awoke sometime in the night. Hushed voices in the shed made him reach carefully for his pistol. His eyes barely peeking, he tried to make out what was happening beside his mule.

"Oh," she said, and he recognized her voice. It was the cross-eyed girl's. She and someone kissed in a deep embrace. He could see a part of them in the little starlight filtering inside. It didn't look like the swallowing boy either.

"That boy ain't got but a wet noodle, girl," her suitor said.

"He ain't got a wife like you have," she replied impatiently.

"I swear, Pearlie—"

"Lower your voice. That stranger is sleeping in here somewheres."

"All right, all right. Turn around and bend over. They'll be missing us before long."

"Don't you be so rough this time either," she said.

Grissum could see the moons of her butt, then the guy stepped up and blocked his view. She gave a little exclamation and then her partner got to pumping her.

"Aw, Pearlie darling, listen. Don't marry him—" He finished with a deep grunting strain.

"Hush, damn it, you'll wake that man."

"Ah, hell, darling. You'are the best." He staggered around as she hurriedly straightened and dropped her dress.

"Get your pants fixed, Carl. And don't act so damn dreamy, they'll know what we've been doing out here."

"Yes."

"I'm going to marry him, anyway."

"You do, and I'll tell him about us."

"You do that, Carl, and you won't ever get no chance at me ever again."

"I won't tell him, I promise, darling. But I'll come see you." He laughed aloud.

"You better shut up or we'll wake that man."

"I know. I know."

Grissum smiled, remembering Margaret's body. He should have stayed there another day. He hoped he found Broome and that wench at Boonesboro. With the side of his finger, he rubbed the itch on his upper lip, and then he huddled under the blankets and went back to sleep.

XXIX

ZEKIAL SPLIT THE LOGS FROM his clearing project into twelve-foot long rails. He paused to rest in the warming sun. The drying stacks of rails fanned out and grew larger. He nodded, satisfied that, by spring, his supply would easily fence the bottomland he would crop.

"You sure cut them rails long enough," she said, coming back from the creek with a pail of water.

"No need to make small ones."

"I guess not, but you stacking them up." She smiled with pride and rubbed her stomach.

"Anything wrong?"

"No, but I think he's going to be a big boy. Why, he's got months to go and I swear he is stretching him out a big den, in there." She frowned at her slightly bulged stomach.

"Don't reckon there is anything I can do about that." He turned back to his axe.

"You going to teach him to read?"

"Sure, why?"

"They going to still say, he be black. High yellow maybe, but he be black. In Alabama, they got laws says you ain't supposed to learn no black to read."

"You seen anyone from Alabama around here?" He glanced around like he was looking.

She rushed over and hugged him. "No, and I sure hope I never do."

He mussed her short wiry hair and kissed her on the mouth. "Don't worry. Ain't no one from Alabama coming here, let alone telling me what to do with my own children." He hugged her thin form to his chest.

"Someone's coming," she said. He straightened and listened to a bawl-mouthed dog hurrying up the creek.

"It's a hound," he said and tried to see if anyone accompanied it. The white and black hunting dog came over to them acting suspect and wagging his tail.

"Here," she said and knelt on her knees to coax him to her. Soon she began to scratch his ears. The dog's tail beat a tattoo.

"Who you reckon—"

"His master's coming." Zekial went to pick up his rifle where it leaned against a large stump.

Under a weathered felt hat, the man appeared, dressed in rags with two more hounds at his side. He carried an ancient flintlock piece and stopped looking down at her and the dog.

"Done found you someone to scratch your old ears, huh?" he asked the dog.

"What's his name?"

"Thunder."

"Hi, Thunder," she said in his face and the other two came crowding in for her attention.

"Zekial Broome, sir." He extended his hand to the man, whose long beard was matted and tobacco stained.

He stuck out an unwashed hand and shook Broome's, looking around curiously. "Booster Bradshaw. This your place?"

"Yes, that's my wife, Tilly."

"Proud to meet 'cha, Mrs. Tilly." He removed his hat and made a bow that embarrassed her.

"That's fine. That's fine," she said.

"What brings you up the creek?" Zekial asked.

"Following my dogs. Figured it were warm enough I might strike a bear."

"I haven't seen one in a few weeks, but I've stretched a few hides this season."

"I'd not come up here and tried to kill none of your bear."

"Bears are bears. I don't own them."

"Yes, yes. But some men do get funny ideas about what they own, you know, Mr. Broome?"

"Hunt to your heart's content up here, Mr. Bradshaw."

"You could call me Booster, I wouldn't answer to no Mr. Bradshaw."

"Zeke would suit me."

The man smiled, shaking his head. "You fixin to make you a home here, huh?"

"I hope so. You know anything wrong with that?"

"Just be a helluva lot of work." Bradshaw grinned big and tobacco juice ran out of his mouth and down his chin before he made a swipe at it with a tattered sleeve. "I believe I'll hunt, instead. Thunder, Blue, Jiminy, get over here. That woman's got her work to do."

"You ever get some pups from Thunder, I'd buy a few," Zekial offered.

"Say, I'll do that." He waved his hat and started on up the creek.

"You come back at dark, I feeds you," she said after him.

Then she glanced up at Zekial for his approval. He nodded agreement.

They watched Booster walk away in his jaunty style until he disappeared in the cane breaks. Zekial had found several like Booster on the frontier. No belongings, no home, free to wander about the land, hunt some and exist. A man could chase rainbows all his life and never have a thing to show for it.

———

BOOSTER NEVER CAME BACK FOR supper. No doubt his dogs hit a track and took him over another range of mountains. Zekial sat studying the dancing shadows cast by the fire. Her rich supper of venison and cornbread settling in his stomach, were interrupted by the sound of a horse.

He grabbed his rifle and headed for the entrance.

"What is it?"

"There's a rider out there."

"Zekial, Dick Hogan!" the man shouted from the base of the bluff on his hard-breathing horse. He could hear the animal's rasping breath and see it had been run some distance. Something wrong, for Dick to do that to his horse.

"Get down and come up here." He turned and told Tilly who had ridden up.

"I fix him some food," she said happily at the return of their friend.

"What makes you come on the run in the dark?" he asked as Dick joined him.

"The Osage are on the warpath. They've been attacking the Cherokee and outlying white people." Dick drew a deep breath and scowled at him.

Zekial shook his head. "No sign of them up here."

"I have word from a scout for the army at Fort Gibson. Not long ago, he was in their camps and he said they had big plans for the yellow hair and his buffalo woman in the canyon. Don't that sound like you?"

"I guess," Zekial said, impressed by the man's words. "Where can we go?"

"Boonesboro is the closest settlement."

"But Grissum McCord," he lowered his voice to not alarm her. "Has he come through there?"

"I'd say, if he's still alive, he's been through there by now."

"How long do we need to stay there?" he asked displeased at the interruption. "That could be ages. I have work to do here."

"You can't fight a whole band of them yourself."

"You're right." He exhaled sharply, angry at the turn of events.

Dick nodded, seeing his argument hit home.

"Here's you some food," she announced serving Hogan a large bowl of her venison and corn cakes.

"Absolutely wonderful," Dick announced, taking himself a place on the deer-skin spread around the fire ring. "I've sure missed your cooking, Tilly."

"Ha. A man runs all over without no woman, he learns," she said and then busied herself with the sewing she'd been working on.

"Thanks," Zekial said at last. "I know you came a far piece to tell us about them."

"No problem. I simply want you to survive, so I have a place to come eat Tilly's great food." Dick laughed out loud at her expense.

She shook her head and pulled the needle through on the long thread. "Plenty good women you could have."

"Not one like you, though," he replied.

Both men smiled to themselves as she made a face of disapproval and acted engrossed in her sewing.

———

AT SUNUP, ZEKIAL GATHERED HIS stock in the sharp air. Dick came along, and their breath rolled out in great clouds. Something told him he must take her to safety, but it went against the grain. Maybe the military would send the Osage packing, but he doubted they would do more than chop wood on the Arkansas. The soldiers he had seen did not look capable of much. He was glad he'd went with real men to New Orleans with Ol' Hickory.

He slipped a halter on the gray mare, swung up on her back and headed across the shallow creek. His mule brayed and came on the run, afraid to be left behind. Red came out of the green briars and followed her obediently back across the creek.

"They call this place Boonesboro?" she asked him, making another trip down from the cave. She already had more things stacked about than he could pack on five animals.

"We going to have to leave part of this," Zekial announced.

"I don't aim to leave all my things here for them savages to mess up."

"They may not even come."

"Why we in such a hurry then?"

"Dick heard a serious rumor about us from an Indian scout over there."

"What they be saying?" She rushed over to confront Dick.

"Well—"

"Tell me."

"Word's out, they want his buffalo woman."

She made a face at him. "What you mean buffalo woman?"

"Indians think black people and buffalo are related because of their hair."

"Don't make no sense. I ain't come from no buffalo. Crazy devils ain't got no brains is all. I'm going to walk there, and you can load that on that mare. I ain't leaving nothing for them."

"I swear we won't ever get to Boonesboro if you keep on," Zekial said.

"I don't care. They ain't getting my things." She marched around with her arms folded on her chest and stomped her bare feet.

Dick tried not to smile, but Zekial could see it proved difficult. At last, the man took his gun and horse to ride up the canyon and look for any sign of the renegades.

XXX

HIS HEART CAUGHT IN HIS throat and cut off his wind. Grissum silently cursed the Indians with the mule's muzzle clamped tightly in his hands. If he'd been ten minutes sooner, he would've run straight into an entire war party. From his place in the brush on top of the bluff, he watched them parade by below across the river. Only their colorful blankets and feathers gave them away against the snowy background left in the shade of the bluff.

At the sight of the first Indian, he had leapt from the mule and quickly secured its mouth with both hands, lest it brayed at them or their horses.

McCord's heart beat at the top of his breastbone and impaired his swallowing. He peeked from time to time as they passed. It was one thing to run into a small band, but below him and across that shallow river, rode an entire war party. Men rode their dancing ponies, with feather-like manes and tails that fluttered on the soft wind. Grissum could even hear the copper bells on their leggings. Only a handful of women, too, no children. Enough squaws to do the camp work. That meant they were out for blood and not just meat hunting. If they were hunting, they'd have the whole tribe with them.

For a long while after the band went up the valley, he waited to be certain they'd all gone. Satisfied the mule wasn't going to bray, he released his muzzle.

His knees were weak, and he needed to empty his bladder. Grissum's breath came short as he stained the melting snow with his urine. He'd have to be a lot more careful or he'd not live to make it to Boonesboro. No bounty was worth losing his hair over.

Weak from standing so long in one place, he swung up on the mule and headed for the crossing. The shallow rushing water glistened over the rocks in the bright sunshine. He twisted around in the saddle seeing Indians behind every tree. It was no joking matter.

He judged that he must be close to halfway to his destination. He'd lost a lot of daylight just waiting for them to clear out and he wanted to make up time. He hurried his mount across the wide, shallow ford and up the hill westward bound.

He loped the mule for the next mile and noticed a plume of smoke in the sky. Black smoke. They'd burned someone out. He pressed the mule on, deep dread in his heart at what he would find. When he finally topped the ridge, he could see ahead, what was left of a cabin's walls. The roof had already collapsed inside.

Carefully, he scanned the fields beyond the rail fences for any sign of life or enemy. His heart strangling off his breath with the rifle clamped in his sweaty hand, he drove the snorty mule up close.

One man lay on the ground. They'd taken his clothes, obviously carved on him, his stark white skin bloody as he lay face down. McCord cringed when he observed how savagely the man had been scalped. He rode on around the yard.

A dead infant lay on the ground, skull crushed. He tried to keep down the gall rising behind his tongue. Dead hounds were scattered about the yard, pin cushioned with arrows. The bodies of two dead oxen lay not ten feet apart. Arrows bristled from them like a porcupine.

A woman's lifeless corpse lay outside the yard. Stripped stark naked and sprawled on her back, her blank eyes stared at the sky. He turned his head from the sight of her. Injuns did cruel mean things. Smoke from the log fire burned his eyes and they teared. Nothing he could do for them but press on. He checked all around to be certain the raiders were gone and then hurried the mule away.

He rode until dark before he dismounted. On foot, he led the mule several more miles until the moon rose. His soles itched to reach Boonesboro and he didn't know how much farther he must go. His distance gauge was messed up by the day's unscheduled stops.

Without a fire, he camped off the road in the timber. No need to tell the bloodthirsty red bastards where he was. They'd probably find his mule tracks soon enough if they were scouting around. Huddled and cold under his blankets, he wished he had never left Margaret's cabin at Carrolton. He was a day closer to his goal or he'd have ridden back come first light. Maybe he'd find Broome and that wench in Boonesboro and his problems would be over. Grissum pulled the blankets tighter and shivered.

Somewhere up on the mountain above him, a wolf howled, and another answered. He shook his head. Wolves avoided fires. He sure hoped they avoided him without one as well. Damn, he swore to himself. If the red bastards didn't get him, then the wild animals would.

——

AT FIRST LIGHT, HE ATE the last of the greasy bear meat. He should reach Boonesboro by evening. He squinted in the cold morning air to be certain no Indians lingered around. Nothing moved in the ghostly gray trunks of the tall white oaks.

He found no sign of anything when he crossed another ridge and looked over the valley below. Buffalo dotted the grassy basin, a good two dozen, counting some large calves. First ones he'd ever seen. But he wasted no time riding through the grassy prairie. The buffalo stampeded at the sight of him and the mule. Didn't matter, he followed the two ruts that Fancher called a wagon road. Maybe someone had driven a cart over it once or twice. Anyone who hauled a wagon over it deserved a medal.

He hit a rise and pushed the mule into a short lope. Nothing comfortable to ride, but his mule had a great constitution and could go a lot harder and longer than any horse he'd ever owned.

——

MIDDAY, LOOKING OVER HIS SHOULDER uneasily, McCord spotted a brown and white hound. Good-looking dog. Where was its owner? He reined the mule around in a circle. Must belong to someone. After three days of his own company, he was anxious to see another friendly face.

The bearded man in brown clothing came off the mountain in great strides, dressed in rags, not clothes. He carried a rifle and had two other hounds with him.

"Seen them Osage?" the hunter asked.

"No, but they killed a man, woman, and child, back a way on this road."

"Shame. That would be Elton Broyles and his woman, Simah. Where you headed?" The man looked around wildly and tried to see back up in the timber from where he came.

"You got them savages on your trail?" Grissum grew upset by the man's actions. The mule acted nervous, too. He sawed on the reins to control the animal's fidgeting.

"There's been a handful on my back trail since daylight," the man checked his rifle, then searched the hills again.

"How many?"

"Four maybe."

"We can whip four, if that rifle of yours is accurate," Grissum said, dismounting. "I can't stay long, but I'd help you for a short while. How far is it to Boonesboro?"

"Five or six miles."

"Why don't we go there and hold them off?"

"They've got the place surrounded." The man swallowed hard. "I tried to go there this morning and they jumped me."

"Grissum McCord," he said by way of introduction, slipping from his mule and pulling down the crotch of his pants.

"Booster." The old man set his rifle up straight to lean on it, his hand grasping the barrel. "Them Osage are on the war path. They've killed several settlers and the rest I guess are holed up at Boonesboro."

"You been in there lately?"

Booster shook his head, then spit and wiped his mouth on his ragged sleeve. "No, I been hunting in a wide circle."

"You ain't seen a buckskinner with a black wench, have you?"

"Yeah, one."

"Where?" Grissum asked, barely able to contain himself.

"Down on a branch of Lee's Creek. I kinda thought they were married." Booster shook his head as if the whole matter was too much for him.

"They ain't, I can assure you of that. How do I get there?"

"Be hard to go down there now. We better try to get to Boonesboro first. After these Osage leave, I can take you there. He's making him a claim."

Grissum nodded and mounted up. "Get up behind me. We're going to run their blockade."

"I'd hoped to slip in, but I guess this mule will do." The man climbed up. He smelled worse than a hog, but company was company and Grissum was determined not to complain.

———

H E SET THE MULE INTO a trot. They headed southwest. Both men rode warily when they crossed the open grassland, seeing several more plumes of dark smoke in the sky

"They've attacked some more folks," Booster said. "Sure do hope them people made it to Boonesboro."

"How many men there?"

"Maybe twenty or more and they all have arms."

Grissum leaned back as the mule descended into a creek. Booster grabbed him with his free arm when the animal rushed up the other side.

"It's over the end of that mountain," Booster pointed and twisted in the saddle. "We got company, McCord! There's a mob of them red bastards on horses coming after us."

"Hang on!" Grissum said and went to whipping the mule. If that mule ever needed to run, he better have lots of reserves. When he looked back he could see the Injuns out of the corner of his eye. He aimed to make as much space as possible between them. Their screaming wasn't making it any easier.

The mule ran a good race, but the mountain that Booster spoke of was too far away. As the animal slowed, Grissum knew even riding him single, he could not go much further.

"Mule's done for. We better get off and go on foot" Grissum looked back at the raging Indians on horseback that came into view. A fearsome sight as Booster slid off and Grissum dismounted. This might be the last day of his life, the last minutes in fact. His stomach curdled at the thought.

"Here they come," Booster said.

Booster's dogs were all upset, barking and baying. Grissum wanted to kick them, but he needed to save his energy to fight the savages. He used a tree for a rest and took aim. He waited for Booster to fire the first round. The smoky report took a lead rider down. Damn good shot.

He laid his barrel on the tree, allowed a little for height and squeezed off the round. Another Indian fell. Pistol in his fist, they drew closer and he blasted away. From the scream, he knew he hit a horse. The downed rider scrambled for his life and was soon out of range

Booster shot again, but missed.

The Indians were milling around on their ponies out of range. Reloaded, Grissum took a chance and his long shot picked the leader off his horse. The elaborate headdress was there one minute and gone the next.

"Good shot. Let's move," Booster said. "They're checking on that chief I shot."

Grissum caught the lathered mule and led him. He looked over his shoulder. Obviously, the downed Injun was some kind of holy man. If there was any way he could, Grissum wanted to save the mule. He'd need him later on. Out of breath, he hurried after Booster.

Osage bucks dogged them the next hour. The pair half-ran and fired enough at them, every once in a while, to hold back their charge. Grissum and Booster kept moving. At last, the two men reached the top of the pass and Booster pointed to the watercourse.

"We don't lack a mile," Booster panted.

"Good, I'd like to be in a camp of white men."

"I only hope they're still there and didn't run off."

"So, do I. Where would they go?"

"Fort Smith."

"Hey, look there!" Booster pointed to the dozen Indians on horseback that rode up and blocked their way.

"We can kill three or four of them," Grissum said over the noise of the three dogs barking.

"I guess we can and what's left, won't be nobody anyway."

"That's right." Grissum mounted up on the mule. "Want a ride?"

"I'll be right beside you," Booster said and fired a shot at the Indians advancing on them. His bullet struck the lead buck in the chest. His arms flew in the air and he fell off his horse. The screaming grew quieter and Booster nodded. It pleased him.

Grissum pressed the mule right at the lead Indian. He wore a long headdress that probably took some squaw over a year to bead and sew the eagle feathers in it.

Grissum steadied the rifle the best he could on the mule's back. Aimed and fired. His bullet struck the chief in the quilled vest and he flipped off his horse like a struck ten pin. The others stopped to stare.

"Come on!" Grissum shouted to Booster. The man was only a few yards behind the mule traveling at a long lope with his rifle in his hand. His damn hounds barking so loud Grissum could hardly think.

Out of nowhere, the sharp sting of several arrows struck Grissum's leg. He glanced down. Lobbed in from a distance, three feathered shafts were stuck in his calf and thigh. The mule screamed and dove sideways as two more feathered projectiles struck him in the shoulder. It unseated Grissum and he was forced to grab the saddle to stay aboard. The arrows in his leg hurt like fire when he swung down and dropped to the ground to reload. The mule rushed away.

On his knee, he loaded the rifle and had it to his shoulder when the Osage, his face a mask of orange paint and rage, came charging at him with a tomahawk raised. He recalled squeezing the trigger and the ring of smoke smarting his eyes.

XXXI

ZEKIAL WATCHED DICK HOGAN STOP his bay horse, whirl him around, and then bring him back toward the two of them. Dick reined up and the scowl on the man's face told Zekial something was wrong.

"We've got some trouble ahead."

"That smoke we been seeing?" Zekial twisted in the saddle to check the timbered slopes above them.

"I figured that's some settlers cabins being burned. Worse, we've got a small war party up ahead that aims to ambush us."

Tilly stood up in her stirrups. "I ain't seen them. How you see them?"

"You ain't had any Blackfeet after you," Dick said. "They'd make these Osage look like green kids."

Zekial nodded. The Blackfeet were the most treacherous he'd ever dealt with. But, at the moment, he regretted packing so much on the mule and their horses. He glanced over at her and the loaded down gray mare she rode. He could think of how to do lots of things better—main thing for them was how to get by this party of savages and not endanger her life.

"We can't go around them," Dick said. "I guess we can hope that they're young bucks and we can teach them how to die."

Zekial agreed with a solemn nod. "Teach them something."

"You stay in the saddle," Zekial said to her. "And you get a break, you ride that gray mare out of here. Leave all that junk you have piled on her for them bucks. Hear me?"

"I's hear you good." Tilly's face was a dark mask as she pursed her lips. Her eyes narrowed, and her hands tightened on the reins.

"Go to Boonesboro," he spoke under his breath looking hard to see any of them on the bare timber slopes that hemmed them in.

"I will, if'n I find it."

"Which way is it, Dick?" He watched closely for any movement in the old-growth hardwoods.

"Another mountain range over and north more." He sliced the air with his hand to show her the direction.

"I find it. You be careful, too," she said quietly.

The gray danced and Red began to sidestep, no doubt feeling the tensions of their riders. Zekial shot a glance at the mule. He hadn't smelled them yet or he'd have been braying. The wind was to their backs, so he probably wouldn't catch a nose full of them until it was too late. He rose in the stirrups and flexed his tight back muscles.

"On the hillside across the creek." Dick motioned and Zekial looked, too late to see the buck advance downhill.

"They two on the left," she said under her breath and tossed her head to the slope beside them.

"They're only clumsy boys," Dick said. "The real fighters are under that creek bank straight ahead."

"You see them?" she asked with a frown.

"No, but trust me, that's where they are." Dick set the bay into a faster walk.

Zekial agreed. The young ones were up on the hill to get their attention, then the real warriors could charge out from their cover and strike them.

"We need to charge them and kill as many as we can shoot," Dick said.

The plan suited him. Zekial pushed Red up ready to try the attack method.

"We'll ride up, slide to a halt and shoot as many of them hiding in the creek as we can," Dick explained his plan.

Zekial agreed and rose in the stirrup to unstick his leather pants from his butt. Only one pistol in his belt, he wished for the other one he'd discarded. No time to worry about it now. He nodded to Dick and they both screamed at the top of their lungs. The horses responded and raced to the high bank.

Sliding to a stop a few feet from the edge of the drop off, both men flew off their saddles and readied their rifles. The shots deafened his ears and the gun smoke blinded Zekial for a minute. A mass of surprised Indians in the creek shouted and screamed in panic and pain. Zekial took aim with his pistol at point blank range. He shot a raging buck in the face as he reached in desperation for his feet.

The others fled up the far bank, the fight gone from them.

Zekial reloaded his rifle, and out of breath, Dick joined him.

"That's three less Osage." Dick tossed his head toward the prone bodies in the creekbed.

Zekial agreed and took Red's reins from her. The younger Osage were racing off in the timber. Good, might be less fight in them after this failure.

"We can't waste time here," Zekial said and swung up.

"Right, we need to get there." Dick caught his bay and they were on their way. The mule coming close behind.

Near dark, they rode into the barricaded village. A cheer went up from the armed men when they passed the over-turned wagons in the end of the street.

"Have any trouble getting in here?" a tall bare-headed man asked, shaking their hands. "I'm Prior Cane."

"You the captain here?" Dick asked. "I'm Whistling Dick Hogan and this is Zekial Broome and his woman, Tilly."

"Nice to meet you" Cane ran a long hand over his high hairline and patted the gray streaked remains down flat. "We can use all the rifles we can get. Are you hungry? We have plenty of food over there and that black girl can go around back and get her some."

"No need in that," Zekial said. "She's with me. We can both go around back."

"You misunderstood, sir," Cane said, rising to his full six-foot height.

"I said—"

"She goes where I go." Zekial pushed past the man.

"Sir," a woman called out to him. She carried a plate of food and stepped off the porch.

A tall, handsome woman of thirty with brown hair and a ramrod straight back. Her dark blue dress looked out of place among the shabbily-dressed men that stood about in the street leaning on their rifles.

"Good day," she said and started to hand the plate to Zekial.

"Take it," he said sharply to Tilly.

His wife frowned at him.

"Oh, yes, miss, take it." She handed the plate to her without a flinch. "You all must have run a gauntlet of those Osage to get here. I knew you would be hungry."

"We have much more food," an older woman said and brought two more plates for the men.

"I'm Geneva Lock," the woman in blue said. "Come sit on the porch."

"That's Tilly Broome and I'm Zekial Broome." He pointed to their companion. "They call him Whistling Dick Hogan."

"A pleasure ma'am," Dick said, taking a hard bite off the chunk of fresh bread and managing his rifle, plate and all.

"Did you gentlemen have much resistance?" she asked.

"I was going to ask them the same thing, Mrs. Lock," Cane said, joining them.

"We fought one war party." Zekial dropped down and sat on the log stoop. Then he busied himself with eating.

"They've been attacking settlers," Cane said.

"We saw the smoke coming from where they'd burned some out," Dick waved his knife to indicate in the east. "You sent for the army yet?"

"What could they do?" Cane shook his head in disgust.

"Well," Dick said with a slow headshake. "We either have to whip the Osage and drive them back north or do something."

"We ain't soldiers," Cane complained. "But the soldiers they've got around here ain't either." He shook his head to dismiss the military as their salvation. "We lost a good man this afternoon, too. Just outside of camp. Booster would have fought with the best of them."

"He that hunter with the three dogs?" Zeke paused in his eating.

"That's him. God rest his soul. Those savages got all those dogs, too. Killed every one of them and Booster, too. And they made a pin cushion out of that guy with old Booster too."

"Hmm," Zekial said, enjoying the rich deer stew. "Booster was alone when he came by our place a week ago."

"These two met on the way here, I understand. Yes, sir, that other man is still alive, but I don't know if he'll make it." Cane shook his head ruefully. "Doc Wentworth amputated his right leg early this morning to save his life, but I don't know—"

"What's his name?" Dick asked, looking up from his plate.

"Grissum McCord."

XXXII

GRISSUM SCREAMED THROUGH HIS TEETH. He reached down for his aching leg and his hands grasped the bandaged stump. My Gawd, they'd cut it off! They'd cut the damn thing off above the knee. No, he wasn't a man anymore—if they had cut it off, why did the part that was gone hurt so damn bad? Oh, it ached like holy fire. He drew his hands back. His fingers stunk of blood and something else. It was all over his hands, sticky stuff from the bandage.

They should never have taken it off. He'd have been better dead than half a man. No way for a one-legged man to chase down runaway slaves. A one-legged man could never plow. What would he do? He shoved his hands down to his crotch and felt for his manhood. Carefully he fingered it, then his balls. It was still there and all right. Lucky, they hadn't cut it off, too. Who did he hate the worst? The damn doc who cut his leg off or those screaming Osage who shot him full of arrows? He hated both of them enough to kill 'em all.

"You want some more whiskey?" the old woman asked, coming from her rocker to check on him.

"Gallons of it." He lay on his back in a cold sweat, too weak to raise his head.

"I got some. You better drink a lot. I'd say the real pain is just catching up with you." She shook her wizened head and went shuffling off to get it.

"Did Booster make it?" Last time he recalled seeing the man, they were fighting side-by-side and hand-to-hand against the painted-faced bucks.

"No."

Damn shame. That man fought hard. Grissum closed his eyes at the thought
of the old woman's warning about his future pain. His fingers closed on the
upper portion of his amputated limb and squeezed to drive out the fire within.
He'd need to drink lots of whiskey.

She held up a cup for him. "Here."

He half rose, and to her dismay, he drank it like water.

"You sure can down that stuff." She shook her head and turned to refill it.

"Bad as I hurt, I could drink gallons of it."

"Guess so." She went for another cupful.

———

WHAT WE GOING TO DO?" Tilly asked. "McCord be here!"

Dick actually chuckled. "Don't sound like he's going to be doing any
slave chasing on one leg."

"We sure can't run out in the arms of the Osage either." Zeke considered the
matter hard. "He leaves us alone, we won't bother him."

Dick agreed with a nod.

"I sure won't sleep none in the same town with that man. Where that Judson
be, if McCord's here?" she asked. Her dark eyes flashed around in the twilight to
check each and everything in the street.

"I'll go check on that." Dick hefted his rifle. "Someone will know, and I won't
raise any suspicions by asking."

"Good idea. Cane said we can sleep in the loft of the barn."

"Be good. They have plenty of folks to put up, must be over a hundred folks
gathered in here." Dick acted awed by the number. "Why this whole country
will be plumb occupied in a few years at this rate."

"More folks coming in." Zeke stood up and watched two wagons and out
riders arrive.

"Them's Cherokees coming in those wagons," Dick said.

"I figured that they'd be safe from attack," Zeke said.

"No," Dick shook his head. "They're civilized Indians—live in cabins. Them Osages are savages. They hate each other. At Fort Gibson, I heard that was the reason the Osage were down here on the warpath was because they didn't like the fact that the government gave this land to the Cherokees. They wanted to drive them out as bad as they did the whites."

"What's the army going to do about it?"

"I figure they won't do nothing and hope the two tribes kill each other off."

Zeke nodded. He knew there were vast differences in the tribes scattered over the west, from friendly to unfriendly. Obviously, by them coming to the village, the Cherokees were feeling the wrath of the Osage, too.

Dick set off to learn about Judson's whereabouts and the two of them went to put up the horses and set up their bedding in the barn loft. Tilly twice almost jumped into his arms as they led their animals to the nearby log barn. Once when a small pig ran out from under a cabin and went snorting off in the fading light—the second time, when a large friendly hound came and brushed up alongside of her.

"Oh," she shuddered and looked around warily "I sure be glad to know where that other one, Judson, be."

"You're safe with me."

"I knows, I knows. I just upset about them being here is all."

"They won't take you from Dick and me."

She drew a deep inhale up her nose. "I'll try to act better."

"Good," he said and began to unsaddle Red.

Later, Dick returned with the word Judson had not come with McCord. Zekial hoped that settled her some and they went to sleep in the loft.

Both men stood guard duty for a shift during the night. In the morning, Tilly cooked deer meat and corn dodgers over an open fire behind the barn. Cane joined them and squatted on his boot heels in the chilly air.

"There's a Cherokee here called Billie Moss. They say he can read signs. I wondered if I could impose on you two to help him in scouting some and see where these Osage are camped at and how many of them there are out there."

"Can she stay with the white women while we are gone?" Zeke asked.

"Of course," Cane said.

He exchanged a look with her, and then nodded to the man. "We can do that."

"If we can find out how strong they are, then perhaps we might raise up a party and go take them on. We all need to get on with our lives. Our food and stocks will soon run out here."

"We'll try to bring game back," Dick said.

"Good, everyone has stayed so close. How many do you think are out there?" Cane asked them.

"I don't know. Maybe less than fifty bucks."

"This man McCord said, of course, he's delirious with pain and whiskey, that three days ago he saw close to a hundred bucks pass going south near the White River Ford."

"He's lucky to be alive," Dick said.

"He said so, too. Almost rode into the whole band of them."

"He going to make it?" Zeke asked idly.

"He's a tough man. Doc says only about one out of four ever survive an amputation. But he thinks that McCord is tough enough to make it."

Zeke acknowledged the man with a nod.

"You two be ready to go in an hour?" Cane asked.

"Yes."

"Bring her up to the store. We'll be sure she's safe."

"Good," Zeke said, taking comfort in the man's words.

Billie Moss was a short, barrel-chested man with a dark face of aged copper. He wore a black felt hat and white man's clothing. His brown eyes flashed, and his smile was infectious. He shook hands with the two of them when Cane introduced them in front of the store and church.

"You have any notion where they are camped?" Dick asked.

"Maybe on the next creek?" Moss replied with a head toss to the east.

"Guess we'll know more when we look," Dick said.

Zeke took her aside. "I won't be back for maybe a day or so. You stay close to those women."

"They not going to like that."

"I don't care what they like. Stay close to them. I'll be back."

"I know. I know." She turned, and with her head down, went off toward the store.

Zeke watched the tall woman in the blue dress come out and speak to her.

She extended her hand and took Tilly's. Satisfied, he quickly turned and mount-ed Red. The other two were already headed out of town.

They stopped on the mountaintop east of the village and looked for telltale smoke. Moss climbed on a tall, house-sized rock and scoped the valley. He came down, took the reins to his brown horse and remounted.

"Nothing here."

"They were near the wagon road when they got after McCord and Booster. Maybe they're north?" Dick offered.

Moss agreed and they headed across the mountaintop in that direction.

"You guys have claims?" Moss asked.

"Zeke has one down on Lee's Creek. I ain't staying that long. You have one?"

"Yes. Until they burned the cabin and my last year's corn."

"Hurt anyone?"

"No, my wife and kids were at her sister's. All I could do was run. Too damn many Osage." Moss shook his head. "That's why all of us came to Boonesboro until they leave."

"Who's the Osage Chief?" Dick asked, leading them off the mountain.

"They say, Blue Heron is his name."

"Don't know him. I knew some Osage up at Chouteau's trading post on the Kaw and Missouri," Dick said and twisted in the saddle to look at Zekial. "You recall a Blue Heron?"

Zekial shook his head. "The only Osage I knew up there was an old drunk they called Dog Boy."

They rode in silence for an hour. The signs they found were old ones. One old campfire they found looked to be over a week old.

Zeke began to be encouraged by the lack of sign. They reached the rolling blue stem prairie and rode abreast headed for the road. No signs and no smoke in sight.

By noon on the sun clock, they reached the road. Trotting their horses, they reined up at the sight of someone staggering down the road. The person was white and naked. Each man checked his rifle, then booted their horses toward her.

The hairs rose on the back of Zeke's neck. What the hell was a white woman doing out there—naked? That must mean the Osage were close by.

He leaped from his horse. She stared at him cross-eyed and shook her head as if the matter was hopeless.

"They killed them," she mumbled, and her knees buckled.

Zekial caught her in his arms while Dick fought to free a blanket from behind his saddle. Hardly more than a teenager, her long straight hair was full of trash and leaves. Her body was dirt-caked. Sometime recently, her small breasts had been clawed and showed dried blood in streaks on them. She smelled of wood smoke and bear grease, probably from the Indians who'd so savagely defiled her.

Dick shook out the blanket for her while Moss circled his horse around looking for signs. They kept their rifles close as they wrapped her in the blankets.

"They killed them," she mumbled deliriously. "Oh, don't touch me, please?" Her hands went to clamp over her crotch. "Don't touch me, please. I am so sore."

"About out of her mind, too." Zekial stood his rifle up and lifted her up for Dick to carry in the saddle.

"We need to take her back to Boonesboro."

Moss had ridden across the small stream with only a trickle of flow and gone east on the road. They looked up when he came back at a lope.

"No sign of any others," Moss said, reining up. "How is she?"

"Delirious," Dick said.

Moss jerked his head back down the road. "They must be camping in the large grove north of here. There are some springs and plenty of firewood there, too."

"You two take the girl back and I'll scout it," Dick offered.

"No, both of you scout it. I'll take her back," Zekial said. "The two of you are both good at this."

"What if you run into a raiding party?"

"I'll either outrun them or hide."

"Be careful," Dick cautioned

"I will. Guess I'll have to carry her." Zekial wondered how that would work.

"They killed them!" she shouted and sat up straight.

"Can you ride a horse?" Dick asked.

She let the blanket fall away despite the cool air, like it didn't matter who saw her naked. Perhaps she thought she was dressed. Zeke was unsure they could even reach her. He knew one's mind sometimes shelters the terrible pain and shock in an obscure way.

"Can you ride a horse and hang onto Zeke?" Dick asked her.

"Don't let them touch me," she said so pained that her eye lids narrowed. Her hands defending her crotch.

"No one will touch you." Dick pointed to Zekial. "Can you ride a horse behind him?"

"Don't let them—"

Hogan sighed. "She ain't going to wear that blanket. Zeke, mount up and I'll put her on behind you."

Unhappy with the situation, Zekial nodded and caught the sorrel horse. When he was mounted, Dick helped the girl to her feet and boosted her up behind him. He handed Zeke the blanket and shook his head as if the matter of her nudity was beyond him.

"Hold on to me." Zeke told her over his shoulder. Her hands clasped his waist and she hugged him tight. He looked back to his companions. "See you soon. Be careful."

He set Red off at a trot. She didn't faint, or fall off, and so long as they didn't run head-on into another war party—they should be fine. Her arms wrapped around him, the side of her face on the back of his buckskin shirt, they headed back to Boonesboro.

He crossed the wide pass and was headed downhill when the sound of horse's hooves made him twist.

"Is it them?" she asked in a shrill voice. Her hold on his waist tightened and her face dug deeper in his back. Obviously, she was afraid to look. "Oh, don't let them touch me."

"No worry, it's only Moss and Dick."

"I don't want to—I don't want to—tell them that."

"I will."

When he arrived, he shouted for the women to come out. Several of them rushed outside, led by Mrs. Logan. He helped the girl down and one of the ladies quickly covered her with a blanket.

"She been through hell." Zekial shook his head when they asked where he found her. The concerned women took her toward Doc's house. Tilly waited until they were on their way then she stepped close to him and he smiled tiredly at her.

"Where she come from?"

"War party killed the others. I don't know. We found her like that on the road," Zekial said to her quietly. "She didn't even know that she was naked."

"I better go help them."

"They treating you all right?"

"Ain't nothin to complain about." She nodded and took her skirt in her hand to hurry after the other women.

Cane called for a war council of the leaders. Moss and Dick had found the camp in the grove on the prairie. They estimated there were forty bucks, or less by their count. The Osage were lounging around their camp as if they had plenty of time.

Dick had a suggestion. "Let's take twenty good men with rifles, march over there by night, over there and when the sun comes up, shoot the Indians."

"We can't leave the village unguarded," Cane complained.

"How many good men with rifles do you have?"

"Twenty-five, counting you three."

"Five can stay here. We can be back in three hours easy."

Cane's face turned red. "If there are other camps, they could attack the village while we're gone."

Dick clenched his jaw and crossed his arms. "You have a choice. Do you want those heathen bastards to keep holding you hostage and killing parties on the road or do you want to lead normal lives?"

"The women and children, though—"

"I say we go wipe them out or we'll never be safe in these hills." Other voices chimed in with various forms of agreement.

"We leave at eleven tonight, on foot." Dick pointed at Cane. "You pick out who stays."

Cane blew out a breath, obviously frustrated. Finally, he shook his head. "Fine. But I appoint you and Moss as our captains. I'll stay and man the guard here with four others. Some of the older men can stay here with me. Lacy has a broken leg. He can stay, too."

Dick looked around at the other men gathered around them. "Okay, boys. Eleven o'clock tonight, have your powder and lead ready. We meet here."

That matter settled. Zekial and Dick headed for the barn.

"You figure we can take them?" Zeke asked under his breath.

"I know we can, if the men will listen to my orders. The Osage have gotten too smug. They think every white man in the territory is trembling in fear and hiding in this village. They're picking off the stragglers."

"How did she get away from them? The girl?"

"Crazy in the head, I figure. They don't like crazy people. Worries them or maybe they were through with her."

"Tilly is helping the women take care of her, so maybe she'll know more about her condition."

They took their blankets outside in the sun to get some rest. It would be a long night.

XXXIII

GRISSUM LOOKED UP THROUGH HIS bleary eyes. He blinked in disbelief at her crossed eyes peering at him.

He screamed.

Doc rushed into the room. "What's wrong man?"

"Her! Where did she come from?" Grissum demanded as his perspiration turned to ice.

"She's a victim of an Injun raid," Doc said and put his arm around her. "Here, you come sit in the rocker and leave Mr. McCord alone now."

"Thought I'd died when I saw her eyes." McCord wiped his sweaty face with his hand. Everything inside him was all atremble.

"Don't let them touch me!" she said plaintively.

"We won't let them," the doc said. "You sit here, little lady."

Grissum pushed himself up. It was hard to pee sitting on the edge of a bed, nothing else he could do. What was that girl from the tavern doing there?

"Her family got wiped out coming here near as we can tell." Doc scooted the night jar out from under the bed for him to use.

"What about her?" Grissum asked, ready to pull up the night shirt and relieve himself.

"She isn't all there in the head," Doc said to dismiss her presence.

"Her father made whiskey and ran a place over east of here. I'll never forget her. Them crossed eyes." He shook his head in disbelief. It was her all right. He sure hoped she didn't cast a spell on him. Bad enough to only have one leg—let alone be cursed.

"She never said her name. Injuns must have repeatedly raped her. She is very defensive about it."

"I'll think of her name. She was going to marry this clod when I left there about a week or so ago. They may have been on their wedding trip." He finished and eased himself back with some wincing at the pain. Exhausted, he laid back, weak as a kitten.

"You going back to Alabama when you heal up?" Doc asked. "You mentioned it several times when you were delirious."

"I don't know. I left there on two legs. I'd hate to crawl back on one."

"Life has to go on." Doc gave a shrug of his thin shoulders.

"Yeah, but you got both legs. You can say that."

"They maybe going to avenge your lost leg for you. Them new buck-skin-ners and a Cherokee called Moss are going to take a small army from here and raid the Osage's camp."

"Buck-skinners, huh. Who are they?"

"Ones called Whistling Dick, the other's Broome, Zekial Broome."

"This Broome guy got a black wench?" He sat up on his elbows.

"Yes, he does. She's the one that helped make that dress for the poor girl."

McCord dropped back in bed and stared at the underside of the cedar shakes. The two of them were there and nothing he could do about it. Whis-tling Dick, he knew them. The same man put him and Judson on the Car-rolton road. He was here, too. What could he do about her? The deep ache in his lost leg grew worse and he tried to crush the pain out with his thumbs dug into his upper stub.

"I need some whiskey, Doc."

"I believe you do."

———

THE SMALL ARMY GATHERED IN the dark street under the far-off stars. Dick spoke to each man, his breath coming out in vapors. "Everyone got plenty ammunition, knife, hatchet or a tomahawk?"

"Got them."

"I'm ready."

"I've got mine."

At last, they started to leave the dark village. Women wearing shawls against the cold stood on the sides of the street in silence watching their menfolk leave on their mission. They faded back inside as the small army marched away.

Moss had scouted all evening long and reported there was no activity near the village. Zekial knew the Cherokee's report had encouraged Dick more. His thoughts on the Osage being smug sounded correct.

In the rear, Zekial kept an eye on the army's back side. They crossed over the pass and turned east, using the road to speed their travels. Without a moon, they made their way in the dark, which also covered their movements from afar. Dick demanded silence and they kept it. Only the shuffle of shoe leather cut the night's stillness.

A mile from the Osage camp, they could hear camp dogs yipping, but Dick explained the matter in a hushed voice while they all squatted down on the ground. The dogs barked all the time and were not a warning to the Osage.

"Zeke, you and three men take the horse herd further away. They're west of the camp. Captain Moss will take six men and slip around to the north. The rest will be with me and cover the south and the east. The less Indians get away the better. Any questions?"

"When are we attacking?"

"When they get up at sunup. Don't get itchy-fingered on the triggers and warn them before that. Is that understood?"

Quiet replies in the affirmative answered him.

Zeke wondered about these men. Many had never seen such action before, but they were tough to be there. Like the men who went to New Orleans with Jackson, they were men who ate by the gun. He tapped three men on the shoulder. Each rose and followed him.

Moss had directed him. The Osage horses were in a wide basin west of the grove along a creek with steep banks. Boys herded them, and they would be asleep at this time of night for the Osage feared no one in this land. The hard part would be to locate the herders and not stumble over them in the dark. Zekial used the North Star to guide him.

Zekial raised his arm in a signal to stop. Two stallions argued in the night. Their shrill screams and attack carried across the chest high bluestem. Zekial spotted a fire glow. The herders had a fire.

He pointed it out to the others. "We need to sneak up and surround them without a shot."

Squatted in the grass seed stems under the starlight, the men agreed.

"Got to go slow and not alert them when we sneak up. I will hoot like an owl twice, then we'll take them," Zekial said. "None of them can escape or lives will be lost."

The sound of stallions' hooves flailing each other rang across the land. More squeals and grunts shattered the night. The men headed out in a crouch.

At last, Zekial drew close enough that he could see the camp.

Three boys in blankets huddled at the fire. One rose from his place when the stallions began to fight again. He must have sworn at them, for his voice cut the night, but the studs still fought beyond the camp.

Zekial caught sight of the man on his right, then another on the left. They were there and ready. He could smell the acrid herders' fire and could see their faces in the orange light. Mere boys, but deadly as their grown-up counterparts.

He hooted, and one horse-herder looked around. Young and inexperienced, he never heeded the strange call. It gave enough time for Zekial and his men, who were on them in seconds. They dispatched each one with their hatchets. Swift and quiet, except for the thuds, the matter was handled. The still bodies of the young herders lay on the ground as the men warmed their hands at the fire.

"What now?" one of them asked.

"Move the horses across the stream and further away and do it quietly."

"What about those stallions?"

"They're a good thing. The noise of their fighting is a normal sound to them and should cover our movement. Drag these dead bodies into the grass so if someone comes they'll think the boys are out herding."

His order obeyed, they spread out in the twilight to move the horses westward with low whistles. They soon had the individuals filing down the dark cut of the creek and up the far side.

The stream was a shallow trickle and the men re-crossed it coming back. Zekial satisfied himself that the horses were far enough away not to offer the Osage a quick escape.

He spread his men out west of the camp in the tall grass and they waited. In the predawn, women began to stir their cooking fires. Smoke carried on the east wind to his face as he bellied down on the damp ground and waited. Snow was gone and the temperature moderate, though it had dropped all night. Cold enough for Zekial to give a small shiver in his position on the ground

When the women went out of camp to relieve themselves, they were taken and quickly dispatched. The sounds of one struggle to the north of his position raised the hair on Zekial's neck. Then a thud and silence. He settled back down on the grass and waited.

The purple streak in the east told him time was drawing near. All the men must be tired of waiting. Moving the horse herd had been a good thing for him and his men to use up part of the night. A red ball of fire was coming up in the east.

A shot shattered the morning quiet and dogs went to howling. A woman grabbed a lance and prepared to defend the camp. The blast of another rifle struck her in the chest and she fell. Warriors streamed from tents screaming at the top of their lungs. They were answered by withering rifle fire.

After his first shot at a figure, Zekial reloaded and shot at another buck coming around the closest tepee. The man was hit and fell but was on his feet in an instant and raced around the other way to be shot again.

A raging Indian came running pell-mell from the camp in only a loincloth with a hatchet in his hand. Zekial used his pistol and fired at point-blank range. The man fell on his back. Zekial dispatched him with his own tomahawk. He rose up in time to see a knife wielding Indian come screaming at him. The buck's charge was cut short by a rifle blast close-by. Zekial nodded in gratitude to the shooter and reloaded his own rifle.

The men mopped up the survivors with hatchets and knives. "How many escaped?" Zekial asked Dick.

"Maybe a dozen, but part of them is wounded."

"McQuire has a knife wound," one man reported.

Dick frowned. "Serious?"

"Naw, he'll live."

"Good, any others hurt?" He looked around. "Zekial, go see about his wound."

"What we going to do with all this stuff?" one man asked Dick.

"To the victors go the spoils," Dick said with a laugh and the others cheered.

Zekial found the wounded man on his butt. His shirt torn to the shoulder. Two men were busy bandaging him.

"You, all right?" he asked.

"Yeah, ain't but a deep scratch. I'm alive and still have my hair." The man grinned, and they helped him to his feet.

Zekial went back to see about the horse herd. They would need several travois to carry all the furs and loot from the camp.

Dick called him aside and motioned to a dead Indian lying on his back. "Look at this," he said and swung a silver medallion before his eyes.

"This is a Jefferson peace medal. I figure that pot-bellied buck over there is Blue Heron. He was wearing this."

"Sure, might be. What we doing with the bodies?"

"Throwing them on the fires when we get the lodges cleaned out. We'll burn a few of them full of their corpses."

"Look here," one man said, waving a woman's corset around. "I found this."

Zekial wondered what had happened to the contents. Probably were slaughtered by these savages. They would not do anymore killing and they'd think twice before they came down into the western territory and tried it again. This would be a great loss for the Osage. Their prime warriors were dead all around him.

Good. This matter settled, Zeke was anxious for him and Tilly to go back home and work on their place. By mid-morning, the stench of burning hides and bodies filled the air with gagging smoke. Many horses heavily loaded with packs or travois loads, the victorious army headed for Boonesboro.

"Some good animals in this herd," Dick pointed to a large mule. "Few arrow scars, but he's a stout looking devil and well broke."

Zeke agreed. He rode a small roan pony up and down the line. Men led some and drove others. The hiss of travois poles filled the air. They raised a great cloud of dust as they headed home, the victors.

'The Osage will not be back soon." Moss rode bareback and pushed his small mount in close to visit.

"Suits me, maybe we can get on with our lives," Zekial said.

"Let's hope for many years of peace."

"Yes, and it didn't take the army either," Zekial said.

"Oh, they would not have done it in this fashion." Moss shook his hand and thanked him. "You ever need anything, you send word to me. My people will be your people."

"Same here."

"Good."

Cane and several others from the village warned by the dust came out to meet them. There was much whooping and hollering over the victory.

Zekial rode ahead to find Tilly and share the news with her.

She rushed out of the store into his arms and hugged him.

"You, all right?" he asked, concerned.

"I'm fine." She bobbed her head.

"The Osage are dead. We can go home."

"Good. I be ready."

"Is he still alive?" Zekial tossed his head toward the physician's house.

"They say so. They say that his man, Judson, already be dead somewhere."

"No matter. I intend to go see him."

"You do?" She frowned. Worry etched in the set of her brown eyes.

"I'm not fretting all my life and looking over my shoulder wondering if he's going to come to our place."

"You be careful. I better wait here."

"Fine." Zekial strode to the Doctor's cabin and rapped on the door. He wanted this matter between him and McCord settled, once and for all. He had no intention of spending the rest of his life looking over his shoulder for this man. On his way, he glanced around at the dry leaves being rolled around in the fresh wind. Spring wasn't far away.

A small stoop shouldered older woman answered the door. "Yes?"

"Is Mr. McCord awake?"

"I believe so. Who may I say is calling?"

"Never mind, I'll tell him myself." He let her move aside, walked in the room, and spotted Grissum in the bed. The slate faced man with beads of sweat coming down his face blinked at him. This was the terror, Zekial had dreaded. This blanched-looking invalid sprawled on his back, obviously emaciated from his former self by the trauma of his leg loss.

"McCord, if you live, don't you ever darken my trail. I will kill you on sight. Am I clear?" He glared at the man and waited for his answer. If need be, he was prepared to simply kill him right there.

This matter between them, about his woman, was ending right then.

The man nodded, then turned his gaze to the wall. "You come threaten a man when he's down."

Two swift steps, Zekial reached out and grasped a fist full of Grissum's nightshirt and roughly hauled him up to a sitting position.

"I just got through helping kill two dozen Indians. Taking your worthless life wouldn't bother me one bit more." He jerked him up close enough to his face he could smell his foul breath.

"Am I clear to you, McCord?"

"Perfectly."

Zekial released the man and stepped back, exhaling sharply out of his nose. This matter between them, for his part, was settled. The rage ebbed away inside him. This slave chaser was through hounding him or her ever again. Zekial turned on his heel, nodded to the stone-faced woman and left the cabin.

Grissum settled back down on the bed. The sharp pangs of fear that clutched his heart slowly drained away. Broome would kill him. He had no doubt. Not much he could do one-legged, either. For certain, he couldn't stay much longer in this place. He listened closely as the man in leather stomped out of the house. Grissum closed his eyes to the pain in his stump.

XXXIV

GRAY MORNING LIGHT SHONE ON the muddy ruts in the street. Shake roofs glistened silver with frost. Their horses were already loaded with supplies, a precious sack of seed corn amongst their things and the plow handles sticking out each side of the horse. Zekial shook hands with Dick and clapped him on the shoulder. His friend wanted to head back west. Too many folks in this land for him. Neither man wanted to talk about it. They'd meet again, if fate allowed. The unspoken partings as strong as if they had said them aloud. Goodbye, old friend.

Zekial turned and undid the lead rope from the hitch rail. The roan horse he had claimed for his portion of the loot was under a pack. Time for them to go, too. Filled with pride, he looked toward his wife. A good thing had come into his life with her. Tilly sat on the gray mare and talked to the lady in blue.

"I sure will come back and see you," Tilly promised her. Zekial exchanged a nod with his woman. He mounted up and they rode out. Men raised rifles in a salute to them, everyone else waved and shouted goodbye. At the edge of town, he turned and asked, "You and that white lady getting along?"

"She's mighty nice. Going to loan me a crib for our baby. You got to come get it this fall."

"I'll do that," Zekial said. He had plenty to do before fall. A cabin to build, fields to get ready and crops to raise. There were lots of things for him to do.

From the stoop of Doc's cabin, Grissum McCord watched Zekial and the wench ride out that morning. He leaned on the crutch under his arm. He still wasn't staying in Boonesboro any longer, Broome leaving or not. One thing, he knew, though, was that he could never go back to Alabama. Not one legged. Not only part of a man. He'd have to make a home somewhere else.

At least he had a pretty good idea as to where, though.

He observed the cross-eyed girl while she packed his bedroll and things out to the mule. Doc had some men fix him up with a travois for him to ride on behind her. No way could he sit on a horse yet. She loaded his gear on the rig and then looked up at him.

"Get your things too, Pearlie," he said to her and tried not to look into her crossed eyes. "Time for us to go."

"I will," she said.

The short distance to the mule that stood in the shafts of the travois, proved to be more exhausting than he realized. He paused twice to rest on his new crutch. Out of breath and weak, he finally reached the mule's side.

"Can you get on him by yourself?" he asked, standing beside the conveyance.

"Sure," she said, tying her sack of things on the saddle.

"Now, you take it easy with him. We've got to go clear to Carrolton. Ain't no rush, we can take several days to get there."

"You sure that woman is going to take us in?" she asked with a pained expression on her face. She lifted the loose hair from her forehead with her hand and forced it back over her head.

"Margaret? Yeah, she'll have us." He gingerly took his seat on the travois and pointed. "Get my rifle."

"Those Indians burned everything down," she mumbled, handing him the long gun. "They killed everyone... but me."

"I know that, Pearlie. Now, you get up on that mule and go slow. I don't want to be turned over or have a wreck back here. You hear me?"

"I hear you. What're we going to do for this woman for our keep?"

"Scrape bear hides. She'll have lots of work we can do. Now, go mount up." He waved her away not wanting to look at her crossed eyes again until later.

Laid back, Grissum listened to the hiss of the poles. His stub leg hurt on every jolt when a pole came off a rock and jarred him everywhere, those parts he had and those he didn't have, but he figured it would always be like that. Margaret would have work for them. He hugged the rifle and tried to squirm around on his butt to be in a more comfortable position on the travois. No use. It would always pain him.

AUTHOR'S NOTE

THE STORY OF ZEKIAL BROOME is a dark, raw, adult insight into earlier times in American history. This is a novel set during the early 1800s on the then-frontier most writers these days leave out. It confronts head-on issues of slavery, racial superiority, sordid vice, and wallows in the muck of raw individuals who bullied their way through life and got away with it due to a lack of law enforcement institutions and the vagaries of transport and communications on the wild frontier. There is little left out about the harsh life and times of the men and women in this story, nor the complexity of their relationships with the peculiar institution of slavery. It is as historically accurate as I can make it, and while it may offend, it is my belief that we can't make things better unless we understand just how bad they truly were.